HOTEL EVER AFTER BOX SET

LIZA PENN

Copyright © 2016

The novellas in this box set were originally individually released in 2016, then re-released in 2021 as a Box Set with some edits.

All rights reserved.

No part of this book may be reproduced in any form or by any electronic or mechanical means, including information storage and retrieval systems, without written permission from the author, except for the use of brief quotations in a book review. For permission requests, contact lizapennbooks@gmail.com

Publisher's Note: This is a work of fiction. Names, characters, places, and incidents are a product of the author's imagination. The town of Fairhaven and the characters are entirely fictional. Any resemblance to actual people, living or dead, or actual locations, hotels, or other businesses, is entirely coincidental.

PREFACE

Welcome to the world of Hotel Ever After! Each story promises a happily ever after, a sexy twist, and a hint of a fairy tale set in a very modern world. These are not straight re-tellings of the classics—the Beast is a hotel tycoon, the tower is the penthouse suite, and the wicked stepmother may not be the best, but she isn't literally a witch.

Each of the novellas in this series is short—only about 75 pages long—perfect for an afternoon tryst!

Want to stay in touch? Follow Liza on Facebook or subscribe to her newsletter at https://rarebooks.substack.com/to be the first to find out about new books!

Up next is a new series retelling classic super hero tales! Liza has joined with bestselling author Natasha Luxe to create a sexy twist on superhero stories in the new Heroes & Villains series—check it out now!

BETTE & THE BEAST

CHAPTER ONE

There was nothing Bette Franklin loved more than her little bookshop. She'd saved everything she had for years to be able to afford the place, even though it wasn't in the best condition. But condition didn't matter—Happily Ever After Bookstore had *class*.

Well...it used to have class, back when it was first built in its beautiful art deco style. Now... now it had a few creaks. A spot in the store room where she couldn't store books because it leaked whenever it rained. Peeling paint behind the bookshelves. And, Bette strongly suspected, some mice that liked to nibble pages in the historical section.

So, maybe not class. But the Happily Ever After Bookstore *did* have character, no one could deny that.

Just like they couldn't deny the bills piling up daily. Bette sighed as she sorted her mail. Quotes for aesthetic improvements, like painting and restoration of some of the carved art deco features on the walls could be ignored for now. Some of the maintenance could be too. No one has actually *seen* any mice...maybe a few traps could delay calling the exterminator.

But some bills couldn't be ignored. The foundation of the building *had* to be examined, that sagging floor was getting worse. And if Bette didn't pay the publishers for the books she'd ordered, she'd lose her stock for the store. And then there was the roof. Happily Ever After Bookstore was at least a decade overdue for a new roof, but Bette just didn't have the twenty grand to drop for new tiles.

She sighed heavily. Something had to give. And it couldn't be the store.

At the bottom of her stack of bills was an envelope made of heavy linen paper. Bette didn't bother opening it. She knew exactly what was inside. Another offer to purchase Happily Ever After right out from under her. The Dickson Hotel Corporation had already made three such offers, but Bette had no intention of selling.

Ever.

The offer was fair, true. It would solve all Bette's money problems, and she could easily use the profits to go across town and open a new store, one that didn't have mice or a saggy roof.

But the Dickson Hotel Corporation wanted nothing more than to tear down the whole building and replace it with another bland hotel for people with too much money. Bette tossed the unopened envelope into the rubbish bin.

She couldn't let that happen to her Happily Ever After.

She just couldn't.

"You could, you know." Bette's best friend, Aria, came into the back office.

"Could what?" Bette asked, pushing her glasses to the top of her head.

Aria reached down to the trashcan and picked up the linen envelope. "You could at least *consider* the offer." Aria's voice was sweet and melodic, but her words were hesitant. This was definitely a hot-button topic for them both.

"No," Bette said flatly. "No, I could not."

"It's more than even your father could get you on the open market," Aria said.

"Since when did you become a real estate expert?" Bette shot back.

"Well...never." Aria shuffled her feet. "But your father *is*, and he said as much to me..."

Bette's eyes widened. "You *didn't*. Please, *please* tell me you didn't tell my father that someone's offered for the store!"

Aria refused to meet Bette's eyes. "He's *worried*."

"He shouldn't be!" Bette leaped from her chair, the cheap plastic bumping against the old wooden wall. "This is *my* place, and I got it *without* him!"

"He just wants to help." Aria's voice became quieter and quieter with each word.

Bette frowned. Her passion for books had made her far touchier that she normally was. Aria was always quiet, and while she loved books, she didn't love the store, not the way Bette did. But it wasn't fair to take out her frustrations on her best friend and only employee.

"Let's open up," Bette said, giving Aria a half-hug. "What's done is done, and it doesn't matter anyway, because no matter what Dad says or what the dicks at the Dickson Corporation offer, I'm not selling."

Aria nodded and left the office to go unlock the front door of the bookshop while Bette opened the register and made sure the check out desk was ready for customers. She tried not to wonder just how many customers she'd have. Most of her clientele was older, people who hated online shopping. Every Saturday morning she always had a big crowd for children's book hour, but most of the parents just used the time to have someone else watch over and read to their kids, and they rarely bought the books.

After unlocking, Aria went into the back to check stock. A local author was doing an event at the store later that week, but while they'd ordered fifty books, only three customers had confirmed they would attend the event.

Bette wandered up and down the rows of shelves. The store wasn't a cookie-cutter box store like most cities had. Fairhaven, the little town tucked among the towering redwoods of Northern California, deserved a better bookstore than this.

But this was all Bette could offer.

The row of sleigh bells attached the front door jingled as someone came inside. "Hello and welcome to Happily Ever After," Belle said cheerfully, then her smile vanished. "Oh, it's you."

"Hello my darling daughter," Tom, Bette's father, said, striding over to her. He dropped a whiskery kiss on her forehead.

"I'm not selling," Bette said immediately.

Tom's bushy eyebrows shot up. "Who asked you to?"

Bette narrowed her eyes. There was a reason why her father was such a good real estate salesman, and it lay in his charming demeanor. He could talk a nun out of her habit, but instead he went around shuffling buildings to different owners like he was dealing cards at Vegas.

"Don't even try anything, or I'll kick you out," Bette warned.

Tom raised both his hands in mock defeat. "I give, I give. But I'm not here for that. I'm here for a favor."

It was Bette's turn to raise her eyebrows. "A favor?"

Tom leaned over the old mahogany counter of the bookshop, his fingers idly dipping into the little bowl of luck stones set beside the cash register as an impulse buy. "I have a very prestigious client coming in from out of state, and he's a bit…a bit flashier than Fairhaven is used to."

"A copy of *People* magazine is flashier than Fairhaven is used to," Bette muttered.

Despite being in California, home to the stars, Fairhaven was closer to Oregon than LA. That's what Bette loved the most about the little town—it was large enough for good Wi-Fi and three different indie coffee shops, but small enough that only a few minutes' drive took you to either the towering redwood forest or the shores of the Pacific. Their coastline was beautiful—a gorgeous combination of rock and white sand, with enough warmth and fair weather for perfect swimming and boating in the summer, followed by rainy, gray days ideal for reading in the fall and winter. The coast was an undiscovered gem of the Pacific—which Tom had been trying to turn into a profit for years.

"Bette, this is really important to me," Tom said. "A sale like this could mean retirement for me."

"Yeah, right," Bette said. Tom was never going to retire. He loved the game too much.

"Still, it would be a huge deal."

"So what do you need me for?"

Tom turned from fidgeting with the luck stones to toying with the tasseled bookmarks on display, handmade by Aria. "He may have seen a picture of you in my office," he said reluctantly, "and he may have asked if you'd be up for a date…"

"You're setting me up with your client?" Bette said so loudly that Aria came in from the back room to check on her. She waved her friend out; she definitely didn't want her hearing this conversation.

"No, no, no!" Tom protested. "It's not like that! He just—he wants to have dinner with you. Just one evening. You can tell him what a great real estate agent I am, and flirt a little, and next day, we can sign some papers and I'll have snagged the deal of a lifetime."

"You mean *I* will have snagged it," Bette growled.

"Come on, my darling girl, don't be like this," Tom pleaded. "Just one night. One dinner. You don't have to talk about anything but your dear old dad."

"My dear old pimp."

"Bette, please," Tom said, dragging out the last word in an almost childish tone. When Bette's mother had died more than a decade ago, Tom had been inconsolable. He'd quit his job as a teacher, where he'd met

Bette's mother. The romance between the science teacher and the history tutor had been legendary. But when it turned tragic after a failed battle with breast cancer, Tom had done nothing more productive than get out of bed for a year. A late night infomercial on real estate had changed all that, and he'd thrown himself into the work in a way Bette hadn't believed was possible. The competition of real estate kept him alive, and Bette just couldn't deny him that.

"Fine," she said. "*One* date. That's it. At least I'll get a free meal out of it."

"Excellent!" Tom crowed. "I'll set it up. He can pick you up here, at the store. Around seven?"

"Tonight?" Bette asked, shocked.

"Great, tonight!" Tom said, and he left before Bette had a chance to evaluate what had just happened.

CHAPTER TWO

"What was that about?" Aria asked as the door to Happily Ever After jingled closed behind Bette's father.

Bette sighed. "He set me up."

"For what?"

"A blind date."

A sly grin spread across Aria's face. "A da-ate?" she said in a sing-song voice.

Bette threw a wad of paper at her friend. "At least it's tonight; it'll be over soon enough."

Aria rolled her eyes. "Oh, you're so romantic," she said. "Come on—why not *try* to make this fun?"

"Fun?" Bette laughed. "For one night?"

"*Yes!*" Aria said. "Yes! For just one night!" She leaned over the front desk and grabbed her friend's arms. "When—honestly, *when*—was the last time you had fun? For one hour, let alone one night?"

Bette couldn't help herself, she turned back toward the back office. Through the door, she could just see her desk and the stack of bills she'd had to prioritize on what to pay first.

Aria squeezed her arms, forcing her attention back to her. "Just one night," she said softly. "Forget about it all for just one night."

Bette dared to smile.

"Go home," Aria said. "Relax, then get ready."

And just like that, she was back in reality. "Ha!" Bette said without a trace of humor. "I don't have time for that! The children's reading group will be here in an hour—"

"Cancel it!" Aria cried. "They never actually *buy* the books, and last time they ruined three copies of *Goodnight Moon* with something that was either Nutella or something far, far worse."

"—And then there's the Whine and Wine book club right after that, and I've not even set up the refreshments, and somewhere in all that, a plumber's coming to inspect the pipes in the bathroom."

"I can handle it," Aria said. "Go home."

Bette shook her head. It's not that she didn't trust her friend, it was just that she knew this bookstore was held together with little more than a lick and a prayer, and if she wasn't there, it would all come crumbling down. The children's readings weren't always profitable, but last month they helped pay the electricity bill. Whine and Wine was a small group, but they always bought hardcovers at full price from Happily Ever After. Bette couldn't risk them going elsewhere if she flaked on their day.

"When's the date?" Aria asked.

"Around seven."

"The store closes at seven today." Aria's voice held an accusatory note. "So when are you going home to change?"

Bette looked down at her clothes. Her brown hair was in a messy bun, and while her t-shirt wasn't exactly date-worthy, but it wasn't that bad. The cover of *The Little Prince* was on the front, and it may be a little faded, but it wasn't worn out by any means. "This is fine for dinner," she said.

"Oh my gosh, you are hopeless!" Aria said, smiling. "But don't worry. I've got this."

She spun away from the counter, cell phone in hand.

"What do you mean?" Bette called after her. "Aria, what do you got?"

~

*T*he children's reading group went better than usual. Bette and Aria had learned: no snacks for the children that were sticky, had nuts, had sugar, or could stain anything. Peanut butter crackers always landed peanut butter side down on top of the most expensive picture books in the store. Grape juice always spilled. *Always.*

Instead, Bette set out little paper cups of animal crackers and water, and read *Jumanji* to the six eager children. She did all the right animals sounds in all the right places, and the children were the best audience, gasping and shouting and cheering.

Bette smiled as the parents herded the children away. This—*this*—was what it was all about. Not the sales, not paying the bills. Having a child scream with glee at her lion's roar, seeing the story come alive in their imaginations...Bette knew that every story like this would turn these kids into life-long readers.

She checked the clock. Soon the Whine and Wine club would arrive. Aria was being very cagey about whatever phone calls she'd made before, but Bette did her best to push it from her mind as she wandered up the aisle of books.

This was her home, far more than the apartment she rented. Books were her home. She shut her eyes and breathed in the scent of ink and paper—but also the store, the lemon oil she used on the gleaming wooden art deco touches in the corners, the dust that always clung to the carved ridges of the patterned ceiling no matter how much she tried to clean them, the slightly salty fresh air that clung to everything in Fairhaven.

This was what she would never give up, not for any price, no matter what she had to sacrifice.

Aria pulled the cork out of a California Riesling and started to pour it into six little plastic wine glasses. She already had a plate of cheese and crackers ready.

"Looks good!" Bette said, swiping a piece of cheese.

"Thanks."

The bells on the door jingled. The ladies of the Whine and Wine club poured in, as well as—

"Ursula?" Bette asked.

"Ursula!" Aria said, running forward. "Thank you, thank you!"

The Whine and Wine club pounced on the cheese plate, and Bette followed Aria's excited hand waving to her friend. "Hi, Ursula," she said, eyeing the long black garment bag and makeup case in her hands. "What are you doing here?" she asked suspiciously.

Ursula was, hands down, the most gorgeous woman Bette knew. She had silky, long brown hair to match her silky, long brown body, and she moved with a confident grace that had men falling at her feet. She was the exact opposite of Aria, but the girls roomed together in a small cottage by the sea and, for the most part, seemed to get along great. Still, Ursula didn't exactly move in the same circles as Aria, and Bette had only met her a handful of times.

Aria clapped her hands excitedly. "I've already talked to the Whine and Wine club," she said. She waved over at the ladies, who were circling their chairs, ready for their book talk.

"Have fun, dear!" old Mrs. Henderson called back, returning Aria's wave. "We've got everything covered!"

"What did you do?" Bette said, dragging out the last word in a pleading tone to Aria.

"Sula is going to help you get ready," Aria said.

"Don't bother trying to fight it," Ursula said, her painted red lips turning up. "Where can we go?"

"Back office." Aria started leading the way. When Bette hesitated, she turned back, grabbed her wrist, and dragged her into the office. The ladies of the book club giggled as they passed.

Ursula shut the office door with a flourish, then spun around, sending the garment bag fluttering. "Strip," she ordered.

Bette raised her hands defensively. "I do *not* need to get dressed up for this!" she said. "It's not a big deal, and there's no point—"

"Strip," Ursula said again, smiling toothily.

"Best not to fight her," Aria said. "Sula is...headstrong."

"But—"

Ursula raised one elegantly sculpted eyebrow.

Bette sighed and pulled off her t-shirt.

"Oh, thank god I brought this," Ursula said, opening up the big case she'd brought with her. Bette had assumed it was all make-up, but while there was make-up inside, there was more than that. Including lingerie.

"I'm not wearing that!" she said as Ursula pulled out a lacy black bra with a tiny red bow. "Or that!" she almost screamed as Ursula tossed her a matching pair of panties.

"The clothes you wear that no one can see are more important than the clothes you wear that they can," Ursula said. "You could put on those old jeans again and be ten times sexier with those panties on beneath them."

Bette stared down at the lacy bits of nothing in her hands. She could imagine how they would feel against her skin...moving with her as she danced with a handsome stranger... She didn't own anything like this at home—it was all cotton and sensible—but maybe she *should* get something sexy.

"But gross," she said. "I'm not wearing your underwear!"

"Oh, shut up, they're new!" Ursula protested. "I asked Aria what size to get."

Bette glanced at the price tags still on the underwear. "How did you know my size?" she asked Aria.

Aria smiled. "I'm crafty. Now strip!" she said gleefully.

Bette turned around, took off the rest of her clothes, and slipped into the new lingerie. She should be cold, but instead, Bette felt way too hot. The little windowless office was stuffy and Bette knew her whole body must be pink from blushing.

Aria whistled as Bette turned around.

Bette meanwhile, groaned. "Not my desk!" she cried. All her carefully organized stacks of bills and papers had been shoved into one corner as Ursula had set out three different dresses on display.

Aria rushed over. "One night," she said softly. "Forget about it all for one night. We can take care of the rest tomorrow."

Bette sighed, but she forced her attention away from the disheveled papers and toward the three dresses Ursula had set out for her.

"No, no, and no," she said pointing at each one of them.

"No and no," Ursula said, pulling off two of the dresses. "You're right. Red is too harsh for you, and this one would never fit your boobs."

Bette crossed her arms over her chest.

"But this one." Ursula swept the last dress off the desk. It was a short black number, and had only a little more material in it than her t-shirt had.

"*No,*" Bette said.

"Yes!" Aria and Ursula said at the same time.

"And besides, I have your other clothes," Aria said. "And I hid them. It's the dress or nothing."

CHAPTER THREE

The Whine and Wine ladies started clapping and whistling the second Bette stepped out of the office. Bette blushed furiously, but she had to admit that their admiration and approval meant a lot to her.

Ursula stood in the doorway, wiping her hands together like she'd just finished a heavy duty construction project. And, to be fair, it had been just about as much work as one. Bette's normal messy bun was now a wave of light brown curls with a glimmer of gold hairspray to add sparkle. She wasn't used to much more than Chapstick, but Ursula had applied a dark pink stain to Bette's lips, and a series of different shades of gray to her eyelids for something she called a "smoky eye." Bette suspected that smoke had far less glitter.

Despite Bette's reservations, the dress fit her like a glove, moving over her body just enough to remind her of the new lingerie. The only thing that didn't fit was the hemline—the knee-length dress came up to the middle of Bette's thighs. And fortunately, none of Ursula's heels fit, so Bette was given the luxury of her regular black ballet flats.

"All right, ladies, that's our cue to leave!" Mrs. Henderson said, snapping that month's book selection shut.

"No, no, you can stay!" Bette cried. "You're my favorite book group!"

Aria slipped behind the register. "I've got this," she said as the book club lined up to purchase next month's books. "You've got a tall, dark stranger to meet."

She nodded toward the big front windows of the store. A man was outlined in the glass, his face not quite illuminated from the lights spilling from the window.

"That might not be him," Bette said, her voice oddly quiet.

The man moved toward the door. Oh, god, it was him. It had to be. And he was about to come into Happily Ever After and meet the entire Whine and Wine book club, a wickedly smiling Ursula, and Aria, who couldn't stop giggling to save her life.

Bette raced to the door, swinging it open just as the man reached for the handle.

"Hi!" she said, slightly breathless.

"Hi," the man said. "I'm looking for Bette?"

"That's me; let's go," Bette said, pushing him out the door.

The man tried to look over her shoulder. "I can wait—I'm a little early. Don't you have to close the store?"

"My friend has it covered," Bette said hurriedly.

The man lingered, a slightly wistful look on his face. Did he actually want to go inside the store? There as *no way* she could let that happen— they'd never leave, and the Whine and Wine club would be writing sexy fan fic of them before the night was over, and if they were very, very lucky, they wouldn't narrate it to everyone before they left.

"So, um," Bette said, "I'm Bette. You know my dad from a real estate deal?"

For the first time, the man paid more attention to Bette than to Happily Ever After. His eyes widened slightly as he took her all in, from gleaming hair to scruffy ballet flats.

"I...yes," he said, flustered. "My name's Richard."

Bette stuck her hand out. The man looked at it, surprised for a moment, then shook it.

"So, where are we going?" Bette asked.

Richard looked down the street. "I was told Baiser was the best here."

Bette's lips turned up—he said the name of the restaurant with a perfect French accent. "You're right," she said. "It's about our only good restaurant. And it's only three blocks from here."

Richard didn't seem sure of where to go, so Bette took his arm and steered him south. Baiser was tucked away off the main street, but the whole town was lit up in beautiful strings of light, sparkling from the trees that lined the sidewalk.

"This town is charming," Richard said.

Bette didn't answer at first. She wasn't sure if he was making fun of Fairhaven or not. It *was* a charming place, but that was often a code word for "rural" and "quaint" and "boring." But Richard didn't look as if he was insulting her hometown.

"I love it here," she said. "The whole time I was at Berkley, all I wanted to do was come back here. Fairhaven is...it's authentic."

A deep rumble of gentle laughter escaped Richard's lips. "Authentic? That's an unusual adjective for a town."

Nope, nope, nope, he was *not* allowed to be this handsome *and* know his grammar. That was entirely too hot.

Bette distracted herself by coming to a stop in the sidewalk. "It's a good word for Fairhaven," she said. "The town works to stay modern, but at the same time, we preserve what we have. Take most of the buildings on this street. It was built in the 1890s, in the Spanish Eclecticism style. And the houses are obviously Victorian—it's a combo that always reminds me of *Lady and the Tramp*."

Richard smiled indulgently, then tucked Bette's hand back in the crook of his arm as they continued toward Baiser. "And what about your bookstore?" he asked. "That doesn't quite match."

"It's art deco," Bette said, her voice ringing with pride. "Designed by George Hoorton. One of his last remaining buildings, and the only building he designed in California. He retired here after living in New York."

Richard made an appreciative noise. "That's quite impressive. All this history in one little town."

Baiser didn't approve of neon signs—if Bette hadn't known it was there, it would have been easy to walk right past it. In fact, Richard almost did. She tugged on his arm, and he smiled sheepishly as he turned around.

"This is it?" he asked.

"Welcome to Fairhaven's finest."

Richard opened the door for Bette. Despite this being the nicest restaurant in town, Bette felt ridiculously overdressed. She tried to tug the hem of her dress down.

Richard whispered words to the waiter, and he changed course, leading them to a table tucked in the corner, lit with candles. Rather than chairs, the table featured a corner booth seat. Richard sat down and scooted close to the middle. Bette hung by the edge of her side, but her knees touched his. She slid closer, so they were side-by-side, which somehow felt more natural.

The waiter handed them a menu printed on tan parchment, explained the specials, and left to give them time to think. Bette watched him walk away, wondering if there was a way she could get him to stay. Walking down the street had been one thing, but being wrapped up in this booth right next to this man she barely knew, in a dress that barely covered her new lingerie... she could feel the heat rising in her cheeks.

"Are you okay?" Richard asked, dropping a hand to her knee. She was wearing elegant silk stockings, held up with old-fashioned garter belts, but his hand felt as if it could sear her skin.

"I'm fine," Bette lied. She inched away under the pretense of facing Richard. "So, I have to ask," she said, gaining confidence as she moved further away, "why did you ask Dad to set this date up?"

Richard stared out over the restaurant. From their vantage point, it was like they were behind a two-way mirror. They could see everyone, but unless the others in the restaurant specifically turned to see them, they were invisible. He watched the dozen or so couples in the restaurant for several long moments before he answered Bette.

"I don't know anyone here," he said, his voice soft, "and I thought I should know someone who loved this town before I decided to invest in it."

"And have you?" Bette asked. "Decided to invest, I mean."

His eyes were intense. "I think I've found exactly what I came here to find."

CHAPTER FOUR

*B*ette's mother always said French food was intoxicating. Baiser had been her favorite restaurant; Bette's father had proposed to her mother at this very restaurant.

Bette had never really seen the appeal. French food relied too heavily on cheese and olive oil for her taste.

But now, as the waiter set down an immaculate chocolate soufflé, Bette felt like maybe, just maybe, she finally understood what her mother had meant about French food being romantic. She pressed the fork down into the soft chocolate, and it gave way as easily as she did around Richard. Bette was naturally shy, but there was something about Richard that made it easy for her to talk to him.

The waiter silently poured more merlot into her glass. Maybe it wasn't Richard. Maybe it was the wine.

Either way, this was the best date of her life.

"So, your name," Richard said, leaning over and stealing a bite of Bette's soufflé.

"Yes?" she asked. She couldn't take her eyes off his mouth as he licked the chocolate from his fork.

"It's a bit old fashioned for a modern girl like you."

Bette giggled. "My dad likes old rock. When I was born, he used to sing 'Bette Davis Eyes' to me."

Richard raised an eyebrow. "I now understand completely."

"Ha!" Bette said, perhaps a bit too loudly. "I'm nothing like the girl in the song. That girl is..." Bette looked down. "She's not me." Bette thought of the lyrics to the song, her fork dropping by the soufflé, forgotten. In the song, the girl's a man-eater, teasing guys and getting them to do anything. Not exactly nursery rhyme material. And nothing at all like shy, bookish Bette.

"Oh, I don't know about that," Richard said, leaning closer. He hummed a few bars of the song, then whispered in her ear, "You definitely 'unease me,'"

She could smell the chocolate and wine on his lips, and it made her feel far more drunk than the wine she'd actually tasted that night. She struggled to think of something—anything—to say to dispel the suddenly intense energy crackling between them. He had commented on her name...she should comment on his. But all she could think of was that people named Richard were sometimes given the nickname "Dick."

And that just made her giggle.

Richard leaned back. "Something funny?" he asked, genuinely curious.

She couldn't stop giggling. "No, no!" she said, grabbing her wine glass and sipping the rich, red liquid as quickly as she could to stave off her laughter. *This is so silly*, she thought. *Why can't I be normal around him?*

"Let's get out of here," Richard said.

"And go where?"

Richard slipped some bills into the black folder containing their check for the meal. He hid it from her view, but she could tell he was leaving a hefty tip. "Why not take me to that bookstore you love so much?" he asked casually.

Nothing could have melted her heart more. The bookstore was the one place she loved more than any other and anyone who wanted to go there was immediately bumped up in her book.

They didn't speak much as they left the restaurant and strolled back to the bookstore. Bette was filled with delicious, savory food, and even more delicious, savory wine that made her feel warm and comfortable, like a cat next to the fire. But Richard beside her was strong and incited a warmth in her that was entirely not comfortable at all.

As they rounded Main Street and Happily Ever After was in view, Richard paused. His eyes scanned the buildings on the block, drinking them all in.

"What do you see?" Bette asked, moving closer to him.

"Potential," Richard said gruffly. "There really is so much Fairhaven has to offer. It's a diamond in the rough."

"And you want to make it shine."

Richard turned his attention to her, and she could see the passion in his eyes. "Exactly," he said.

"Come on," Bette said, pulling him down the street. "Let me show you inside my store."

It was darker now, the strings of lights in the trees that lined the street glittering like stars. When Bette pushed her key into the store's lock, the jingling of the door bells was one of the few sounds on the whole street. There weren't even that many cars. Light spilled in from the streetlamp and the strings of lights, and as Richard stepped behind her, all warm and dark, Bette didn't want to turn the lights on. Turning the lights on would remind her of the water stains in the wood she couldn't afford to fix, the shelves that weren't quite full, the dust she could never entirely reach to clean.

Lights would ruin the magic.

She pulled him inside and closed the door.

"Isn't it a bit dark?" Richard asked.

The giant windows in the front of the store gave just enough of a glow from outside to make everything inside feel magical, surreal. In the bookstore, Bette could be anyone. Any of the characters in any of the books. She could be brave, here, now, in the dark.

So she leaned up on her tiptoes, and kissed Richard.

She could feel his hesitancy—for just one moment. His chest muscles hardened beneath his dark suit, his lips were tense. But then he melted under her touch, just like the chocolate she'd eaten earlier, and his lips parted. Their kiss deepened. His hands moved up her back, and down again, lingering on that spot just where her back curved into her buttocks, and he pushed her closer to him. She came willingly, and his back bumped into the door, making the bells on the handle jingle.

Neither of them cared about that.

One of Richard's hands slid up her back, his fingers tantalizingly sending sparks up the bare skin between her shoulder blades, then cupping the back of her head. His fingers tangled with the immaculate curls Ursula had teased from her hair.

Alarm bells went off in Bette's mind. *You only just met him,* she thought. *This is going too fast.*

But then he whispered her name against her lips, and she quit thinking all together.

Richard lifted her up, his arm supporting her back as his lips trailed from hers, down her chin, her neck. She sighed and leaned back, granting him access to the skin her little black dress exposed. He growled and held her tighter. She was deeply aware of every inch of him beneath his immaculate suit—his hard chest muscles; his strong thighs, supporting them both; the growing hardness in his pants that made Bette realize that they had trailed onto dangerous ground.

A sudden flash of light flooded the bookstore as a lone car traversed Main Street. It broke the spell of the kiss and reminded Bette of reality. She stepped away, her breath shaking, then reached around Richard and flicked the lights of the store back on.

"I—I'm sorry," she said.

Richard adjusted his coat and shifted his weight, trying to adjust the other parts of him that were probably just as desperate for satisfaction as Bette was.

"Think nothing of it," Richard said graciously, his voice an octave deeper than it had been before.

"I should..." Bette looked around desperately, trying to think of something she should do other than throw this man on the floor and take him right there. Her eyes landed on her office door at the back of the store. "I should change out of this ridiculous dress," she said. "Stay here; I'll just be a minute."

Richard looked as if he very much wanted Bette to stay in her dress— or perhaps to help her take it off—but he remained by the door as she practically raced to her office.

She closed the door and leaned against it, her heart pounding. This wasn't *her*. This wasn't the way she acted. This is the way beautiful women like Ursula acted. Not Bette. Never Bette.

It was this damn dress. It had to be. She shimmied out of the thing as quickly as possible, then began rummaging around, looking for her old clothes that Aria hid. She found them neatly folded in her second desk drawer. *Classic Aria,* Bette thought, looking at the pile of black cloth where she'd dropped Ursula's dress.

Bette tried to unclasp the sexy new bra, but her hands dropped away, then raised again, running over her own breasts, gasping as she touched her hard nipples. *Just the cold,* she lied to herself. Her cotton panties and serviceable bra were there in the drawer, too, but she couldn't bring herself

to take off the sexy lingerie. Ursula had been right—it made her feel...
different. And she liked it.

Before she could talk herself out of it, Bette threw on her t-shirt over
the black lacy bra and tossed on her pants. She stabbed pencils in her hair
to hold up the messy bun. She didn't bother with her shoes. If Richard
wanted to see her, let him see her as she really was: t-shirt and jeans,
sloppy hair, careless about her appearance.

She padded out of the room, barefoot, her heart in her throat. She felt
just as foolish now, in her old clothes, as she had before, in the hot dress.

Bette moved silently past the cash register, down the aisles of books.
She found him in the travel section, flipping through a guide on Paris. But
his eyes weren't on the book. He shelved it without really paying it any
attention. His fingers trailed along the bookshelf, and his gaze wandered
up, to the ornate art deco carvings in the ceiling. He had a strangely
contented look, one that mirrored Bette's own when she entered the store.
This place was home to her, and it seemed as if Richard had already found
something he loved inside.

When her shadow crossed his, he jumped, surprised, and turned.

Bette smiled at him nervously. That look of loving admiration that he'd
had for the store didn't fade a bit as he looked at her.

CHAPTER FIVE

"I love your store," Richard said, and Bette could feel the sincerity in his voice. "It's so unique."

"It's vintage," Bette said, grinning at him.

"And—how did you put it? Authentic."

Bette loved the way that word sounded from his lips.

A small frown marred Richard's face. "I just can't figure you out," Richard said softly.

Bette's lips quirked up in a half-smile. "What's to figure out?" she said. "What you see is what you get." She lifted her arms a little, as if her body was evidence of who she was.

"What you see is *never* what you get," Richard said, moving closer to her. "That's true of this building—there are secrets in these walls, a history we'll never know—but it's also true of people. Which Bette is real? The one in the sexy black dress who kissed me in the dark, or this one, in a t-shirt and jeans? The only the thing the same about you is your Bette Davis eyes."

That wasn't quite true—Bette still had on the sexy lingerie, reminding her of who she could be—but he didn't know that.

"Maybe...maybe sometimes it's better to not know," Bette said, her voice dropping an octave. "Maybe there's something to that whole 'strangers in the night,' sort of thing."

Richard looked behind him, but there were no visible windows from this aisle. "It is night," he said. "But the lights are on now."

Bette bit her lips. "So? We're in the travel section," she said. "See?" She reached past him and pulled off a tourist guide to Las Vegas. "What happens here, stays here," she said, a devilish smile creeping up her lips.

"Is that so?" Richard asked, taking a step closer.

Bette nodded, her heart racing. She had never done this sort of thing before, but...if this is playing with fire, she wasn't sure she'd mind getting burned.

Richard came even closer, close enough for her to feel his warmth. "It's warm in Vegas," she muttered, tugging his heavy woolen suit jacket off his shoulders.

"Very warm," Richard muttered, sliding his necktie down.

"Downright hot." Bette started to slowly unbutton his shirt. With a guttural growl, Richard stepped back, ripped his shirt off, and threw it on the ground next to his coat.

Bette took a moment to admire the hard outline of his pecs. This was no random real estate investor her father had discovered—this man was chiseled from granite. She reached out to touch his bare skin and noticed her hand was slightly trembling. She pressed her palm over his chest, leaning into him slightly.

She lifted her eyes to his. He was watching her carefully, as if he was a beast and she was his prey.

Bette's hand slipped down his chest, lingering on the line of hair that led from his ripped abdomen down to his belt...past his belt. Her hand slipped into his pants. She met his eyes fully, not looking away. *She* would be the beast. Just this once.

Her fingers wrapped around the hard length of him. He sucked in his breath, but he didn't tear his intense gaze away from hers. She let just her fingertips trace up and down his shaft, enjoying the way it made him tense up. But there was hardly room to do more.

Richard dropped his head to her neck, kissing turning to nibbling, a groan fluttering from his lips down the skin of her throat. Her fingers tightened around him, and he grabbed her back, clutching her. His hands flattened, roaming over her body, moving from her back to her waist, under her shirt, up, up, cupping her breasts. He teased her nipples with his thumbs, and it was her groaning now, her pressing against him.

Bette stepped back, pulling her t-shirt up over her head.

Richard stared at her, his eyes widening at the lacy black bra. Bette was deeply, deeply glad that she hadn't changed out of it when she'd changed her clothes.

"I told you so," he said, his voice husky. "I certainly wasn't seeing all of you before."

"You're still not," Bette whispered, but she wasn't sure if he heard her.

She unbuttoned her pants, then waited until he unbuttoned his. They moved in rhythm—shimmying her jeans down over her hips as he loosened his belt and let his pants drop. She slipped out of her ballet flats, and he kicked off his shoes. Their clothes piled up at their feet, creating a little nest between travel books and photography how-to.

"You're—" But whatever she was, Richard didn't have the words for it. He could just stare at the little lace nothings covering the parts of her that no one had ever seen, not like this, not in the middle of her bookstore, with the lights blazingly on. She should feel ashamed, but instead, all she felt was *need*.

"Do you have—?" she asked.

Richard nodded, tossing his drawers in the pile of clothes, and then rooting around in his pants, producing a condom. He ripped open the foil, but Bette took it from his hands.

"Let me," she said. She wore only the lacy black bra and panties, but they were her armor, giving her the mask she needed to pretend to be someone else, someone brave enough to do this.

She placed the condom on the tip of his penis, then used her mouth to slide it over his shaft. He groaned aloud, his fingers convulsing in her hair. Without taking her lips from him, Bette reached up, yanking out the pencils that held her hair up. It tumbled around her shoulders, and Richard fisted it, his fingers telling her of the same aching need he felt.

Bette withdrew slowly, then quickly slid her mouth back around him, all the way to the hilt, her tongue flicking up and down the long, hard expanse of him. She pulled back again, but before she could repeat the motion, Richard stepped back.

"Not like this," he said. "I want to feel more of you than this."

He knelt down in front of her, staring into her eyes. The two of them, kneeling together in a hidden aisle of her bookstore.

She would never look at the travel section the same way again.

"This is okay with you?" he asked, brushing a stray lock of hair away from her face.

She nodded. "Yes," she said. "I want this. All of this."

He bent down over her, dropping heated kisses along her neck. As he came closer to her breasts, his mouth became more urgent, hotter, wetter. He slipped the bra straps off her shoulders, pushing the flimsy cups of the bra down and flicking his tongue over her nipple. Bette gasped, arching back to give him more access to her breasts. His strong arms held her against him, almost lifting her up off her knees as he buried his face in her chest, licking and nibbling at the sensitive skin.

One arm still held her as she arched back, her hair swinging, her breath gasping. His other arm slipped lower, lower. His hands cupped her butt, caressing the soft curve, but then his fingers trailed over the top of her lace panties, skimming between the waistband and her skin. She could barely think; her heart was pounding so hard in her ears.

His hand slid down the front of her panties. She could feel the material straining against her skin to accommodate his hand.

"You're so wet," he said, slipping one finger against her clit. He toyed with it gently, barely touching, then the pressure intensified, and his finger slid lower, deeper, lingering at the edge and then thrusting inside of her.

Bette moaned, the muscles in her stomach quivering with anticipation. Richard's thumb circled her clit, rubbing slowly at first, then harder, faster. A second finger joined the first, thrusting inside her. Richard's left arm held Bette up as she arched against him. His mouth claimed her nipple, biting and sucking as his thumb rubbed her harder and harder. Bette shivered, moan after moan escaping her lips. She could feel her body tightening around his fingers. It was so good, so hot, so right.

Almost...almost...*almost*...

"Not yet," Richard whispered, withdrawing his hand. He lowered her gently to the nest of clothes on the floor, pulling her panties off and then nudging her legs apart with his knees. He cursed appreciatively. "I am so glad the lights are on," he growled as he positioned his thick shaft against her entrance. "I want to see every moment of this."

"Oh, god, please," Bette moaned, lifting her hips up to meet him.

A cocksure grin smeared across his face. "You want this?" he asked, his voice deep.

"Yes, yes!" she cried.

He inched closer, just the tip of him inside her. She squirmed, trying to get more, but he wouldn't give it to her, not yet. He leaned over her, propping his muscular body up with his left hand while he trailed his right hand—fingers still slick with her essence—up and down her body, over her too-hard nipples, down her side, gripping her hip.

He met her eyes, and she knew—*this is it.*

Without breaking eye contact, Richard pushed against the entrance of her, sliding inside, moaning as he thrust all the way to the hilt. He was so big, but her body adjusted to his, clutching at the long length of him, shuddering in delight.

"Are you—?" he stared to ask, concern on his face, but she clenched around him and thrust her hips up, confirming that she was far, far more than okay. His eyes grew hooded, full of lust and desire, and he pulled back, then slammed in her again, hard, forcing a cry of pleasure from her lips.

The pleasure mounted inside her as he thrust again and again, both hands on her hips, pulling her up into him. The agonizingly sweet tension built stronger and stronger inside of her, and she could feel herself tightening around the hard length of him. He was driving her to the brink, his thrusts so hard that she couldn't think, she could only feel, and what she felt was so hot, so passionate, more than she'd ever felt ever before...

He slowed. "No," she gasped. "More."

He grinned wickedly, letting go of her hips. On hand went to her breast, teasing her, but the other dropped lower. Her body clenched as she felt his thumb rub against her clit, softly—but it was already so aching with need, with desire. She cried out as he began thrusting again, timing each one with more immaculate pressure against her clit, creating a perfect rhythm of pleasure that built inside her like a tsunami—rising, rising, threatened to overcome her, to drown her in bliss—

With a cry, she came apart in his arms. A moment later, he climaxed, too, his body jerking with relief. He collapsed beside her in their little love nest, tucking her safely in his arms as they both stared up at the books that would keep their secrets.

*B*ette would have liked nothing more than for the world to stop right that instant. But despite their pile of clothes, the wood beneath them was hard, and a button of Richard's suit jacket kept digging into her side. Her sweat was cooling on her body now, leaving goose bumps on her skin. Sighing, Bette rolled out of Richard's embrace. He made a small noise of protest, then a louder one as Bette threw her t-shirt on. Even so, the languid smile didn't melt off his face.

"You look rather pleased with yourself," Bette said, nudging him with her knee. Her jeans were under his bare bottom, and she wasn't sure she needed them back so desperately.

"Today has been rather...eventful," he said.

Bette cocked an eyebrow. "Eventful?"

Richard closed his eyes. "Eventful. And productive."

Bette pushed him playfully with both her hands. "Productive?!" she said. "That's what you call this?"

"No, no," Richard said, laughing. He sat up, but purposefully kept Bette's pants away from her reach. "You were the eventful part of this. The productive part was this morning, with your father."

"That sounds *very* dirty," Bette said, smiling.

"Not like that! With the real estate meeting this morning!" Richard passed a hand over his face. "Sorry—I have issues turning off from work."

"You didn't have those issues an hour ago."

"No." Richard's smile was wicked. "No, I did not."

Bette knew she should get up—she shouldn't get attached, not here, not now, not like this. But she couldn't resist. She snuggled down against the warm embrace of Richard's arm. "So what was this all important real estate meeting that was so 'productive' and possibly 'eventful?'"

"I had been discussing the possibility of remodeling some of the old buildings here in Fairhaven," Richard said. "Your father seemed to think the locals wouldn't like it, but I have a feeling they won't mind."

Bette snorted with laughter. "So is that what this is? You were just seducing the locals so you could come in with your fancy development plans?"

"You seduced me!" Richard said. His voice grew serious, though, as he stared up at the ornately carved ceiling of the store. "But you've made it clear that the people here care about class and tradition. They don't want a boring-same-thing-you-can-get-anywhere type of hotel, and that's not what I'd provide for them."

At that word—*hotel*—a cold feeling washed over Bette. She sat up fully, leaning away, but Richard didn't seem to notice her shift in mood.

"I'm going to take the entire block. Keep the facades, but gut the interiors. Turn them into a truly boutique hotel, one that captures the essence of Fairhaven."

"Richard *Dickson*," Bette said, biting out the words.

"Yes?" Richard said.

"Your last name is *Dickson*."

"Yes." He sat up too, finally noting Bette's sudden stiffness and angry. "Didn't you know?"

"Richard Dickson who keeps trying to buy my store out from under me."

Richard put up both his hands defensively. "I feel like there's something going on here I don't know about."

Oh, she was such a freaking idiot. How could she have done this? How could she *not* have known her father would side with the businessman with deep pockets and try to trick her into liking the Dickson Hotel Corporation? How could she have *slept* with this tool who wanted nothing more than to *gut* her precious bookstore?

"How could you?" she screeched, jumping up. "How could you possibly want to change Happily Ever After? If you think for one damn moment I'm going to sell this place to you, you're a bigger idiot than I am for thinking you were a decent guy!"

She leapt up, grabbing his suit jacket and throwing it in his face. "Get out!" she screamed.

"What the hell just happened?" Richard said, standing and clumsily stepping into his rumpled pants. "Why are you so damn mad? I'm trying to *help* your town."

"By killing its soul!" Bette shouted. "Get out!"

Richard bent down to pick up the rest of his clothes, but he kept his eyes on Bette, as if worried that she'd attack him like a vicious, rabid animal at any moment. "I wasn't trying to deceive you," he said slowly. "I asked your father for a chance to meet you in person, to figure out why you were resisting our offers."

"I should have resisted more than your damn offers," she growled.

"I'm trying to make this place *better,*" Richard said, frustration rising in his voice. "I have *no idea* why you're flipping out. Look at this place! It's falling apart! At least let me save what I can."

Bette backed up into the bookshelf. The worst part was that she could almost see the store through his eyes. It was falling apart. After...*after*... when they'd both been naked on the floor, staring at the ceiling, had he only see the dust and the cracks in the wood? Had he not seen it through Bette's eyes, had he not seen the beauty of what this place had been, what it could be again?

Her fingers reached behind her, feeling the spines of the beautiful books stored on the shelf. How *dare* he presume this store was worthless? That was like saying *she* was worthless, her dreams, her hopes.

She ripped off the closest book and threw it at him.

Richard ducked—barely. "What are you—?" he started as a Fodor's guide to France smacked him in the chest.

"Get out!" she yelled. "This store is *not* for sale, and you'll never get it from me. I will *never* let you destroy it!"

"I'm not trying to—" It was a Lonely Planet guide to China this time, a hefty volume. It landed against him and then thudded to the floor.

Richard retreated. He mumbled something else, but it was lost in Bette's barrage of more books—she threw Portugal at him, and South Africa, Australia and Japan before the bells jingled in the door, signaling that he was gone.

Bette stood there, panting, her heart racing. She wore nothing more than her old t-shirt and still held a copy of *Escape...to Paris!* in her hands. She sank to her knees, staring at the rubble of the books scattered across the floor, and the rubble of her life in the clothes scattered among them.

CHAPTER SEVEN

She didn't bother going home.

Outside those doors was Richard. Not literally—he was long gone—but he was somewhere out there and definitely not here, and so she would remain here. She slept on a cot in her office, then dressed the next morning in her same jeans and a store t-shirt she swiped from the shelves.

She had woken up at four in the morning. There was no reason for it— she was exhausted—but she had still awoken. So she dedicated her time into thoroughly organizing her office, then tackling the dust in the ceiling and along the tops of the bookshelves. She was tempted to use Ursula's black dress as rags, but settled for paper towels as she doused every nook and cranny with lemon oil.

"Bette?" Aria's quiet voice carried throughout the silent store.

She stopped her vigorous scrubbing. "Up here!" she called.

Aria approached warily. "Bette?" she asked again. "What's wrong?"

"Nothing's wrong. Why would anything be wrong? Everything's fine."

"Okay, now I know something's wrong," Aria said.

Bette sighed and stared at the dirty paper towel in her hand. The worst part was that Richard had been right. She *couldn't* keep this up. She couldn't save the store. It was falling apart around her.

"Did you know," she said imperiously from her perch atop the bookcase, "that the man my father set me up with last night was Richard *Dickson?*"

It took Aria a moment, then she gasped. "Of the Dickson Hotel Corporation?"

"None other," Bette said. She leaned down. "His name is Richard Dickson, Aria. Richard Dickson. His name is *literally* Dick Dickson. Dick, son of Dick. That's who I went on a date with. A dick, squared."

"Get down here so I can hug you," Aria demanded.

Bette threw her paper towels down. "I can't believe I was so stupid," she muttered, stepping down off the shelf and into her friend's arms.

"You weren't stupid," Aria said into her hair. "Your father set you up."

Bette choked back a sob-laugh. If only she knew just how dumb Bette had been.

"Well, it's over now," she said. "You can just reject whatever new offer he has this time, and he'll eventually take the hint."

Somehow, Bette didn't think it'd be that easy.

"He didn't..." Aria paused. "He didn't try to hurt you, did he?" Her eyes searched Bette's, concern etched on her face.

Bette shook her head. He *had* hurt her, but not intentionally, not the way Aria thought.

"Listen," Aria said. "Whatever happened last night has you rattled. Go home. Take a shower. Take a nap. Quit thinking about it for awhile. I've got the store."

Every instinct in Bette told her to reject this idea. It felt too much like defeat. The store was her life, the one thing she fought for, and abandoning it now was like abandoning a child.

But her heart told her she needed time to heal. What was supposed to be an easy, freeing encounter had left her feeling dirty and sad.

"Are you sure?" she asked quietly.

"Positive," Aria said. "Go. I got this."

Bette impulsively hugged her friend. "You're the best."

"I totes expect a raise for this." She smiled mischievously.

"I'll add it to the tab of all the other things I owe you," Bette said, already practically running back to the office to grab her things. "I may have to offer you my first born instead of cash, that's cool right?"

"I don't want no babies!" Aria called as Bette dashed from the office to the front door of the store. "Diamonds only! Maybe a trust fund. Ooh, or gold bricks! Also, I'd take you paying off my college loans."

The door jangled as Bette waved goodbye to her friend.

*B*ette's apartment was nothing like Happily Ever After. The bookstore was elegant and old. Her apartment—located just off the highway and hidden by a large privacy fence that didn't quite block out the noise but totally blocked out the view—was only about a decade old or so. Just old enough for the paint to lose its gleam and the cheap carpet to start looking tired, but not anywhere near old enough to have a history. Not like Happily Ever After.

If she could have anything, Bette would love a home that mirrored the store. She would love to feel as comfortable enclosed within the warm wood of Happily Ever After in the place where she lived. Instead, her apartment was little more than a bed and a place to store her t-shirts.

"I'm such a freak," Bette muttered, dropping her purse on the floor.

Who loved the place where they work more than their own home? It wasn't supposed to be like this. She was supposed to love coming home. She was supposed to feel safe at home. She was supposed to feel loved.

This place was beyond impersonal. Anyone could live here. The walls were white. The posters on the wall—a print of Van Gogh's *Starry Night* and a photograph of the beach Aria had given her for Christmas last year —could have belonged to anyone. There weren't even any dirty dishes in the kitchen—just empty take-out containers and plastic forks in the trash.

This apartment was as devoid as Bette's life. The only thing she had going for her was the bookstore, and it was falling apart around her.

Bette stripped her clothes off, letting them drop on the beige carpet without worrying about where they fell. It wasn't like Richard—it wasn't like *anyone* was going to come here and see her mess.

She went straight to the bathroom, turning the shower on and watching as the steam fogged over the glass doors. When Bette was first apartment hunting, she remembered being embarrassed by the clear glass doors of the shower. It had seemed so...exposed. But no one had ever been in her apartment, much less her bathroom, other than Aria, a few college friends, and her dad. And it wasn't like any of them would shower with her (or that she would want them to).

Not like Richard...

Bette stepped into the shower, turning her face to the pulsing stream of water and letting the warmth wash over her. She wouldn't think of him. She wouldn't think of the way he made sparks sizzle in her stomach. She wouldn't think of how carefree she'd felt—for the first time in months, in *years*. She had let herself quit being Bette-the-bookstore-owner around

Richard, and instead, she had just been Bette. Bette, with Bette Davis eyes. Bette, with sexy lingerie. Just...herself.

And look where being herself had gotten her. Hurt and alone. Again.

Before...before yesterday, she had been just as alone as she was now. Her apartment had been as empty. Her store had been as broken.

So what was different now?

Now...now she'd had a brief, incandescent taste of how things could be different. She'd felt fire in the hollow places inside of her, filling her up and igniting her soul.

That dumbass who said it was better to have loved and lost had clearly never been laid as good as she had last night. Because having that—and suddenly *not* having that—was killing her.

But it wasn't just about the sex. No...if it had truly been a one-night stand, Bette could live with herself right now. Even though she'd only just met Richard, he had seemed...connected to her. He seemed to love the store as much as she had, and he seemed to *get* what she loved about it.

"I've got serious issues," Bette muttered, grabbing the soap and forcing herself to quit wallowing. She felt a connection to someone because he liked her *store?* What the hell was wrong with her?

What was wrong with her was that she hadn't had enough.

As the soap dripped down her soaking skin, Bette closed her eyes, remembering not Richard, but the way he made her feel. The way her body had responded to his.

Her hands slid over her soapy breasts, her nipples taut despite the warm water. The soap dropped from her fingers, and Bette turned in the water, letting it cascade over her, rinsing away not just the bubbles but also her thoughts.

She leaned against the cheap tiles of her shower, the water hitting her navel and sending warmth down her legs. Her breasts prickled in goose bumps despite the steam as she let her hands glide over her body, mirroring the way Richard's hands had touched her. Here, on her neck, his fingers barely touching the hollow space behind her collar bone. Over the curve of her breasts, trailing down between them, across her stomach, playing around her belly button.

And then lower.

Bette let her fingers play across the mound at the vertex of her legs, then dip into the warm center. She stroked the way Richard had stroked, playfully dancing along the edges of her core and then plunging inside, relishing the way her body tightened deliciously around her finger. She withdrew, sliding across her clitoris, a moan escaping her lips.

The water from the shower started to cool, but Bette just found it more enticing. It reminded her of the way her sweating skin cooled while she was bare and in Richard's arms, naked and exposed in the wide expanse of the store. Of the way he was so insatiable...of the way *she* was so insatiable...

Her fingers quickened their play, sliding over her clit, the beautiful tension coiling inside her, tighter and tighter.

Unbidden, an image of Richard rose in her mind, naked and hot, standing over her, positioning himself at her entrance. Her fingers copied her memory, gently pressing into her center and then plunging inside, again and again, sliding up against her clit, becoming slick not with the water from the cool shower but with her own desire, in and out, faster and faster, the intensity burning her up alive until—

—Release.

Bette's knees shook, but only for a moment. The memory was nice—the memory was great—but it wasn't the same.

CHAPTER EIGHT

After the shower, Bette wrapped herself in her biggest, fluffiest towel and went straight to bed. Good sheets and good towels were the one luxury she afforded herself. Her clothes were crap; she hadn't bought anything more than a t-shirt since college. Her apartment was crap, one of the cheapest places in Fairhaven that wasn't rat-infested. Her car was worse, nearly as old as she was.

But her towels were fluffy and her sheets were silky.

It was her mother's fault. Growing up on two teacher salaries hadn't afforded Bette's family many luxuries. Their most extravagant vacation had been a driving trip for a one-day pass to Disneyland when she had been ten. Their mother was able to make a week's salary feed the whole family for a month. So what if sometimes they didn't have meat and never had soda?

Bette had never been embarrassed by her family's lack of means growing up, not even when she had felt the pressure to get a scholarship for college or when she had to wear hand-me-down prom dresses and graduation robes. Clothes never really mattered that much to her, and she had always been proud of her grades.

She hadn't felt ashamed until she was a freshman in the scholar's dorm. Until she realized that not a single one of her tiny, scratchy towels matched, and she only had one set of sheets for her bed. Her roommate had been nice, but she couldn't avoid the pity in her eyes.

Bette could only afford to go home for the major vacation days—Christmas break and spring break. All the other long weekends off, she had stayed on campus while her roommate drove off, either to visit her parents in the Hills or to go on some weekend trip with her boyfriend.

One day while her roomie was away, Bette had crossed to her side of the room. A set of clean, fluffy, matching towels rested on the foot of her roommate's immaculately made bed. On impulse, Bette had sniffed the freshly-laundered towels, relishing in the feel of them on her skin. Without thinking, she'd take a shower, wrapping herself in the luxurious cotton. She slid between her roommate sheets, feeling the soft cloth with her bare skin and promising to herself that if she had nothing else, she would have this.

For Christmas that year, all Bette asked for was towels and sheets. Her mother had laughed at her—but had given her a beautiful sage green set.

"We have to have one thing that's just ours," she'd said. "One thing that makes us special."

When her mother had died just a few months later, and Bette and her father had been cleaning out her mother's belongings from the house, she found a stack of fancy towels and sheets folded neatly and placed into an oversized gift bag. There had been no label on the bag, but Bette had known: her mother had gotten these in advance for her birthday.

And at the bottom of the bag had been a copy of Dr. Seuss's *Oh, the Places You'll Go!* The little sticker over the barcode on the back signaled that the book had been purchased from Happily Ever After.

Happily Ever After was Bette and her mother's special spot. Her father never liked reading, but her mother cherished words the way some people cherished jewels. She had instilled a lifelong love for books in Bette, from the very first copy of *Where the Wild Things Are* to this last book her mother had purchased for her.

Fairhaven Elementary School was only five blocks west of Happily Ever After. Bette begged her parents for a month to be allowed to walk to the bookstore and wait for her parents to pick her up there rather than wait for them at the school. The bookstore owner—a kind old lady named Linda—had promised it was okay. She set up a little desk, a remnant from when the school had remodeled, in her office, and let Bette read as many books as she wanted, as long as she'd write recommendations on placards for people to see which books she thought kids would like.

Linda always said that Bette sold more books than she did. Her mother said that she had impeccable taste. Her father said maybe the bookstore should start paying her for child labor.

As Bette grew older, her fascination with the store didn't end. Other kids went to parties in the woods with beer and bonfires; Bette went to the bookstore. Linda couldn't afford an employee—the bookstore was struggling even more than it was now back then—but Bette didn't care. She volunteered as much as she could, happily stocking books and talking with customers. People thought Linda was her grandmother, and Bette's mother played the connection up, calling Linda her "second mom."

When Bette left for college with the goal of an MBA, it was with the intention of taking over Happily Ever After after Linda passed it on to her. Even though she had a full ride, including a meal plan and a dorm, Bette worked as much as the kids without a scholarship or trust fund, moving from waitress to manager at a diner, then netting a sales job at Barnes and Noble. While she loved being around books, she missed the hominess of Happily Ever After, the carefully selected stock, and, most of all, Linda behind the register and her mom jangling through the door juggling cups of coffee and tea for them all.

When her mother died before she graduated, Bette started to question if she could make this dream come true. She had almost ten thousand saved, but ten thousand couldn't buy a bookstore. Ten thousand couldn't even cover all her mother's funeral expenses.

At Bette's graduation, she'd invited Linda to take her mother's seat in the audience, right beside her dad. She had posed for pictures and smiled brightly and pretended that there wasn't a mom-shaped place missing beside her.

And she quietly started to tell herself that everything she'd wanted in life—a quiet bookstore filled with the people she loved—was far more impossible than fluffy towel sets.

It was tragedy that changed her life again. Linda passed away soon after Bette's graduation, and she left Bette everything. The store, the stock, the customer database.

And the bills.

It'd been a struggle, but Bette wouldn't let the store go. It represented not just everything she loved, but everyone.

Bette woke up with a start. She hadn't meant to fall asleep after her shower, and she still felt groggy. The doorbell rang again.

"Shit, shit, shit," she said, leaping out of bed and grabbing a summer dress from her closet and throwing a wrap around her shoulders so no one could tell she wasn't wearing a bra. "Coming!" she shouted in the direction of her front door.

The doorbell rang again.

"Hold on!" Bette screamed. She kicked her dirty clothes—strewn over the living room floor—under the couch and yanked the door open.

The only people who had ever come to her apartment were Aria and her dad. And the UPS guy. So there was no real reason for Bette to have expected Richard to be there.

Still, she was disappointed that he wasn't.

"Come on in, Dad," she said, still holding the wrap over her chest.

"Why is your hair wet?" Tom asked as he stepped inside.

"I took a shower. Why are you here?" she asked grumpily.

Her father took a seat on the edge of the couch, not relaxing into the cushions. When he looked up at her, she recognized the guilty look in his face.

"I dropped by the store to see how things went last night," he started. "Aria said you'd be here. I figured if you were taking a day off work, something bad must have happened."

"You set me up."

Tom opened his mouth, but Bette cut him off.

"No, I mean you set me up. Not on a date. To be a fool."

"I didn't mean to!" Tom protested. "Mr. Dickson said he just wanted to meet you. I figured if the two of you could talk face-to-face, you'd be able to reach an agreement that'd be lucrative for both of you..." His voice trailed off as he finally noticed Bette's scowl. "What happened?" he asked bluntly. "That asshole didn't hurt you did he?" He moved to stand back up. "If he touched my baby girl, I'm going to—"

Bette raised her hands, stopping him. "He didn't tell me until the date was over who he even was, and he acted like this was all a done deal," Bette said.

Tom's face showed his confusion. "But the point of the dinner was, you know, to talk about the deal. I knew you wouldn't agree to it if I told you that, but it was *his* idea to try to talk to you one-on-one. About the deal. What *did* you talk about?"

"Just..." Bette's voice trailed off. "Architecture."

"Well, that's not surprising, I guess." Tom leaned back into the couch. "Considering it's in his blood and all."

"What?" Bette asked.

"Yeah, his grandfather is that same guy who built the store. Um, what's-his-name...Oarman?"

"Hoorton," Bette said softly. "George Hoorton."

"Him. That's why he wants the store."

"To gut his grandfather's work?!"

Tom shook his head. "I didn't get the impression that was the plan, but I don't know any more. There seems to be a lot about Richard Dickson I got wrong. He seemed like a decent guy, but if he just yanked your chain all night..."

"No, it was just that..." Bette's voice trailed off. "We had a nice talk. But not about the store. And what he thinks about plans for the store... don't exactly match my plans."

Tom leaned forward. "Bette," he said seriously. "You do realize that something has to change, right? That your plans for the store, whatever they may be, have to include some sort of change. You can't continue the way you are."

"I don't want to talk about it." She didn't meet her father's eyes.

"Bette, the offer the Dickson Hotel Corporation has presented...it's fair. More than fair. They could fully restore that building, and you'd have more than enough money to move the store to a different location, one that wasn't falling apart at the seams."

"I do *not* want to talk about it!" Bette said, standing up. The store was more than just the books and the people. It was the worn spot on the floor where the children's group met, it was the jingle bells on the door that clattered against the wood and glass, it was the smell of the lemon oil and the books and even the dust.

"Bette—"

"Why are you here?" Bette asked, rounding on her father. "Why did you come here today? You set me up on a blind date with an asshole and only bothered to tell me the truth about him after it crashed and burned. In case you didn't notice, I really don't need your opinion. Buildings exist for more than just to buy and sell them, Dad."

Tom stood up, abashed.

"Just...just go," Bette said, sighing. The fight left her. She was so exhausted. So tired of...everything. Of existing. Of caring.

Tom attempted a hug, but it was awkward at best.

As soon as the door closed behind him, Bette wrapped her arms around her chest. Was it true that Richard Dickson was related to the architect who made her store? And if so, why was he so cavalier about it?

She went straight to her table and pulled out her rusty old laptop. After waiting ten years for it to boot, Bette brought up Google and searched for Richard's history. She'd never done this before, but maybe she should have. Wikipedia started her on a rabbit trail of his family's history. Richard's grandfather—who apparently had a heavy hand in raising Richard and his four brothers and sister in the summers for most of their lives—was indeed the same architect who designed Happily Ever After.

A picture popped up of Richard. He may have been eight or so, standing in the center of wooden beams and sawdust, a huge grin across his face with George Hoorton standing behind him, beaming.

Bette was looking at the bones of her store. Her beloved store.

And Richard was standing right in the center of it.

The image was linked to a brief biographical article of the hotel mogul. "The happiest I have ever been in my life," he said in a pull quote highlighted in the first page, "was working with my grandfather on restoring the last building he designed one summer when I was a kid." The building itself was obviously built before Richard had been born, but it had been refinished and remodeled, stripped down and lovingly put back together. Linda must have taken over the store shortly after this.

He was here, Bette thought, her mind wandering from the article. Richard Dickson had been right here, in Fairhaven, when she was just a kid and so was he. They may have met. They may have played together at the park.

He had spent a summer helping his grandfather fix up the bookstore. His grandfather's greatest accomplishment may have been the huge hotels, museum, and buildings in New York, but his heart had belonged here. He was proudest of Happily Ever After.

And Richard had been a part of it.

So why, Bette wondered, *did he want to destroy it?*

CHAPTER TEN

Bette was barely thinking as she got in her car and drove to the address her father had texted her—the address where Richard Dickson had set up a temporary office.

Although to be fair, she was thinking enough to bother getting dressed up. The skirt she wore was a modest knee-length, but the black lace she wore under it was anything but modest. *It's only because it was the first thing I found,* she lied to herself.

Bette blared the music in her car's radio, but quickly turned it off. She wanted to drum out her thoughts, but she needed them.

She needed to decide what to do.

The only thing Bette wanted was to hold the store close to her heart. To protect it the way it had protected her—through her childhood, through her mother's death.

Through the loneliness. Through the walls she built up around herself, stronger than the old oiled wood.

Would selling it be so bad? Yes. But would selling to someone who loved the way the store was, from the bones up, who cared about the architect and the architecture...who was like Richard had seemed to be... would selling then be so bad?

Maybe.

But maybe not.

She had to see more of his plans. She had to know, exactly, what the fate of Happily Ever After would be if she sold.

She had to know what Richard would do to it if she sold.

What he would do to her and to thing most precious to her.

Before she had met him, he had been a faceless monster to her. A beast. But now...maybe he wasn't really as bad as she'd thought. Maybe there was still hope, if only she could reach him.

Richard's office was located past the Main Street part of town, at the halfway point between the textile factory at the edge of the county and the hospital. A few offices lined the four-lane street in a strip-mall type fashion, and, after pulling into the parking lot of the closest one, it only took a few minutes for Bette to locate Richard's office. Through the big glass windows of the bricked building, she could see a pretty blonde woman typing, her desk positioned in front of another door leading deeper into the office.

Bette's hands gripped the steering wheel. Why was this such a big deal? Why was she even here? She knew what Richard wanted to do with the bookstore. Tear it down and make a hotel. That was his deal. He'd been upfront about that from the start. There was no reason to think that one careless night would have changed his mind and made him reconsider tearing down Happily Ever After.

...And it wasn't like he wasn't up front about everything else, either. He hadn't known that Bette's father had been less than forthright with her. He hadn't lied.

Just like the bills didn't lie. Just like the maintenance the building needed didn't lie.

Just like the fact that she was going to lose Happily Ever After anyway wasn't a lie.

Bette unraveled her fingers from the steering wheel. Just talk. That's all she wanted to do. She just wanted to talk to him.

She was out the car and pushing open the glass door before she could talk herself out of it. The blonde receptionist looked up, a smile already plastered on her face. Bette glanced down at the glass placard etched with the woman's name: Zelda Goethe. An old name for such a young woman.

"May I help you?" Zelda asked politely.

"I'd like to speak to Richard. I mean, Mr. Dickson." Bette glanced at the only other door in the room, a closed wooden office door.

"He's not in right now," Zelda said. She twirled a pen in her hand, then poised it over a pink notepad. "Can I take a message for you?"

"Oh, never mind," Bette said, turning toward the glass door. "It's not a big deal." She had known it was a bad idea to come here in the first place. Talk never changed anything. She could see her fate as clearly as if Zelda had written it out on the pink paper: She would have to sell to this man who she had opened up to in far too personal a way, and Happily Ever After would be hidden beneath a bland, boring hotel, lost to the bulldozers and gone forever.

Maybe she could get a job at B&N.

"You're not Bette, are you?" Zelda called as Bette pushed open the door.

Bette turned around slowly.

Zelda smiled, her grin lighting up her whole face. "He told me if you came to make sure you didn't go," she said. "He wanted to talk to you. Would you like to wait in his office?"

"I—uh..." The glass door closed behind her. "Really?"

Zelda hopped up from her chair and dashed to the office door. "Right this way," she said, still smiling. Bette had never seen anyone so perky.

A stab of jealousy at this beautiful, chipper blonde who worked with Richard pierced Bette's heart, but she forced it down as she entered Richard's office. She had no place to judge others, no place to be jealous, and no reason to dislike this woman who had been nothing but kind to her.

Zelda closed Richard's office door behind Bette.

All her other chaotic thoughts stilled. *She was in his office.* This space seemed very personal, very Richard. The furniture was mahogany, and while it all looked really expensive and classy, it was cluttered with blueprints and papers, and there were scuff marks in one corner, as if he spent a lot of time propping his feet up on the desk. Bette ran her fingers over the marks, imaging how much Richard must recline in his chair in order for the marks to already mar the desk. He can't have been in this office for very long—just while he was negotiating the deals to buy the land for his new hotel—but he had already left his mark.

It didn't take long for Richard to leave his mark.

Bette closed her eyes and breathed in deeply, relishing the smell of wood oil, the same smell that reminded her of Happily Ever After. Richard was George Hoorton's grandson, and it seemed as if his legacy resided in him. There were awards for design and architecture littering the bookshelf behind the desk, and photographs of buildings Richard had worked on lined the walls.

Richard clearly loved buildings the same way other people loved art... the same way Bette loved the art deco details of her store. He cared about them in a way that Bette could understand.

If only she could understand *him*.

Bette collapsed into the chair—not the one positioned opposite the desk, but the chair Richard must sit in. She leaned back, propping her feet up where he did. Huh. Not too bad. Actually kind of comfortable.

Bette's arm dropped down, and her fingertips touched paper. She straightened in her chair and looked down. Richard's trashcan was overflowing with torn up blueprints. She wouldn't have cared, but then she saw the words written across the top: *Happily Ever After site redesign.*

Bette pulled out the oversized paper and smoothed it down on the desk. She pulled more of the torn up pages from the trashcan, fitting the three pieces together.

Her heart broke.

Connecting the lines of the torn drawings wasn't so hard. Richard had planned to tear down everything but the front facade, turning her beloved local bookstore into nothing more than a lobby for his overpriced hotel. Many of the windows were gone, replaced with larger and gaudier glass that had none of the charm of the old panes.

And the shelves. All of them, gutted and gone.

Bette gripped the edges of the papers. It hurt more, seeing this plan for Happily Ever After's destruction. Knowing it was imminent, and she didn't really have the power—or the cash—to prevent it from happening.

Before, she had felt rage—at Richard, mostly, but also at herself, for failing the thing she loved most. Now she felt only sorrow and regret.

The office door opened almost silently. Through tear-bleary eyes, Bette looked up as Richard entered the room. He took one look at her, then turned back around.

"Zel, take the rest of the day off, okay?" he said to his receptionist. Then he stepped into the office, closing the door behind him.

"I didn't want you to see those," he said. He carefully pulled Bette's fingers from the torn up pages of the blueprint then swept the papers back into the trashcan.

Bette bit out a sardonic, bitter laugh. "I didn't want you to see this," she said, swiping the back of her hand against her eyes to hide the tears lingering on her lashes.

"I made these plans when I was in New York. When I was focused on the bottom line. Before I saw the old store, and remembered what Granddad was like when he built it." He paused, and when she wouldn't look at him, he turned her chin gently toward him. "Before I met you."

"And now?" she whispered.

Richard turned to the desk, shuffling the blueprints and bringing up one that looked fairly new.

"I've moved the lobby over to the east side," Richard said, pointing to the lines. "And I'm keeping the corner intact. I figured that most hotels have gift shops, right? Well, this one will have a bookshop."

"You're keeping Happily Ever After?" Bette asked, barely daring to hope that it was true.

Richard nodded. "Let me show you."

He sat down at his desk chair—the same chair Bette had been reclining in earlier—and booted up a laptop she hadn't noticed buried under the papers before. In moments, he brought up a fully detailed, colored schematic of what his new hotel could be.

"I had been going for a sort of an Empire State look before," Richard said in his soft, melodic voice. "But once I got to Fairhaven, it was clear that wouldn't fit with the style of the town. Granddad was right—art deco is much more appropriate. It fits the setting."

Bette stared with wonder at the building on the computer screen. It had every detail she had told Richard she loved about the architecture of downtown Fairhaven. He played off the structures that already existed, adding details that made the building look as if it was organically grown in the town rather than a computer generated image of something that didn't even exist yet. And what was more—there was her store. He kept it almost entirely the same, only altering the roofline so he could add floors above it, and removing one wall so it opened up into the lobby of the hotel.

"And it will still be a bookstore?" Bette asked.

"It will still be *your* bookstore," Richard said. "I was just in a meeting with my lawyer to ensure that I can offer you a lifelong lease on the bookstore. Of course, it will be a lease instead of a sale, but then the hotel can provide you with all the maintenance that the building needs, and any updates you'd like to make to the store and—"

"Are you serious?" Bette demanded, leaning back. "Are you seriously going to offer all this to me?"

Richard nodded, not breaking his eye contact. "I don't want to take away your store, Bette," he said. "And..." He paused. "I don't want you to leave."

"What do you mean?"

"If I tore down Happily Ever After..." Richard shook his head. "What I mean is, if I keep the store, and you're still working there, then..." He ruffled his hair, a nervous act that made Bette's heart melt. "I plan on being at the hotel for awhile. I want to oversee its construction, and I want to ensure that it's established. Which means I'm going to be here for awhile. In Fairhaven. At the hotel. If Happily Ever After is built into the hotel rather than torn down, then you'll be there too. Right next door to where I'll be."

"Not next door," Bette said. "A part of the same building."

Richard nodded. His eyes drifted up to hers. "I just...if it takes building a hotel around your bookstore to keep you close, that's not such a bad thing, is it?"

Bette found that she didn't have any words to say. She just shook her head, a huge grin spreading across her face.

"And besides, you were right. That bookstore—it's a part of my grand-father's legacy. It'd be ridiculous to make my legacy be something that tears down his. I'd rather be known as the man who added to Granddad's art than destroyed it."

"I think it's beautiful," Bette said, shifting her attention from Richard to the computer schematics.

"I'm changing the whole theme," Richard said. "A book theme for the whole hotel. Maybe a little kitchsy, but I think it'll work."

"A book theme?"

"The lobby will emulate the same designs as Happily Ever After," Richard said. "Every room will have a mini library accessible to the guests. And the top floors will have themed rooms—a Wonderland, an Oz, a Narnia."

Bette laughed. "I want to stay in them all!"

Richard looked at her very seriously. "I hope you do," he said.

"Thank you." The words threatened to choke out of her voice. "I mean it. This is...it's far more than I could ever ask for."

"I'm only doing what I feel is right."

"Thank you," Bette said again. Her eyes glimpsed at the stylized sign on the schematic. Hotel Ever After. It was perfect.

Richard seemed flustered as he closed the laptop and shifted it to the table behind the desk. As he reached past Bette, his hand brushed along her hip. Shivers rippled up her body. She tried to jump out of his way at the same time as he stood up, clearly intending to move in the opposite direction of her, but just crashing into her instead. They stuttered their apologies awkwardly, laughing and flustered.

"I should go," Bette said at the same time as Richard said, "I'll have my lawyers contact your father with the new offer."

"Thanks again," Bette said, turning to leave, her hand lingering on his desk, her fingers rubbing over the familiar scuff marks he'd made on the corner.

Before she could move, he grabbed that hand, sliding his own calloused fingers under hers and wrapping them around her wrist, pulling her back closer to him.

"I'm glad," he said, staring down at their hands, "that we were able to come to an agreement."

"Me too." Bette made no move to pull away from him.

"I hope—" He looked into her eyes.

"Yes?" She wasn't sure if she spoke aloud or not, but she knew he understood the question.

"—That it's not the last...agreement we can arrange."

A sly smile spread across her face. She remembered the way Richard had dismissed Zelda, his secretary, leaving them alone in the office.

"We *are* going to be working rather closely from now on," Bette said.

Richard moved closer to her, the heat from his body radiating into hers. "Very closely, I hope," he said.

"One could almost call it intimately," Bette said, her voice dropping an octave.

"Could one?"

Instead of answering him, she slid her arms around his neck and drew him into her kiss.

CHAPTER TWELVE

Richard hesitated just long enough for Bette to make the first move. She leaned up, claiming his lips as her own. Their touch was electric, and Bette gasped, parting her lips. Richard responded voraciously, deepening the kiss, his hand cupping the back of her head, his body pressing her against the desk. Richard's other hand fell to the desk as well, and he leaned over her. He growled, his arm sliding under her and lifting her onto the desktop. She was dimly aware that the blueprints on the desk were being crinkled, but then she felt Richard's arms sliding down her body, and she could think of nothing else.

Bette was very, very glad she'd bothered to dress nicely for this meeting. Richard's hands slid down her silk blouse, bunching in the flowy skirt. He seemed very, very glad too.

His fingers caught on the straps of her garters under the skirt, and he sucked in a deep breath, raising lust-filled eyes to Bette's smirking face. "I just prefer them," she said.

Richard's eyebrow quirked up. His hands slid lower, lingering on the silk stocking covering her knees, then they slipped under her skirt, his fingers toying with the straps of her garter, sliding up and down, dipping under the top of her silk stockings, dancing higher and higher up toward the lace of her panties. "You put these on for me to find," he said.

It was not a question, but Bette still denied it. "I just prefer them to regular hose," she said, tilting her head up. "They're..."

"Sexier."

"*Nicer.*"

Richard grinned wickedly. "Sexier," he said. "And you know it."

Bette didn't deign to answer.

"And that's why you wore them for me." Richard said. His voice was getting lower.

"And what if I did?" Bette asked.

"Then," Richard said, his hand sliding up Bette skirt, wrapping around her black-lace covered hips, "you deserve a reward."

"A reward?"

"A reward."

He yanked her forward on the desk, her bottom sliding on the blueprints. Her legs spread apart naturally, encasing his torso, and Bette felt Richard's desire through his suit pants. But he made no move to claim her —not like that, not yet. Instead, he pulled her head to his, kissing her breathless, his lips trailing down the side of her jaw, down her neck, lingering over the low-cut silk blouse, his tongue trailing along the top of her breasts while his hands danced along her torso.

"Lean back," he whispered.

Bette looked at him, confused.

"Trust me," he said, pushing her shoulders gently back, supporting her body as she leaned all the way back against the desktop.

He kissed her silk-covered knees, and she jumped in surprise.

"Shh, shh," he said.

But she was fairly sure what he was about to do would do anything but silence her.

His fingers fumbled with the ties at her garters, and Bette reached down to help, but he swatted her hands away. "I like them," he said. His hands pushed her skirt up the rest of the way, and Richard leaned back, appreciating Bette's black lace.

"Perfect," he whispered, and the word filled Bette with warmth. No one had ever looked at her and said that, in that way.

Richard's fingers slid over the top of Bette's black lace panties, just skimming along the edge, his hand brushing the mound beneath. Richard looked into her eyes as he dipped one finger past the hem of her panties, sliding it along the smooth skin he found there.

He bit his lip, and a predatory look filled his eyes.

Bette shivered.

Richard slid Bette's panties to the side, exposing her to his hungry gaze. His touch was gentle though, as he ran one finger along the side of her vagina.

He hissed. "You really want this," he said, his voice barely audible. "You're so wet already."

Bette moaned in anticipation.

His finger traced the edge of her, up, down...in. She was slick with desire, and the feel of her seemed to buzz in Richard like a drug.

He leaned down. "Do you want this?" he asked, the deep rumble of his voice and his warm breath sending shivers deep inside of Bette.

"Do you?" he asked again.

"Yes!" Bette cried. "Oh, yes—please—Richard—"

Richard made a noise deep in his throat, something like a growl and something like desire, and his mouth covered her mound, his tongue delving inside of her, stroking up, a delicious mix of hot and cold. Bette wanted to scream in ecstasy, but all she could do was struggle for breath, gasping for air as his tongue discovered her clitoris, circling it over and over, sucking gently and then stroking up and down, up and down.

Bette's back bucked up, pressing herself against his mouth, her body begging for more when her voice couldn't. Richard responded in kind and with enthusiasm, humming against her clitoris and swirling it with his tongue. Bette's hands balled into fists, her head thrown back against the desk as her desire rose higher and higher, a tight coil of lust twisting deep inside of her. She was panting as he laved her with his tongue, her breaths coming in short bursts, nearer and nearer to release—

And then he pulled away.

"No, no," she gasped. "Please—almost—"

"Almost?" Richard said, and she could hear the smirk in his voice even though she had no strength to lift her head. "Oh, no, my love, we're nowhere near done."

A moment later she heard his pants unzip. She propped herself up on her elbows to watch as his pants dropped to the floor. She could see the massive bulge of him through this boxer briefs.

"Wait," she said, shimmying off the desk.

"Wait?" Richard growled. "My love, I *can't*."

She didn't protest any more, but she stood before him, her skirt falling back to her knees. His eyes were rapt with hers, and she didn't break that contact as she slowly lifted her silk chemise off, letting it flutter to the floor. She did, however, notice the way his Adam's apple bobbed up and down as he watched her slowly unzip her skirt, letting it drop to the floor.

She kept on her black lace and silk stockings. He seemed to rather like them.

She padded across the short distance between them, reaching for his tie and loosening it. When she was too slow, he jerked it from her hands and yanked the knot down, throwing the tie off his neck. She clicked her tongue at his impatience, and slowly started to undo the buttons of his shirt.

With a roar, he ripped at his shirt, and the buttons went flying.

"Richard!" Bette said, gasping in surprise, but he pounced on her, his mouth covering hers, his body stalking her until they bumped into the wall. Richard grabbed Bette by the hips, using the wall to support them as he hoisted her up. She instinctively wrapped her legs around his waist, and he groaned at the feel of her silk stockings against his sweating skin.

She could feel him through his boxer briefs, but then he slipped a hand between them, freeing himself and shoving her lace panties to the side again. He had a condom ready and struggled to put it on, but she took it from him, using her hands to wrap around his shaft and slide the latex over the full length of him. His eyes questioned her again, and she nodded, burrowing her head into his chest as she felt him at the entrance of her. He thrust forward and up, filling her to the core, and she threw her head back, moaning at the sensation of being so perfectly fit with a man.

Her back slid up the slick, glossy paint as he partially withdrew and thrust into her again. She cried out in pleasure, that gasped in surprise as Richard's hand slipped between them, his finger finding her clitoris and gently probing it. She felt herself clench around him, and Richard growled in pleasure, thrusting deeper inside of her while rubbing his thumb against her clit, perfectly timing each thrust with each stroke.

The coil inside of her wound tighter and tighter as she panted for breath. She tried to tell Richard she was close, that she couldn't hold back, but he seemed to know, without words. He stroked her clit harder and faster, thrusting into her with such force that she felt as if she may break. She panted his name, gasping for air, and he threw his head back and thrust even deeper inside of her. Her body clenched around his dick, and spasms of pleasure rippled up from deep within her, sending her entire body into an electric-like ripple of ecstasy. With a triumphant shout, Richard thrust up once more and released himself, pulsing inside of her.

Her legs slipped down his sweaty back, and she could feel him twitch inside of her. He groaned and sagged against her, sandwiching her between himself and the wall. She was grateful; she wasn't sure she could stand on her own.

She let her head fall against his shoulder, her face nuzzling into his neck.

"You were amazing," she whispered, and she relished in the way goose bumps spread up on his skin at her words and her breath so close to him.

"Were?" Richard laughed. "Oh, love, we're just getting started."

CHAPTER THIRTEEN

*B*ette could hardly believe how quickly things had changed. Almost as soon as she signed the paperwork—a lifelong lease on the store for a fraction of the cost of the mortgage she'd been paying—Richard's team had gotten to work on fully restoring the bookstore. Everything had been taken out while all the electricity and plumbing was worked on and updated, and special sealant was applied to the wood. George Hoorton was a genius architect, but all his other buildings were on the east coast, where he didn't have to think about the constant humidity of the Pacific Northwest.

The thing that surprised Bette the most was the way Richard seemed to change, growing happier and happier as work continued. At first she thought it was just that he liked to be busy, but then he pulled her into the store to show her the foundation of the building.

Etched into the concrete was an elegant, old-fashioned signature.

"Granddad," Richard said, and Bette could make out the elegant capital G and H. She was more distracted, however, by the childish scribble beside it, written with a small finger on slightly darker concrete: R.D.

"Me," Richard said. "The summer Granddad and me worked here.

Granddad knew there were some structural problems with the foundation of the building, and he thought we'd fixed them then."

"They're fixed now," Bette said, thinking of the plan for all the renovations.

Richard kissed her on the top of the head. "This store isn't going anywhere, that's for sure."

After fixing all the basic issues the building had, Richard's workers cut the roof off the building, adding more support and prepping it for an addition. Meanwhile, Bette's old office was opened up to become a coffee bar, with direct access to the new lobby of the hotel, modeled to be a mirror of the same key architectural elements of the bookstore.

There was a ton of work to do to finish the hotel, but one of the first things Richard did was promote Zelda as overseer. While Bette had assumed that Zel was Richard's secretary, it turned out she was much more along the lines of a personal and business assistant who had a hand in everything. Zel easily lifted the reigns from Richard's hands and started calling the design shots.

Richard also got help from his brother, Eric, who flew in from the LA's Dickson hotel specifically to aid in the development of Hotel Ever After. He was still working on the LA division, and could only fly up occasionally, but Zel was more than capable of handling everything.

Bette had wondered briefly if Eric and Zel were an item, but they had a more brother-sister relationship. Which was good, judging from the doe-eyes that Aria kept shooting toward Eric when she thought no one could see.

Bette stood in wonder in the center of Happily Ever After, in awe of how much had changed, and how all the changes had been for the good. The store was safely in her hands and would never face the old threats of closing, the hotel was a glorious monument to both Fairhaven and Hoorton's legacy, and things with Richard seemed to be going amazingly well.

Except...she couldn't help but worry that maybe she was a temporary fling for him, a Fairhaven girl that was fine for right now, but not up to snuff compared to the girls he must surely have lined up in New York City.

"'Up to snuff?'" Zel said, laughing. "What makes you think Richard even *has* girls lined up in the NYC?"

Bette threw the remains of her biscotti at Zel. Aria frowned. While Bette still managed the bookstore on her own, Aria had completely taken over the new coffee shop, including some of the baking.

Zel snatched the piece of biscotti off the table and popped it in her mouth before Aria could protest. "Trust me, Richard was always so career-focused that he never even noticed other girls. I thought he was gay for a long time. Used to think the same thing about Eric, too," she added, casting a look at Aria, "but don't worry, he's definitely not gay either."

"What do you mean by 'definitely?'" Aria snapped, then blushed. "I mean, that's fine, I don't care, it's none of my business."

Zel laughed at Aria, but Bette just frowned at her coffee. "It's just that..."

Zel sobered up. "What's wrong?" she asked seriously.

"It's just that he's been letting go lately," Bette said. "Like passing off the major work of design to you and construction to his brother. There's hardly anything left for Richard to do now that he's distributed all the work, and it makes me wonder if maybe..."

"Maybe?" Aria prompted.

"Maybe he's planning on going back to New York," Bette said. She didn't add, *without me,* but that was her biggest concern. Because...she wasn't going to give up Fairhaven for the Big Apple, and if Richard was planning on leaving now...

Then this was the end.

"I don't think that's the situation," Aria said gently.

Zel nodded her head in agreement.

"I just don't know anymore," Bette said. "I want this to work, but..."

"Hold on," Zel said. She pressed her finger to her ear, listening to whoever was at the other end of her Bluetooth. One of her trademark grins lit up her face.

"You're wanted in the penthouse," Zel told Bette after she disconnected.

"The penthouse?" Bette said. "Who wants me there?"

"Who do you think, doofus?" Zel said. She looked as if she'd throw something at Bette, but Aria was already jumping up to clean off their table.

Bette scooted her chair back, and Zel gave her an encouraging look. "You're not going to your death sentence, you know," she said. "There's no guillotine up there."

Bette rolled her eyes and crossed the hotel lobby to the gold-toned elevators, using the special key card Richard had given her to grant her full access to the top floors. She didn't mean to be so dramatic—she just didn't want this story to end. Not yet. Not with her and Richard going their separate ways.

The elevator zipped up past the floors, dinging rapidly. Very few of the rooms were actually complete, but Richard had started with the top floors, which he intended to be a bit more illustrious than the regular rooms on the floors below. Each of the five top floors had a different theme, and each room was decorated to match the literary motif of the floor.

The penthouse, however, didn't have a theme other than "rich" and "luxurious." Half the floor was dedicated to the rooftop restaurant, a glass encased room with a swimming pool for a roof, overlooking downtown Fairhaven. The other half of the floor was the penthouse suite.

Bette stepped off the elevator to the sound of power tools. The restaurant was no where near completed—only the glass walls were up, even the subfloor was exposed as Zel tried to figure out what sort of tile or carpet looked best. She turned right, past the little alcove designed as a waiting area for restaurant guests, past the restrooms, and toward a bookshelf built into the wall at the end of the hallway.

Most guests would assume the bookshelf was little more than decoration, but Bette had helped design the secret and private entryway into the penthouse. She held her keycard up to the side of the bookshelf, and, with an audible click, the entire shelf unlocked and opened for her.

She entered the penthouse. This room was far more complete than any of the other rooms in the hotel so far. The carpet was thick, a creamy beige that begged to be walked on barefoot. The walls were papered in a solid, textured design, and beautiful replicas of classic book covers served as artwork.

In the center of the main room was a giant king-sized canopied bed with a long, cylindrical pillow across the head embroidered with the phrase "Book lovers never go to bed alone." Richard had let Zel decorate most of the hotel, but he had selected everything for the penthouse himself. Bette had thought that this meant that Richard intended to live there, and she'd liked the idea of having him so close, but she'd seen the plans since then. Richard had no intention of living in the hotel, even in this beautiful suite.

"Richard?" she called.

The curtains by the french doors leading to the balcony shifted as the glass doors opened. "Out here," Richard said.

Bette crossed the room—why were fresh flowers on the nightstand?— and stepped onto the balcony. Richard was leaning against the wrought iron railing, staring past the town and toward the ocean view.

Very few spots in the entire world were as beautiful as this one.

"I have a gift for you," Richard said. He reached down to the small cafe table on the balcony and handed Bette a wrapped package. She could tell immediately by the size and weight of it that it was a book—and she could tell by the wrapping paper that it had come from her store.

She shot Richard a questioning look.

"I bought it from Aria," he said. "Which was rather difficult to do, since you're almost always in the store."

She stuck her tongue out at him and started to peel back the paper. Her fingers hesitated, though. This wasn't a break-up gift, was it? The flowers, the serene setting…if this was his way of breaking up, she'd bash his head in with the book.

"Fodor's guide to France?" Bette asked as the paper fell away.

"Do you remember this?" Richard asked.

Bette shook her head, staring at the strange gift.

Richard leaned in, his breath tickling the side of Bette's ears. "This is the book you threw at me after our first night together," he said.

Bette laughed. "This? You remember that?"

"You don't? I'm wounded!" He clutched his heart playfully.

Bette pretended to weigh the book as if she was going to throw it again.

"Mercy! Mercy!" Richard cried, dashing inside and ducking behind a chair.

"Only if you tell me what this is all about," Bette said.

Richard straightened. "Well, you might have noticed that Zel and Eric have most of the day-to-day operations down for the hotel right now…"

Bette lowered her arm. "Ye-es," she said warily.

"So I thought perhaps a bit of travel would be good…"

Bette looked dumbly down at the book in her hands. "France?" she said, reading the title.

"Open the book."

The tourism guide opened naturally to the middle of the book, where an envelope lay nestled inside the pages. Bette put the book down on a nearby table and opened the envelope.

Two tickets to Paris.

"We'll just start there, of course," Richard said. "But then we can rent a car and go to some of the villages. You'll love the gardens at Versailles. And Nice! There's a little town called Eze nearby that has a perfume factory. And the Riviera…"

"Richard!" Bette cried, still staring at the tickets, "but—we can't! I can't afford this, and the hotel…the bookstore!"

"I've talked to Aria—she can handle the bookstore while we're gone. And Zel and Eric have the hotel." Richard crossed the room in three long strides, and tilted Bette's chin toward him. "All you have to do is say yes, and next week, we're gone. Just us, and all the croissants and macaroons we can eat."

"Yes!" Bette said, laughing and throwing her arms around him. "Of course, yes!"

CHAPTER FOURTEEN

*Z*el waved goodbye as the black Lincoln packed with Bette and Richard's luggage—and Bette and Richard—zoomed from the hotel toward the airport about an hour away. They'd be gone for just over a month, and when they returned, Richard expected the building to be nearly complete.

She ran down the figures in her head, mentally scheduling everything that needed to be done. The top floors, with the restaurant and the themed floors, would require the most work, but she couldn't let the little details necessary for them to distract her from the fact that the rest of the hotel still needed some major decisions.

"Zel?" Aria asked in a small voice beside her. "Everything okay?"

Zel nodded. "It's fine. It's just—Richard's never left me with such a big project before," she said. "I don't want to disappoint him."

"You'll be fine," Aria said with confidence.

Zel smiled, but it didn't quite reach her eyes, and she didn't have the words to belie Aria's statement. Aria had only seen the happy side of Richard, and Zel assumed that as long as Bette was around, that was the only side anyone would see. But she'd seen his beastly side, when project deadlines weren't met, building schedules were delayed, and grand openings didn't go off without a hitch. She'd seen that side of him, and definitely didn't want to be the reason it came back out.

And besides, this was her first major step up. Richard came from a large family, but she couldn't blame him for the spot of nepotism he had here and there, hiring his brother to oversee construction, working with his sister on some of the design projects in New York. Zel knew she had to prove herself, and that she'd be held to a different—a higher—standard than Richard held some of his family. And it'd be worth it, she knew.

As long as she didn't fail.

"You have to make sure to take some time to yourself," Aria said.

"I'll do that when the hotel's completed," Zel replied, a little more snap to her voice than she intended.

"And also?" Aria hesitated.

"Yes?"

"You got a message while you were helping Richard and Bette." Aria handed Zel the piece of paper in her hand.

"Oh, *damn*," Zel said as she read the name scribbled across the top.

"What's wrong?"

"My *mother*," Zel said, heaving a sigh.

Aria tried to question her more, but Zel was already turning to the main office behind the lobby desk. She closed the door behind her, picked up the phone, sighed, put it back down, and picked it back up, punched in three numbers, and then dropped the phone back into the cradle.

She knew what her mother wanted.

She wanted to *visit*.

Fairhaven was at least five hours away from Portland, Oregon, but that was far closer than New York, especially considering how her mother had a fear of flying. And while Zel had promised to come visit at some point or another...she hadn't.

Mostly on purpose.

Okay, fine, *entirely* on purpose.

Zel's mother was just...exhausting.

Her cell phone buzzed, and Zelda glanced at the message that flashed on the screen. Her mother had actually deigned to send a text.

Three words.

"Explain yourself. Why????"

Zelda heaved a sigh. So. Her mother had found out. Not just that she was so close to Portland, but that she had been doing a little investigating on her own, trying to find out who her birth parents were. She hadn't told her mother because she knew she'd take it the wrong way. Her mother always had a chip on her shoulder about the fact that Zel was adopted; she constantly felt as if she had to prove that she was a good enough mother to replace her birth parents. Zel had never tried to make her mother feel inadequate—if anything, the fact that her mother had actually been there to raise her more than proved that she had no need to feel lesser next to her birth parents—but there was no way Zel could have looked into her own adoption without her mother getting upset about the whole situation.

She sighed again. She should contact her mom, assure her that all was well and she didn't love her any less and, and, and.

Zel's head sank in her arms. Her mother wasn't even *here* and she was already exhausted.

Across from her, the newly installed security cameras displayed every public inch of the hotel, from the lobby to the café to the still-in-progress ballroom that was being developed above the bookstore. Zel let her mind wander as she watched the workers buzzing from room to room, installing carpet along the hallways, trucking appliances to the newly tiled kitchens, hanging drapes in the ballroom.

"Well, who are you?" Zel said aloud, straightening her spine and zooming in on the front cameras. A young man was chatting with Aria at the cafe, and Zel felt an immediate stab of senseless jealousy.

He was tall and slim, with close-cut hair and square glasses. He had the perfect combination of geek and cute, with just enough of a careless, unkempt look to his appearance to make him exactly Zel's type.

Using the reflection of the screen, Zelda smoothed down her own hair —pinned up in a bun to keep it out of the way—and grabbed a lip gloss. Aria was right; Zel had put her own life on hold while dealing with the hotel, and it was time she at least took a break for herself.

She dashed out of the back office, past the front desk, and was approaching the cafe as the guy turned around from Aria, a paper cup of coffee in one hand and a tablet in the other.

"Hi," she said cheerfully. "I just wanted to introduce myself; I'm overseeing the design of the hotel."

The guy returned her smile, juggling the coffee and the tablet so he could offer her his hand. "Hi," he said. "I'm your new networking guy. Andrew. Drew."

"Zelda," she replied. "Zel."

They stared at each other, and Zel had a fleeting thought that if they were in a rom-com, this is where the sappy music would start playing.

Instead, a screeching voice shouted her name across the hotel lobby.

"Zelda Amelia Goethe!" her mother said, striding forward.

Zel closed her eyes and wished that the newly tiled mosaic floor of the lobby would swallow her up whole.

"I want to know just what you think you're doing, ignoring your mother's calls," Heather Goethe said. "I have been worried sick about you. I could have been wasting away in a ditch on the side of the road, but *no*, you couldn't possibly be bothered to pick up the phone."

"Hello, Mother," Zel said.

Drew looked at her mother in something akin to alarm. Zel couldn't really blame him. While she was tall and slim, with long blonde hair that reached passed her thighs, her mother was short with wide-set eyes and chin-length graying hair that she sometimes forgot to dye. Heather had adopted Zel when she was in her mid-forties as, she suspected, a way to pretend that she was still in her mid-thirties or even her mid-twenties. Heather did everything in her power, from facelifts and Botox to the latest trends in makeup and hair treatments, to appear younger than she was, but it only served to highlight her age rather than hide it.

And it made her look slightly crazy, especially when she barged into hotel lobbies screeching Zelda's name.

"Mom," Zel said, sighing heavily as she turned to her. "Could you not?"

"Could I not what?" Heather demanded. "Could I not be your *mother* any more? Because that is clearly what you want."

"Let's discuss this in my office," Zel said.

Drew—perfectly handsome, nerdy geek boy of her dreams—looked away from Zel, muttering something about catching her later and disappearing toward the elevators.

And just like that, she'd lost her chance with the first guy she'd had any interest in for ages.

ZEL & THE TOWER

CHAPTER ONE

airhaven was definitely not New York.

New York had a skyline that didn't involve redwoods. It also had more than one pizza place, coffee at every corner, and roughly eight or nine million more people. Which meant that Zelda Goethe had a chance to lose people in New York.

Not so in Fairhaven.

To be fair, Zel didn't want to lose "people." She wanted to lose a specific person.

Her mother.

Instead, Heather Goethe was right there in the lobby of the hotel Zel was overseeing construction of, sipping on a latte and perching on a seat facing Zel's office.

Only a month more, Zel told herself as she fake-smiled at her mom while she stood at the café's counter. In one more month, she'd be back in New York, where she belonged, literally on the other side of the country from her mother.

It was kind of a shame, though. Fairhaven as a town was growing on Zel; it had a certain charm that she found refreshing. And the hotel was her baby, the first project her boss, Richard Dickson of the Dickson Hotel Corporation, had allowed her to oversee the design of while he was off enjoying a whirlwind trip to Paris with his new girlfriend and—Zel smiled to herself with the secret knowledge—soon to be fiancée. And the people of Fairhaven were nice. At least the people she wasn't related to.

"A green tea latte," Zel told Aria, the newly promoted bookstore manager who was currently in charge of the café. This was a part of Richard's design—the bookstore was a historical building and cornerstone of the town that was fully preserved and restored before being integrated into the hotel design, bridged by the cafe that bled into the lobby.

"I'm not sure it's really going to provide you with the 'zen of a fresh day,'" Aria said, reading the label on the tea before handing it to Zel.

Zel glanced at her mother. "Yeah, I don't think anything will."

"We-ell," Aria said in a coy tone. "I can think of at least one thing. Or one person."

Zel groaned. "Drop it, Ari," she said. "He is definitely not interested." Zel had had the pleasure of meeting the networking guy for the hotel—a tall, thin nerdy-chic man named Drew—a week ago. The same day her mother had arrived in Fairhaven after driving down from Portland. Just in time for him to get a full dose of her crazy. And nothing cock-blocked like Zel's mother and her crazy.

After paying for her latte, Zel sat down at the café table with her mother. There was really no avoiding it, much as she wished she could.

"I don't see why I can't stay here," Heather said by way of introduction. This had been her mother's first source of arguments: That she should stay—for free—in the still-being-built hotel.

"No one stays here," Zel said.

"*You* do."

"I work here."

"You could just let me stay with you, love," Heather said, reaching over and twirling a lock of her daughter's hair into place behind her ear.

"Mom." Zel's tone held a warning as she leaned back.

Her mother sighed deeply. "It's just, my darling," she started, her eyes dropping to her latte. "I miss you. It's so rare I get to see you, and you'll be back in New York before I know it..."

Zel sighed.

"And," her mother added, "I feel like you're pulling away from me."

"Mom," Zel said flatly.

"It's just...why now?" Heather cried.

Zel knew exactly what her mother meant, and she knew the answer, but she wasn't willing to give it. Heather would never be able to understand why Zel wanted to find her birth parents. And Zel had no intentions of ever telling her why she had such a sudden and unexpected interest in discovering them, now, when she was in her almost-late-twenties and after she had shown no real interest in ever meeting them before. It wasn't something she felt Heather would ever be able to understand, and it certainly wasn't something that she was going to explain in the middle of an in-progress hotel lobby while the workers for the day were starting to stream in.

"Let's talk about this later," Zel said. "Dinner tonight. My treat."

"No, no," Heather said. "I think it's clear that I should go back to Portland." It was about a four hour drive up to Oregon, and part of Zel did a happy dance that her mother was so ready to leave—and after less than two weeks here.

But she also knew what kind of guilt trip that suggesting this would create.

Behind her, Zel could hear a flurry of motion as the workers started to bring in the carpets for the lower floors. She checked her watch; delivery men would be here with a shipment of tables and chairs for the top floor restaurant any second now. And she had to track down the networking guy —the very nerdy-cute networking guy who thought she was a co-dependent freak, no doubt—and get the routers reset or whatever it was you had to do to make the internet work properly.

"Stay at least one more night," Zel said, starting to stand up. "We'll talk about this at dinner."

"One more night?" Heather asked, a whine in her voice.

"Or more," Zel said. "I don't mean to ignore you, Mom, I'm just really busy right now, and—"

Heather waved her hand. "No, no, it's fine. You don't have time for your mother, but you do have time for..." Her voice caught in her throat. "For finding out who your *real* mom is."

"You are my real mom," Zel said automatically.

"Am I?" Heather's voice dropped. "Because if I was, you wouldn't still be looking..."

Zel dropped her latte on the table and moved around the table, giving her mother a hug. "Of *course*, you're my mom," she said. "My *real* mom. You always will be."

Heather shot Zel a watery smile. Zel hugged her again, and then caught sight of the impatient delivery men standing at the front desk. "I've got to go," she said, already heading towards the desk. "Tonight we'll talk, okay?"

"Okay!"

Zel jogged over to the desk and greeted the delivery men with her trademark grin—which didn't work on them at all.

"I've got a big shipment here," the lead man said. The label on his shirt was emblazoned with the company from which Zel had ordered chairs for the restaurant on the top floor.

"Yes, thank you," Zel replied. "We have workers ready and waiting to accept the delivery at the back entrance."

"Yeah, well, they said *you* had to sign." The delivery man thrust a tablet at Zel. She used her finger to sign in the little box on the screen and accept the delivery.

"Your wi-fi's not working," the delivery man grunted. "Can't deliver until this is sent back to the main office."

"You...can't give us the chairs until you have internet?"

"We got the tables too."

"That's ridiculous."

The delivery man shrugged. "We're paid by the hour," he added.

"I can't help that the internet's not operating!" Zel said. "That's kind of a work hazard when you deliver furniture to *buildings that aren't yet complete.*"

"Well, we don't have a strong enough cell signal either."

"I'll call the main company and confirm delivery," Zel said.

The delivery guy shrugged again. That seemed about all he was capable of. "Can't deliver until the bossman approves."

Zel grunted in irritation. "*Fine,*" she said. "Wait here." She marched into her office and called the delivery company on her landline. After several long minutes of back-and-forth in which she confirmed that it was impossible to send an online form when the building wasn't *online*, the owner of the furniture company confirmed with the delivery guy out front to unload the tables and chairs.

Zel collapsed behind her desk and sighed heavily. If it wasn't one thing, it was always another. And this wasn't the first time that the hotel's lack of internet—combined with Fairhaven's notoriously spotty cell phone signal —caused her trouble. She couldn't very well change the cell phone towers in the area, but she *could* at least get the wi-fi going in the hotel...even if that meant she had to face the hottest guy she'd ever embarrassed herself in front of before.

*I*t took a combination of using the in-house communication system, the landline, and text messaging to confirm that Drew, the networking specialist hired to wire up the hotel was both in the building and working on the problem of no wi-fi. Still, Zel felt like she should be on the problem personally, so after ensuring that she had someone reliable to man the front desk and handle any more shipment fiascos, she strode across the lobby and toward the gleaming brass elevators.

Zel was no specialist in computers and networking. She knew a little more than her mother, who seemed to think that witchcraft and possibly voodoo were involved in working wi-fi, but not that much more. In terms of a complicated project like the hotel, Zel knew that if the internet wasn't working, it was because something was wrong with the computers and routers and other networking things in the main office or because something was wrong with that panel of wires and blinking lights by the penthouse suite.

And that was pretty much the extent of her knowledge.

Apparently today's problem had something to do with the wires and blinking lights. Zel tapped her foot, waiting for the elevator to take her to the top floor. Enough running around. Enough avoiding Drew. Just because he happened to meet her at the same time as he met her (wildly insane) mother, which shot all chances of ever trying to hit him up doesn't mean she couldn't work with him on a professional level.

The doors dinged open, and Zel started to step into the elevator without looking—at exactly the same time Drew started to step out of the elevator. They crashed into each other.

"Sorry!" Zel cried as Drew stepped back.

Drew laughed. "I was just coming down to see what you needed," he said. "I heard on the com sys that you were looking for me?"

"It's um—" the elevator doors tried to shut, but her elbow was in the way. It beeped at her. She stepped into it, Drew followed, and she pushed the *close door* button.

"The wi-fi," Drew supplied for her.

Zel nodded.

Drew reached around Zel and pushed the top floor button, and the elevator zoomed upward.

"What's wrong with it?" Zel asked.

Drew cocked an eyebrow. Dear goodness, why did her mother have to ruin her chances with all the hot men?

"Do you really want to know," Drew asked, "or would you rather I just give you an ETA on when it'll be fixed?"

"An ETA is great," Zel said, smiling in return.

"Soon," Drew supplied. "I'm rewiring a few things, and have placed an order for a stronger router."

The elevator stopped on the fifth floor. A group of workers carrying rolls of carpets stood in the entrance. "We'll take the next one," one of them said.

"No, no, there's room," Drew said. He and Zel moved against the back of the elevator wall, and the workers tried to enter, but the elevator beeped at them in protest. With a shrug, the workers backed off the elevator, and Drew and Zel continued toward the penthouse suite.

"So-o," Drew said, drawing out the word.

"So," Zel said.

"I can't help but wonder if you've been avoiding me."

"Avoiding you?" Zel mentally slapped herself. Was she going to just repeat everything he said?

Drew nodded. But before he could say anything, the elevator gave a weird little jolt.

And then came to a halt.

"What was that?" Zel said, panic already rising in her voice.

"Probably nothing." Drew looked at the display on the elevator wall. "We're three floors until the top level," he added.

"Yes, but we're not moving." Her voice shook.

"Are you okay?" Drew asked, turning to her.

"I will be when this damned elevator starts moving again."

There was a pause as they both waited to see if the elevator would budge.

It didn't.

"I want off this thing," Zel said immediately.

Drew looked at the firmly closed brass door. "I think that will be more difficult than usual."

"This is a nightmare," Zel groaned. She leaned against the smooth metal back of the elevator. "I'm stuck in an elevator with a guy who knows how crazy my mother is and also did I mention the being stuck in an elevator part?"

Drew laughed. "Is that why you've been avoiding me? Because of your mother?"

"You saw her!" Zel cried. Drew had walked up to her just as her mother had confronted her about the paperwork she needed to find her birth parents. Being on the short end of that crazy stick was enough to drive any man away.

"She's a bit...overbearing," Drew conceded. "But that's no reason to avoid me."

Zel covered her face with her hands and sank against the elevator wall. Now was not the time to have this conversation. Truth be told, she knew that she was being silly to avoid Drew, and that he probably wasn't judging her based on her mother. But he was the cutest guy she'd seen in ages, and she just didn't want to set herself up for failure. Again.

But now—with the metal walls of the elevator pressing down around her—was *not* the time to either discuss it with Drew or think about her own feelings on the subject.

"I want off this ride," she groaned again, her head sinking into her knees.

"Hey, are you okay?" Drew asked. His voice dripped with sincere concern. He dropped down beside her, reaching one hand out to rub her back, but withdrawing at the last moment.

"I *hate* being trapped in small spaces," Zel told the carpet of the elevator, squeezing her eyes shut. "I always have. Can't stand it. I need off." She punctuated each sentence with a deep breath.

"You're claustrophobic," Drew said, realization dawning.

"I just don't like small spaces."

"That's what claustrophobic means."

"Call it whatever the hell you want, I need to get out of here!" Zel said, her eyes wild.

Drew put up both hands, as if that would calm her. "Okay, look, my dad used to get these bad panic attacks, okay?"

"I'm not having a panic attack, I just need out of here." The more they talked about how trapped they were, the more Zel's heart rate climbed. She could feel her blood pulsing in her ears, her heart rattling around her ribcage. She struggled to catch her breath. Mentally, she was replaying all the warning signs she'd ignored—the way the elevator door beeped at her protruding elbow, the over-the-weight limit the carpet guys had triggered. She shouldn't have trusted the elevator. She shouldn't have gotten on in the first place, and once she was on, she should have gotten off with the carpet guys. Staying on this godforsaken elevator had been a mistake and now she was trapped and there was no way off and was it her or were the walls closing in on them?

"Listen, I need you to focus," Drew said in a very calm voice. Zel's eyes drifted to him. "I'm going to help you, but it's going to take five minutes. You can time me if you like."

"I don't have five minutes," Zel muttered. Five more minutes here and she'd rip the walls out with her teeth. Or die of heart failure. One or the other.

"Two minutes, then. You got your phone on you? You can time me."

Zel fumbled in her pocket for her cell phone. No signal. Typical. But she brought up the timer and punched in two minutes.

"Close your eyes," Drew said.

Zel cast him a doubtful look but did as he said.

"Okay, I'm going to touch your hand." She could feel him picking up her left hand and gently squeezing the skin between her thumb and forefinger. "This is a pressure point," Drew said. "Now I'm going to touch the back of your neck."

She felt his warm hand at the base of her skull, his fingers sending shivers down her spine as he crept up her scalp, gently twisting in her hair.

"This isn't doing anything," Zel said, despite the fact that it kind of was.

"Just trust me for..." He glanced down at her cell phone in her hand. "One minute and twenty-eight more seconds. Keep your eyes closed."

Zel shut her eyes, focusing on the feel of his hands on her body. She wondered what it would feel like if his hands crept lower, if they were focused on creating a totally different sensation within her, one that had nothing to do with calming her from panicking in an elevator. Zel took a sharp breath when she remembered the way the elevator walls seemed so looming and constraining, but Drew gently added a little more pressure to the back of her neck, and she leaned into his touch, focusing on the slight roughness of his fingertips on her sensitive skin.

Her phone buzzed in her hand. She looked down, a somewhat dazed look in her eyes, surprised to see it was still going.

"See?" Drew said. "I told you it would only take two minutes."

"We're still stuck here," Zel pointed out.

He smiled. He knew that wasn't the point. She wasn't focused on the walls any more; she was focused on him. He gently pulled his hands from her hand and neck.

"You don't have to be so smug about it," she said, bumping into his shoulder.

"It doesn't always work," Drew confessed. "But I'm glad it did this time."

"Where'd you learn how to do that?"

"Just watching my mom helping my dad," he said. "He used to get really wound up and have panic attacks. It helped him to get through just a few minutes. If you can get through two minutes, then you can get through two more. You remind yourself that you'll be okay, and suddenly the problems aren't as bad as they felt like before."

"And I guess hypnotizing your patient or whatever with those pressure points helps."

Drew barked out a laugh. "Oh, those weren't pressure points. Or if they were, that was just an accident. I just had to trick you into thinking it was something more than just a distraction from your claustrophobia."

Zel looked around for something to throw at him and his incredibly cute, smug face.

He looked down at his hands. "It doesn't always work though," he said again, and Zel wondered at his sad look, and the way he casually mentioned his father's panic attacks.

"It worked this time," she said. "Thanks." She glanced up at the blinking elevator screen. "Now if only we could get off this elevator before I need you to do it again."

Drew smiled at her in a lopsided way. "Well, if you need a distraction, I've got better things than fake pressure points..."

Zel cocked an eyebrow. "Oh? Really?"

Drew opened his mouth—

CHAPTER THREE

—nd the elevator doors opened.

Before he could say anything else, Zel leapt out of the elevator. *Smooth*, she thought, looking back at Drew, who seemed a little confused by it all. *Now he thinks your mom's a freak, and you are too.*

But she couldn't stand being in that elevator one more moment.

"I—uh," she started.

"There's just three more flights," he started, looking at the elevator. "It seems to be working fine now."

"I'll just take the stairs," Zel said. She mentally slapped herself. If she wasn't so lame, she could get back on that elevator and go up three more measly flights. It would take just a few minutes. She could last a few minutes.

But the thought of going back into that tiny metal box of death made her want to vomit.

"Okay then," Drew said, and the doors started to close.

And there goes my last chance with super-hot-geek-boy.

Drew stuck his arm between the closing doors and stepped out into the hallway.

"What are you doing?" Zel asked, surprised.

"Taking the stairs with you." Drew looked around. "Or, at least, I would if I knew where the stairs were."

Zel laughed in relief that he was being so chill about her freak out.

"This way," she said. "It's kind of stupid how it's always so impossible to find stairs in a hotel," she added, leading him down the hall. "It's the worst thing about New York. Elevators everywhere you look, but never any stairs."

"I remember stairs," Drew said. "I was in New York for about a year awhile back, and it was stairs all day long. Especially in the subway, when I was bone tired and just wanted to crash in the bed. Nope! Just kidding! You get to go up three flights of stairs just to get back up to the street."

"Maybe my perspective is a little off," Zel said, holding open the door to the stairwell for him. "But all I see is elevators, waiting to trap me."

They started up the stairs. While the halls and rooms of the hotel were still in construction, the stairwell had the same industrial smell of any stairwell in New York—except it was cleaner. Far, far cleaner.

"So, um," Drew started. "You don't have to answer, but you wanna talk about it?"

Zel glanced past the railing, down ten flights of stairs. Funny how heights didn't bother her at all—she never got vertigo—but small spaces drove her batty.

"I think," she said, still looking down the stairwell, "that it was because of the way my mom used to punish me. If I was bad as a kid, she'd lock me in time out."

"Lock you in...? That sounds ominous."

"In a little room in the attic of our house," Zel said. "In her mind, it probably wasn't so bad. There were toys, and it's not like it was a prison or anything. But there was only one window, really high up, too far up for me to see through it, and I don't know, the walls just felt really small to me. It'd freak me out, but she always thought I was just trying to get out of being punished, and so she kept me in there longer, and it just spiraled into this horrible situation where I don't like small spaces where I can't escape."

When she finally met Drew's eyes, she saw that they were sympathetic and not mocking at all. "I completely understand," he said. "Well, I don't really, because I've never felt that way or had your experiences, but I understand how it feels to be helpless to your emotions."

That was a strange way to put it, but it perfectly captured the way Zel felt about it all.

Drew opened the door to the top floor of the hotel with a sweep of his arm. "After you," he said, holding it open.

Zel smiled. It was such a relief that he was so okay with her weirdness.

In the long run, being a little freaked out by elevators and tight spaces wasn't that strange, but still…Drew was remarkably cool about it all.

Or he was acting. She was, technically, his boss after all.

The stairs opened up to the worker's area of the rooftop restaurant. "This way," Zel said, showing him a shortcut that veered around the restaurant—and the workers that were obviously doing something that involved far more hammers than should be banging at one time.

They by-passed the restaurant and went down a tastefully decorated hallway that looked like it contained nothing more than restrooms and a bookshelf. This area was far more complete than many of the other areas of the hotel were, and it was far more silent.

"Mr. Dickson, the hotel owner, designed the penthouse suite to be hidden," Zel said. "The door is there, behind that bookshelf." She pointed to the bookshelf at the end of the hallway.

"No way, really?" Drew said, moving over to the bookcase and examining the hidden door. He spotted the card reader there and lifted his worker's access key card to the slot. A tiny red light blinked near one of the books.

Drew turned around, disappointed. "I've got the key," Zel said, smiling at him. "But the wi-fi panel is over here."

Drew shot her a smirk. "Wi-fi panel?"

"The box thingy with the lights that makes the internet work." Zel moved over to a print of an Ansel Adams photograph and flicked a switch under the frame, allowing it to move to the side and show the networking panel.

"You sound like my mother," Drew said laughing.

That stopped Zel cold. She liked geeky boys, but she admittedly had very little clue as to how technology worked. She didn't like the idea that her ignorance aged her and reminded the hot guy of his *mother*.

Drew looked back at her when she didn't respond, and his face lit up with mirth. "Don't worry," he said in a low, flirtatious voice. "You don't *look* anything like my mom."

"I'm pretty sure I act nothing like her, either."

Drew bit his bottom lip as he looked Zel up and down. "Excellent," he said.

Zel felt the heat rush into her cheeks. Why on Earth did this chiseled man hidden behind plastic-rim glasses and a polo shirt send her heart into such a flutter?

"Zelda!"

Zel's heart immediately turned to ice and sank into her stomach. All the playful banter about Drew's mother had somehow demonically summoned her own.

Zel turned around and felt her heart sink all the way into her toes.

Heather was rushing toward her daughter and Drew with a bright yellow wheeled suitcase in tow. She waved enthusiastically, as if she'd just seen them after months of being apart.

"Mom," Zel said, "what are you doing here? And with your luggage?"

Heather's face immediately fell. "You *told* me to stay one more night," she said. "You didn't mean... My reservation at the budget motel was already complete. I thought you meant I could stay here!" She looked around. "And that nice girl at the coffeeshop, Ariel—"

"Aria," Zel corrected.

"—Said that the penthouse suite was up here, and she said it was totally gorgeous, and I know the hotel owner's not here, so I thought maybe..."

"You can't stay in the penthouse suite."

"No one else is using it!"

"No, Mother."

"But—"

"I guess you can stay the night with me." Zel resisted the urge to see if Drew was upset at all that Zel would be sharing a bed with Heather instead of him.

"At least let me *see* the penthouse suite," Heather said. "Ariel said there was a private balcony and a jacuzzi tub and a secret entrance and—"

"Come on," Zel said, taking Heather's suitcase handle from her. "My room's on the third floor."

She glanced back at Drew, who was studiously working on the network. "I've got this covered," Drew said without looking up. "Wi-fi should be fine throughout the hotel in a half hour or so."

"Thanks," Zel said.

As Zel and Heather walked down the hallway, Zel paused. "You know, Mom, I think I'm going to take the stairs," she said.

"Don't be ridiculous." Heather gripped Zel's arm, steering her to the elevators. "Is this because of your silly little phobia? You are not taking the stairs."

Zel took a deep breath. "Five more minutes," she whispered to herself.

CHAPTER FOUR

Zel was going to kill her mother.

Not in a malicious way, of course. It's just that while Zel had spent the entire day on her feet, running around, putting out one fire after another, organizing the entire hotel and managing all the staff and workers, her mother had been getting in the way. She stepped onto the ballroom floor tiles before they were set. She left fingerprints on the still-wet paint. She fiddled with the designs of the higher-class themed rooms on the upper floors of the hotel. She mis-shelved books in the bookstore and bothered Aria, who she still called by the wrong name.

Which meant that not only did Zel have to do her job, she had to run around behind her mother and apologize for it all as well as fix everything she messed up.

And now—after all that—she was *snoring*.

Zel leaned up in her bed to stare down at her mother's perfectly peaceful—and entirely loud—sleep. She had a pillow in her hand. At first she was just gong to hit her mother with the pillow to wake her up and get the snoring to stop, but now she was seriously considering holding it over her face.

"This is wrong," Zel said to herself. She slipped out of bed. She was wearing a sexy lace nightgown, but only because that was the only bedclothes she'd brought with her from New York. She hadn't expected to share her room with anyone—which meant she usually just slept in her panties—but figured if she did end up with someone in her bed, the black lace would be best.

She hadn't factored in her mother.

Zel threw on the matching silky black robe with tiny pink roses embroidered on the sleeves. She needed some air. She needed some space. Because if she didn't get it, she really might hold that pillow over her snoring mother's face.

Grabbing her key cards and cell phone, Zel tiptoed out of the room. The door closed behind her, and she leaned against it, breathing the cool air deeply.

The door still vibrated with the sounds of her mother's snoring.

A walk, Zel told herself. Just a walk. To clear her mind. Of murder.

Unfortunately, when you're living in a half-finished hotel and wearing nothing but black lace, a walk isn't that great of an idea. She definitely didn't want to run into anybody, and there wasn't anywhere very private...

Her mind flew to earlier in the day, when she'd taken the stairs with Drew. There would definitely be no one in the stairwell this late in the night. She veered left.

The lights in the stairwell were far brighter than anywhere else in the hotel, the light bouncing off the freshly painted walls and bright concrete steps. The air was colder here, too, and in moments she was wide awake.

"Might as well work off this energy," Zel muttered. If she exhausted herself, there was a chance that she might actually get some sleep tonight, snoring mother or no.

Up one flight of stairs, and all she succeeded in doing was raising her heartbeat and bringing to mind a checklist of tasks to start on tomorrow. One more flight had just added five more things she needed to add to the list. By the time she was nearly at the top of the staircase, she was reciting a to-do item with every step she took, her cell phone in one hand, scheduling each task.

"I'm a mess," she said to herself.

She was also dying of thirst. At least the top floor of the hotel had a restaurant, and it was unlikely anyone would be here now. She pushed open the door leading out to the main floor.

It felt weird to not hear the banging hammers or the constant noise of workers. Some may find the silence creepy, far too much like *The Shining,* but Zel actually liked it. She liked hotels in general, or at least hotels like the ones Mr. Dickson worked on. They each had their own personality, and this one was shaping up to be the most unique, most special hotel in his entire holdings. From the bottom floor with the hints of architecture reminiscent of the art deco time period, a reflection on the historical bookstore they built onto, to this floor with the soon-to-be five star restaurant and hidden penthouse suite that promised luxury and the sweetest of dreams...

The penthouse suite.

Holy shit, why didn't she think of this sooner? It was totally unprofessional, but Zel needed her sleep, and there was no way she was going to get it with her snoring mother in her bed. But the penthouse suite was *right here*, and empty, and she had one of the only keys to it...

Zel bounded up the remaining stairs and threw open the door to the penthouse. Her feet padded on the thick carpet, down the winding hallway that seemed to lead nowhere. She stopped at a bookcase at the end of the hall.

A secret door to the penthouse suite wasn't really necessary, but even she had to appreciate Richard Dickson's flair for the dramatic. Zel held her key card up beside the bookcase, pressed against the spine of Shakespeare's *Much Ado About Nothing*. The lock clicked inside the hidden door and the bookshelf slid away, revealing the entrance to the penthouse suite.

Zel breathed deeply as she stepped inside, and the door whisked shut behind her.

Yes. This was exactly what she needed.

The room exuded serenity. Even though she hadn't directed the design of the room, she couldn't help but feel a sense of pride. It was a gorgeous room, and she liked to think that some of her design taste wore off on her boss.

The giant four-poster bed with canopied drapes took pride of place, built on a little platform in the center of the room. Tasteful furniture surrounded it—damask-covered chairs and sofas in ivory and gray, elegant tables with carefully selected books on each surface to maintain the theme of the hotel, gossamer drapes that let in the starlight outside.

Of course, to Zel the best features in the room were the windows. They stretched from ceiling to floor along the wall opposite the door, and beautiful French doors led out to a private balcony. Zel crossed the room and swung the doors open wide, breathing the cool night air deeply before stepping out onto the balcony.

It was chillier than she'd imagined it would be, but the view was gorgeous. Just stunning. The mountains stretched out in the distance to one side, a jagged, dark line that blotted out the stars. She could just hear the sound of the ocean roaring to the west, and she could smell the saltwater. Fairhaven was perfectly located between mountains and sea, and even though it was in the middle of nowhere and not exactly a tourist destination, Zel had no doubt that Richard Dickson would be able to turn it into one. Who wouldn't want to be in this tranquil piece of heaven?

Zel was startled out of her reverie by the sound of a door slamming shut.

The wind had blown the balcony doors shut, the loud bang ruining the mood. Ah, well—time to go in now anyway...

Zel crossed the small balcony. The metal handle felt like ice on her fingertips. She pushed down...

It didn't budge.

"No," Zel said with authority, as if her command could change the fact that the door had automatically locked her out. "*No.*"

But the door didn't open.

Zel's hands were so cold she fumbled with her key cards, but it was useless; the balcony didn't use a key card. It used the pretty little ornate key that was sticking out of the other side of the lock. Zel could see it through the gauzy drapes, mocking her.

At least she had her phone. She tried her room first, hoping to wake her mother. She didn't want to tell Heather where the spare universal key cards were, but better her mom found her on a balcony in a thin night-gown than someone else.

But of course, her mother didn't pick up. "Probably snoring too loud to hear the phone ring," she muttered.

Aria then. She'd be sympathetic. Zel scrolled through her contacts and dialed Aria's cell phone.

Straight to voicemail—her phone was turned off. And while she knew Aria lived in a cottage nearby, she had no idea what that number was.

With increasing panic, Zel scrolled through her contacts. Most of them were friends in New York—no help here, on the other side of the country.

A warning flashed on her screen. Ten percent battery life left. *Dammit.* Heather had unplugged her phone so she could charge her own.

A car honked on the street below. Zel dashed to the edge of the balcony. They were thirteen stories up, but the night was still and calm. Zel could just make out the workers from earlier packing up in their van and leaving.

Shit. Should she try to get their attention? How bad would it be if floor tilers and carpet installers had to break her out of the penthouse suite in her nightgown?

...How likely would it be that she'd lose her job?

Before she could decide, the van sped away, its taillights twinkling red before it turned down the street.

Zel loved that Fairhaven was a sleepy little town, but at least in New York, *someone* would be on the street who could help—and probably not care that she was hanging around outside practically naked.

And then, from well below her, she heard someone moving on the sidewalk. The unmistakable sounds of metal-on-metal drifted up. Zel peered over the balcony and saw someone wrapping up a bicycle chain. He threw his leg over one side of a gleaming white bike. He turned, looking down the street, and Zel realized who it was.

Drew.

In a moment he'd be gone.

"Drew!" she shouted, no longer caring about propriety. The only worse thing than having someone come rescue her now would be if no one came to rescue her at all until morning.

Drew stopped, looking around, clearly confused. But he didn't look *up*.

"DREW!" Zel shouted even louder.

He got off his bike. Zel breathed a sigh of relief. But rather than go inside to the lobby and the elevator, Drew walked to the corner, looking down the street. Even from up here, Zel could see him shrug, giving up.

"Son of a—" Zel started. There was only one way to get his attention. She gripped her phone, hating that she was about to throw away a thousand dollars for something this stupid, and she threw it.

It smashed on the concrete sidewalk by Drew's bike. And he finally —*finally*—looked up at her.

CHAPTER FIVE

"*W*hat are you doing?" Drew called up.

"Help me!" Zel shouted. "Locked out!" There was no way she could explain everything from thirteen floors above him.

Drew nodded and ran into the lobby. Zel stepped away from the balcony, leaning against the cold, glass doors. Minutes ticked by. *He's getting the universal key card,* she promised herself. *He's coming for me. He'll save me.*

She wrapped her flimsy robe tighter around her. It was so cold.

How could she have been so stupid? She was *Zel.* Zel didn't make mistakes. Zel was poised to take control of any hotel in the Dickson line. Zel was put together. She was *not* the kind of girl who wound up half-naked on a penthouse balcony she wasn't supposed to be on.

She groaned, her head thumping against the door. Here's hoping she could cover all this up without her boss finding out.

Or my mother... the thought came unbidden into her mind.

Zel heard muffled sounds on the other side of the room and leapt up, straining to see through the gauzy white curtains. A shaft of light filled the room and then disappeared—Drew had opened the secret door! In moments, the balcony doors were flung open.

"Zel?" Drew asked as she rushed inside, slamming the door behind her.

"It's *freezing* out there!" she said, wrapping her arms around herself.

And then an entirely different chill washed over her as she realized just how little clothing she was wearing...and the way Drew was staring at her, mouth slightly open. His eyes snapped away from her long legs and back to her own gaze, and she saw the unhidden appreciation and lust in their clear blue depths. The chill left her, replaced with a heat she couldn't explain.

"What...um..." Drew said, attempting to replace their awkward silence with words.

"What was I doing out there?" Zel stepped further into the room, away from the door. "Trying to escape."

"Escape?"

"My mother."

Drew looked at a loss for words.

"She snores," Zel added.

Drew bit back his smile.

"I was going to sleep here—just for tonight!"

"Who could blame you?" Drew asked, looking around at the ornately beautiful room. His eyes lingered on the bed. "So, uh, how did you end up out there?" Drew nodded toward the balcony doors.

Zel shot him a sheepish smile. "Just wanted to see the view. It *is* pretty nice. Want to see? I promise to take the key with me."

Drew shook his head mutely.

"No, seriously, I'm not so dumb as to get locked out there a second time." Zel strode back to the doors and swung them open.

Drew, however, actually took several steps back. "I...hate heights," he said finally, avoiding her eyes.

Zel laughed. "Really?"

"They're my elevators."

Well, she could understand that. "But you didn't have any trouble before," she said, thinking of the casual way he climbed the stairs and worked on the top floor of the hotel.

"No windows."

She retreated from the balcony and closed the drapes. Drew's tension visibly left him.

"So this is the infamous penthouse suite," Drew said, moving in a slow circle as he inspected the room. "I can see why your mother wanted to stay here."

Zel imagined she could still hear her mother's snoring, ten floors below. "Let's not talk about her now," she said.

Drew gaze fell on her. "Yeah," he said, drinking in her lacy nightgown.

Zel wanted to do nothing more than let the robe fall away and take her chances on this incredibly handsome hunk of man in front of her. Instead, she tied the belt a little tighter. She was his boss. It wasn't right.

But it couldn't be *that* wrong...

It all felt so serendipitous. Zel had nothing in her schedule that allowed time for a fling with the networking guy at the hotel, but here she was, in the pristine penthouse suite, in the dead of night. And she was certainly dressed for the role.

"I should...go," Drew said, drawing out the last word so that it was more like a question.

"I'm..." Zel let her own voice trail off, weighing her options. *Damn the options,* she thought. *I've worked hard enough. I deserve this.* "I'm going to stay," she said. "Just for tonight."

Drew's mouth worked as his eyes dropped lower again, unable to rip them away from Zel's nightclothes. She didn't readjust the silky robe this time.

"Would you like to stay too?" she asked.

His eyes snapped back up to her face, uncertain and questioning. He found whatever answer he was seeking there.

"Just for tonight," she repeated, somewhat hesitating.

"Then I better make sure tonight counts," he said with a feral look in his eyes.

CHAPTER SIX

Zel untied her robe slowly, letting it drop to the floor. Drew watched, his eyes huge, and Zel could see from the way his pants tightened that she clearly had the desired effect on him.

She left the robe on the floor and padded over to the bed, releasing the gauzy drapes from their rope ties and letting them flutter closed. Ever since she was a little girl, she'd wanted a fairy tale bed like this one. As the drapes swirled around the bed, Drew made his way to the bed, too, shedding clothes as he went, ripping off his shirt, kicking off his shoes, and throwing his pants to the ground until he stood before her in nothing but boxers and his glasses.

Zel knelt on the crisp white duvet, the perfect height for Drew as he approached. His arms wrapped around her like he was a starving man, and he feasted on her lips, his kiss voracious and unrelenting. Her fingers clutched at his back, pulling him closer to her. His kiss slid down her jaw, his lips lighting a trail of fire along her neck, and then lower down, nestling in her cleavage. He ripped his glasses off his face and threw them across the room so he could more fully worship her breasts.

Zel dipped her head to his earlobe. While Drew seemed as if he could never get enough of her, Zel pulled back, teasing him lightly, just grazing the back of his neck and tugging at the little hairs there with her fingers. She let her lips brush along his skin, lingering at his ear, and she gently bit his earlobe.

His reaction was immediate and volatile—he sucked in his breath and crushed her against him, biting down on the top of her breast in response. So his ears were extra sensitive. Noted. Zel smiled evilly and licked the outer edge of his ear. He groaned aloud, riding his hips forward so she could feel the full hardness of his erection through his boxers.

"Do you have a condom?" she whispered.

With a lustful sound of impatience, Drew pulled away from Zel, scrounging for his long-forgotten pants and fumbling for a condom. While he looked for it, Zel lifted her lacy black nightie off her body. Her nipples were hard and tight, and goose bumps prickled her skin.

Drew looked up, triumphant with a condom in one hand, and then froze at the sight of her.

Zel smiled slowly, relishing the way her naked body filled him with such insatiable desire. She reached languidly up to her hair, bundled up in a loose bun, and she pulled the pins out, letting her long, blond locks tumble around her shoulders. She loved her long hair, but usually kept it bunched up and out of the way. She shook it out now, arching her back toward Drew.

He took the invitation, rushing to her. He buried his face in her breasts and entwined his hands in her hair, his mouth exploring her body. His lips wrapped around her nipple and he sucked on it, letting his teeth graze along the sensitive flesh in the same way she'd nibbled on his ear. She shuddered in delight and would have fallen back against the bed if his strong arms hadn't been wrapped around her.

Scooting back, Zel took the condom from Drew's hands and let her fingers slide under the waistband of his underwear. She playfully teased her nails along the little hairs leading from his stomach down, down, and then she wrapped her hand around his fully hard cock and squeezed.

"Zel," he groaned.

She looked up at him wickedly. She tugged his drawers down, and he kicked them impatiently away.

"Shh," she whispered. The more eager he was becoming, the more she relished in his desire. She stood up, pulling him down to the bed, and as soon as he was sitting on the edge, she dropped to her knees.

"Zel, oh god..." he said, his voice choking as Zel ripped the condom out of its package and positioned it at the tip of his penis. Rather than rolling it down over his shaft with her hands, she leaned over him and used her mouth to put it on him. He lost all ability to speak, moaning and bunching the duvet in his fists. His entire body was taut, needing her for release.

Zel stood up again, smiling demurely, and started to shimmy out of her lacy black panties. With an animalistic growl, Drew leapt up. He ripped the panties off her, almost shredding the delicate fabric, and then in one swift, fluid motion, he picked her up and carried her to the bed, dropping her amid the pillows. She shrieked with delight, and then he turned his attention to her, and the sounds in her throat became lower, more lustful, moaning with desire.

He paid her back for all the teasing she'd given him. Starting at her knees, his lips trailed along her inner thighs, moving in an achingly slow way closer and closer to the apex. Zel writhed on the bed, her long blonde hair fanning out behind her, gasping for breath as Drew's lips got closer and closer to the center of her desire.

And then he kissed her there, his tongue barely dipping along the edge of her, and her back bucked up, eager for him to take far, far more than just a taste. He responded in kind, spreading her open and lathing her with his tongue, moaning against her clitoris with his own desire. She gasped with pleasure as the tension inside her wound tighter and tighter. Drew's tongue tickled her clit, his teeth barely pressing into the painfully sensitive flesh. He moved higher up, biting her hip as his arms wrapped around her and pulled her closer to him.

"Done teasing me?" he asked, staring at her with hooded eyes.

She lifted her hips up towards him in response. "Please," she begged.

Drew knelt between her legs and positioned himself at her center. He rubbed his penis just along the edge of her, letting it glide smoothly over her clitoris. Zel panted his name, begging inarticulately for more, pushing her hips up toward him, undulating with desire. He leaned over her, eagerly taking her mouth and driving his tongue inside of her at the same time as he entered. He swallowed her gasp as he pushed deeper inside of her, thrusting into her hard.

His mouth dipped lower, and his lips claimed her nipple again, his tongue swirling over the sensitive flesh. At the same time, his hand slipped between them, his finger sliding over her clit as he drove himself into her again and again. She struggled for air as she gasped with desire, the tension inside of her coiling tight.

"Drew," she moaned.

Saying his name seemed to drive him over the edge. He thrust deeper and deeper, harder and harder. Her body clenched around him, and he groaned, finally releasing as she climaxed, descending into shudders of bliss.

Zel stirred in her sleep, and her hand connected with something warm and hard. Her eyes flew open, and for a moment, she couldn't locate where she was—the gauzy white curtains, the luxurious bed—or who she was with.

And then she looked over and saw Drew's sleeping face.

Warmth flooded her body, and she immediately felt a longing ache for him again. Drew was...he was much *more* than she had ever imagined. More skilled in bed, yes, but more...more kind. More gentle. Seeing him now was like seeing his true self. His face prickled with whiskers that needed a shave, his mouth slightly twitched up in a smile.

Zel's eyes trailed south. His shoulders were broad and strong, far more muscled than she'd imagined under his plain polo shirt. He didn't look like an IT guy, not when he was naked.

Zel could feel the aching want in her body growing, and part of her wanted nothing more than to sweep aside the white duvet and mount him again.

But just past his shoulder was a clock.

Zel bit back a groan. Last night had been a fairy tale—her prince had saved her when she had been locked up in her tower—but now...

Now she had a job to do.

Zel slipped out of bed, hissing slightly under her breath as the cold air hit her naked skin.

Shit. She had come here with nothing but a black lace nightie and panties, and while no one had seen her in the dead of night, it was well past time for the workers to have arrived throughout the hotel. There was no way she would slip by undetected this time.

Zel dashed to the bathroom. She paused on the marble tile, looking at the huge jacuzzi tub with regret. It was big enough for both her and Drew to have rather a lot of fun...and there was a bottle of bubble bath just calling for her...

Zel shook herself out of that delicious reverie and grabbed one of the oversized, fluffy white bathrobes from the closet. Thank goodness this room was already stocked. A big bathrobe wasn't exactly professional attire, but it was huge and covered everything and would get her back to her own room, no problem.

When she stepped out of the bathroom, Drew was awake, sitting up in bed. The duvet slid down his hip, exposing his thigh, tantalizing Zel with the possibilities of what was still hidden under the covers.

He eyed her in the bathrobe.

Zel clutched it tighter around her body. The thick terry cloth was her protection. Her armor was back up.

Drew smiled, but there was a little something sad about it.

"Just one night," he said, repeating her words, but there was a question in his voice, as if hoping she'd take them back.

Her fingers clutched the robe so tightly that they were starting to cramp.

Just one night, she should say. No need to let this draw out forever. No need to turn it into something...else. Something it couldn't be. Something he didn't want...did he?

Before Zel could say anything, though, she could hear something just outside the room. The door to the penthouse was hidden, but most people at the hotel now knew it was there. But none of the workers should be messing with it. This room was done.

Zel shot Drew a look, and he grabbed his clothes and fled to the bathroom. Zel strode across the room, letting the mask of authority settle on her face. She flung open the door and saw—

Her mother.

"Mom?" she asked, surprised. And then she took in Heather's face. The red-rimmed eyes, the tear tracks down her cheeks. "Mom?" she asked again, gentler, concern filling her voice. "What's wrong?"

Heather walked into the room like a dog walking inside from a thunderstorm. She held out a file folder to Zel.

Zel's mouth tightened. She recognized that file.

"I know I shouldn't have been snooping," Heather started.

"No you should *not* have," Zel growled. "Mom, how could you?"

"I woke up, and you were gone!" Heather said, her voice threatening more tears. "And I felt so lonely and sad!"

"So you went through my briefcase?"

Heather waved her hands as if this detail was unimportant. "I had hoped that seeing me...that if I came here...I had hoped I'd be enough," Heather cried. "I want to be mother enough for you!"

Zel pinched the bridge of her nose and snatched the file folder out of her mother's hand. How could she explain to her drama queen mother that Zel wanted to find out who her birth mother was because...because she was curious, because she felt incomplete, because she wanted answers? It had nothing to do with Heather. Heather Goethe was the one who raised her, was the mother who was there for her, who remembered her birthdays and bought her Christmas presents. Heather was the one Zel called when she needed something, even if all she needed was to hear her mother's voice. Zel wanting to know more about who she was and her own past had nothing to do with whether or not Heather was a good mother. It was about Zel, and what she wanted—needed—in her life.

"Why are you in a bathrobe?" Heather said, the tears gone from her voice as she squinted at her daughter, inspecting her.

Zel's head whirled from the emotional whiplash.

Heather's eyes drifted from Zel's bathrobe to the bed. To Zel's panties wadded up on the floor, to the nightie flung across the room. Heather's eyes narrowed, and Zel could tell that her mother was looking for evidence of what had happened last night.

"I came here to sleep," Zel said, perhaps a little too loudly, drawing her mother's focus back on her. "You snore." She glanced down at what she was wearing. "And I was about to take a shower."

"Oh, I see how it is!" Heather wailed. "You didn't even want me to stay in this hotel, but you pass me off to a smaller room while you sneak up here!" She held her arms out, indicating the expansive penthouse.

"Mom, I—"

"Don't you 'Mom,' me!" Heather said. "You don't even *want* me as your mother! You can't wait to replace me with the woman who gave you up!"

The words hurt Zel more than they should have; she should be used to her mother's penchant for drama by now. Still, they stung—both that her mom would think she'd replace her, and the blunt way she talked about how her birth mother had abandoned her.

"I just want to *know*, okay? Is that so hard to understand?"

"You hate me!" Heather said. "And if you go to meet that...that *woman* —that just proves it! It proves how much you hate me!" Heather's shoulders hunched over, shaking.

"Mom, I don't *hate* you," Zel said.

"Prove it!" Heather pointed at the file folder. "Throw that away."

"Mom—"

"I was never good enough!" Heather cried. "I tried, and I tried! I gave up so much for you! But I was never a good enough mother!"

"Mom, you were good enough—"

"I *was*! But not now! Is it because I'm older?"

This was a huge source of insecurity for Heather—she'd adopted Zel when she was 45.

"No, Mom—"

"But it was something! Something about me—" she waved towards her body dramatically "—makes me not good enough!"

"*Fine!*" Zel roared. She stomped to the trashcan by the door and tossed the file inside. "Fine! If I have to *prove* my love to you, I *will*."

Heather stared at the file in the trashcan. There was a look of triumph on her face, but also something deeper, real sorrow that Zel couldn't quite place.

"Zel, honey," she started, but Zel cut her off.

"Let's go." She pushed the door open for her mother, but before she followed her, she looked back. The door to the bathroom was still shut. She trusted Drew to leave, and she hoped that he could pretend like this— all of this, from last night to now—had never happened.

And a little piece of her heart broke at the idea of leaving both him and the file behind.

*H*eather seemed to realize that something snapped within Zel at the confrontation. She usually liked to relive her drama, play-by-play, but she was uncharacteristically silent. She didn't even comment when Zel swerved immediately to the stairs rather than taking the elevator down to her room.

"I'll, uh, meet you at the café?" Heather asked as she pushed the button to call for the elevator. "Breakfast? My treat?"

Zel nodded and pushed open the stairwell door.

Back in her room, she picked her most severe outfit—a black business suit with a pencil skirt that came tastefully past her knees and a silk blouse that didn't show a hint of cleavage. She sat down in front of her makeshift vanity. That was the worst part of living in a hotel room—no real place to put on makeup. As much as she tried to convince Richard that women travelled too, he ascribed to the traditional room layout, at least for the rooms on the lower floors, the "normal" rooms: bed, desk, chair. Zel had an entire suitcase dedicated to her makeup battle station, and had long ago converted the desk to her needs. A lighted magnifying mirror in the center, high-end makeup neatly stacked in a U-shape around it.

Zel washed her face; she had no time for a proper shower. Then she sat down at her battle station.

To her, makeup was an art. It was impermeable, gone by the end of the day, but that made it more interesting to her. She could create a look, and it could be fabulous, but it would be gone in 24 hours.

She started with her eyes, creating dark smudges at the corners and adding a hint of silver to the center of her eye. Then winged eyeliner, extra sharp. Zel's hand lingered over a bright red lipstick. Had her mother not interrupted her, she would have worn that shade, and she would have made sure Drew saw it. Instead, she opted for a tasteful nude.

By the time she met her mother in the café, Heather had recouped whatever abashed feelings she'd had before.

"I just want you to know," she said before Zel could even order her green tea latte, "I *need* you to know, I'm your mother, and I care for you, and I only worry about you. What I do, I do out of love."

You do out of selfishness and insecurity, Zel thought, her eyes narrowing on her mother.

It had taken Zel years to work up the courage to start searching for her birth mother. She'd used every connection she had, every tiny memory and piece of knowledge. She'd been adopted when she was a little less than a year old, and all Heather ever told her was that her mother was "unfit," and that Heather had gone straight from her birth mother to Zel in a closed adoption—not a usual situation. Zel had gone back to their old hometown near Camden, New Jersey, interviewing social workers and knocking on the doors of neighbors as she built her file up.

And finally, *finally* she had a lead. She'd called her mother before coming to Hotel Ever After to meet up with her since Heather lived far closer to Fairhaven than NYC. She'd felt it was only respectful to tell Heather in person that she intended to meet her birth mother.

And now that file—and her birth mother's address—were in the trash.

She wanted to hold onto her anger. Heather was more than dramatic sometimes. Sometimes her drama was so self-serving it would put Regina George to shame.

But Zel loved Heather. Even when she was mean. Because no matter what insecurities Heather had about being an adoptive mother, Zel knew they were unfounded. Heather was her mother, blood relations be damned.

Heather watched Zel intently, a whisper of a smile creeping on her lips when she noticed Zel's face soften. "I love you," Heather said, her voice a whisper. She reached out and grabbed Zel's hand.

Zel shook it from her grip. But she said kindly, "I know. My usual," she added as Aria approached.

"I just worry," Heather added, not taking the hint. "I don't want you to be disappointed."

You don't want competition.

"Drop it, Mom," Zel said.

"I just—"

"Drop. It."

Heather looked down into her mug of coffee and nodded. "So what are we doing today?" she said brightly as Aria handed Zel her latte.

"Well, *I* am going to work," Zel said. "I've already had a late start."

Heather pouted. "I thought you could take me on a drive along the coast. It's so pretty here."

"Mom, it's Tuesday. I have to *work*."

Heather's pout intensified. "But *Zellll*," she said. "Baby, I'm only here for a few more days—"

"Days? You were ready to leave yesterday."

"Yes, but wouldn't it be lovely if—"

Zel stood up. "I love you," she said, seriously. "I really, really do. But I have a job to do." She rooted around in her purse and plopped her car keys on the table. "If you want to go for a drive along the coast, use my car." She turned around and headed to her office.

"Zel!" Heather called, but Zel didn't stop.

That's the thing about her mother. A weekend visit turned into a monthlong vacation. What Heather wanted, Heather got.

Zel thought about the file upstairs.

Her fists clenched.

Not this time.

~

*I*t had only been an hour since she'd left the penthouse, but surely Drew was gone by now. Surely.

Zel shifted the fresh linens in her arms. They were surprisingly heavy. But she didn't want to make the newly hired maids clean this room. Not when she was the cause of its dishevelment.

Zel pressed her key card against *Much Ado About Nothing* and opened the door. The scent of fresh lavender wafted up to her.

The room was spotless.

Zel dropped the linens on the chair and inspected everything. The bed was perfectly made, not a pillow out of place, the sheets fresh. She peeked into the bathroom; the bath robe she'd taken had already been replaced.

Drew must have asked one of the maids to come clean up after them. On the one hand she was grateful; he was thinking about how to help. On the other hand...

"No," Zel whispered. She darted back into the main room.

The trashcan by the door was empty. Her file was gone forever.

CHAPTER NINE

*H*er first thought was to Dumpster dive. She could piece back together the information in the file, but it would take time, weeks or more. She should have backed everything up. And all the electronic files she had *were* backed up. But it didn't include everything. It didn't include the address, which she'd hastily scribbled on a piece of paper and filed safely in the folder.

But then the plumber came to the front desk, saying he wanted to close down the water main for a week, and the head interior designer peeked at the tenth floor luxury suites and screamed that the wrong carpet had been installed, and some of the chairs that had been delivered yesterday had damaged cushions, and the head chef who'd just been hired was demanding a chance to inspect the kitchen as soon as possible and, and, and.

And Zel decided she could let the file go. It may not even be salvageable. She could repair the work...eventually...and maybe then Heather would be okay with her continuing her quest to find her birth mother...

And maybe it just wasn't worth it anyway. Sometimes, we just don't get what we want, no matter how much we want it.

From the front desk, Zel saw her mother get up after paying Aria, car keys in her hands.

And part of her wanted to go with her. Maybe on the coastal highway they could hash out just what made Heather so insecure and resistant to

Zel meeting her birth mother. Maybe they could just have a day without arguments. That would be nice.

Zel looked at the lights blinking on the hotel's main phone line, the computer flashing with new email messages, the workers lined up at the desk, needing her to put out fires.

"Just one moment," she started, putting her finger up and shooting a sympathetic smile to the interior decorator. She dodged out from behind the front desk and headed toward her mother.

But when her eyes scanned the lobby, they drifted right over Heather. And landed on Drew.

It was like electricity sparking, a bolt of lightning shooting from her gaze to his. She froze, and so did he. Her mouth parted, her tongue swiping along her bottom lip, tasting the words she *wanted* to say. Because if she was going to do something selfish, something just for her, it wouldn't be to go on a drive with her mother.

It would be to go nowhere at all with Drew.

Her heart thudded, the blood pounding inside her like rocks falling. She should tell him. Tell him that she wanted more than one night.

But before she could say a thing, he turned his back on her and walked away.

~

"*N*o, he *didn't*," Aria gasped.

Zel nodded. She stared at the bagel sandwich Aria had just put in front of her, but out of the corner of her eye, she watched the front desk. It was already two, but she hadn't had a chance to eat anything all day aside from her green tea latte earlier.

"He just turned away from you? Maybe it was an accident."

"You're sweet," Zel said, shooting her a tired smile. "But no. He met my eyes, he clearly saw I wanted to talk, and he turned the other way."

"After—after a night of..." Aria's voice faded away, and her cheeks flushed red. Zel couldn't help but smile. Aria would be eaten alive in New York.

"Yeah. I mean, we both went into it knowing what it was, but still." Still, her heart hurt at the totally emotionless way he rejected her. "He wouldn't even *speak* to me."

"Maybe," Aria mused, drawing the word out, "he saw your mother? And that's who he was avoiding."

Zel snorted and took a bite of her sandwich. "Yeah, maybe that first time. They were both in the lobby. But then he just turned his back on me and got in the elevator. Not a word to me. And then..." She took another bite, filling her mouth with food rather than words.

"Then?" Aria prodded gently.

"Then I saw him again, working on the network on the second floor."

"And."

Zel shrugged. "He wouldn't even meet my eyes."

Aria tried to find the positive in the situation, but she came up empty.

"And I saw him again. On the penthouse floor. By the penthouse."

Aria gasped and Zel smiled. "The main networking panel is right there, Aria."

"Oh. Yeah."

It's not like he was lingering near the room where they'd...

Well. He didn't seem to care about any of that.

"And he ignored you again."

"Barely nodded at me. Just total ice."

Aria frowned.

Zel ate the rest of her sandwich in silence. Aria was one of the most optimistic, positive people she knew, but there wasn't a good spin to this.

She'd had a one-night stand. Not the first one she had, but the first one she wished would have lasted more than a night. But Drew clearly didn't. They were in that awkward stage, where they had to forget what had happened before they could meet each other's eyes. And since the hotel was nearing completion, there wouldn't be a chance to ever move past that stage.

"Soon enough I'll head back to New York," Zel mused aloud. And Drew would still be here.

If they couldn't make it in the same hotel, there's no way they had a chance at anything three thousand miles apart.

____

CHAPTER TEN

____

$\mathcal{Z}$el didn't have a chance to face her mother until that evening. Heather was sitting at Zel's makeshift vanity, staring in the mirror, examining her wrinkles in the magnification.

"Hey," Zel said.

Heather started, looking ashamed at being caught.

"Want dinner?"

Heather opened her mouth to speak, then closed, then stood. "Yes," she said finally, grabbing her large purse.

"It's okay," Zel said. "We're just going upstairs."

But Heather didn't put her purse down.

"The new head chef," Zel chuckled. "Well, she's a firecracker. She's got silver hair and nerves of steel. Anyway," she said, taking a deep breath and walking past the door that led to the stairwell and heading to the elevator. "Anyway, she said she'd cook us a sample dinner of some of the dishes she plans on using in the main menu."

"That's nice," Heather said quietly. She stopped as Zel pushed the elevator call button. "Darling, you hate the elevator. Let's take the stairs."

Zel's eyes widened. She hadn't wanted to board the tiny box of potential death, but she was certainly not used to Heather volunteering to take the stairs.

"Is something wrong?" Zel asked as they turned back down the hall to the stairwell.

Heather shook her head, clutching her purse a little tighter next to her body. She held the door open and they started upstairs.

"Mom?"

"I'm just..." Heather's eyes were on the steps. "I wanted to apologize. I'm sorry for the way I acted earlier."

"It's okay, Mom," Zel said. "I'm used to it." Her mother was a storm—wild and screaming one minute, calm the next.

"Really," Zel added when her mother didn't say anything. "It's really okay."

They climbed the rest of the stairs in silence.

The top floor of the hotel was designed for parties. Aside from the penthouse suite, there were no guest rooms. Instead, there was an expansive restaurant that spilled out into a glass-walled balcony overlooking the infinity pool. The Hotel Ever After may never be used for conferences or conventions, but the parties it hosted would be...magical.

Half the restaurant's roof was made of glass, curving down to form a wall of windows, giving the room the feel of a Victorian conservatory. Ivy and trailing flowers hung from the ceiling, strung around twinkling fairy lights on copper wire. Paper lanterns flickered along the ceiling, each a different size and hung from invisible thread creating a beautiful optical illusion that made it look as if they were disappearing into an endless sky.

"Hey! Finally!" a voice barked from the kitchen, ruining the effect.

"Hello, Wilhelmina," Zel said, smiling as the head chef emerged.

"Mina, just call me Mina." She wore immaculate chef's whites and carried a huge knife.

"This is my mother," Zel said, pulling Heather closer. Heather was being unusually reserved, and she had no idea why.

Mina, however, didn't care. "I've got the first course already ready. You're late." She leveled Zel with a glare.

"Sorry." This woman should be grandmotherly, but she was more intimidating than Mr. Dickson was.

Mina nodded, accepting the apology. She turned on her heel back toward the kitchen, barking an order at the red-headed sous chef as she pushed through the swinging doors.

"Over here." Zel lead her mother to a table near the kitchen. There was still work to be done in the restaurant—the trim wasn't painted, the glass wasn't polished, and there was an exposed electrical panel on the other side.

"Did you go for a drive?" Zel asked. The silence from her mother was growing unnerving. Heather usually carried far more of the conversation than her share, but now she seemed closed up and hidden, and Zel didn't know what to say to make her open back up again.

Heather's eyes shifted to something behind Zel. Zel turned in her seat as Mina opened the kitchen door, bearing two dishes. At first, Zel thought that her movement had drawn her mother's gaze, but it was something—someone—else. Drew hung back against the wall, nodding quickly at them before moving over to the electrical panel. Zel was a little surprised to see him working this late, but he knew how important it was for the hotel to remain on schedule, and she appreciated his dedication.

Heather's eyes were glued to the table as Mina explained the food—deep fried capers and grilled shrimp as an appetizer. Zel's mouth watered at the sight, but her mother barely heard Mina and twirled her fork absent-mindedly.

"Mom?" Zel asked. The capers crunched, bursting with salt in her mouth, paired with the lemony shrimp. "Oh, man, you've *got* to try this."

"Zel," Heather said, putting her fork on the table. "I want to apologize."

"I already said, don't worry about it. You're my mother; it's not worth it to me to upset you."

"No." Heather's eyes flicked over Zel's shoulder again, then met her gaze. "No, this is important. It was wrong of me to try to stop you from finding your birth mother. I was unfair and-and dramatic."

Zel squinted her eyes. It was unusual for her mother to stutter over her words, to hesitate like this. And yet she seemed sincere, deeply so.

"I don't understand why you want to meet your birth mother, but that's okay. It's not for me to understand. It's for you to experience. So..." She bent down and hauled her giant purse into her lap.

Zel wasn't sure what to expect any more, but it wasn't the file folder with all her birth mother's information.

Heather slid the folder across the table toward Zel. "You don't need it, but you have my...my blessing."

Zel stared at the folder. How did she get it?

Why did she get it?

Heather's eyes flicked back over Zel's shoulder. Zel twisted in her seat, and she caught a glance of Drew walking out of the restaurant. The electrical panel was exactly the same as it was before, and it only now occurred to Zel that panel had nothing to do with the network, and there was no reason for Drew to be working on it.

He did this. She didn't know how, but she was certain of it.

Zel threw her chair back and headed to the door.

"Hey! Next course coming!" Mina called.

"I—I'm sorry!" Zel said, truly apologetic, but not enough to stop.

She burst into the hallway and caught a glimpse of Drew heading to the elevator. Without thinking twice, she dove into the tiny elevator with him, the doors sliding shut behind her.

"It was you," Zel said, breathless.

"Me?"

"You got that file back for me."

Drew's gaze intensified. "It was important to you."

"More than you know," Zel whispered.

And then she realized she was in the elevator and the elevator wasn't moving. She felt her heart rate spike, and her hands fumbled for the wall behind her.

"It's because we didn't hit any buttons," Drew said, pointing. "If we do, it'll go."

Zel met Drew's eyes. "I'm not sure I want to go anywhere."

Drew quirked his eyebrow up. "You want to stay in the elevator forever?"

"I meant—with you, stupid! I meant I want to stay with you!"

Drew leaned over and pushed a button on the panel. The elevator doors slid open. Zel stepped back, breathing the non-claustrophobic air with relish. Drew followed her back into the hall.

"Just one more night?" he asked.

"One more," Zel said. "Let's start with dinner."

She led Drew back inside. Mina stood at the kitchen door, glaring at the empty table Zel had left. Her mother was gone, the file folder alone on the table.

"So now it's you two?" Mina growled.

"My mother—?"

"Said she'd leave you to it."

Zel glanced at Drew. "Then yes. Now it's us two."

CHAPTER ELEVEN

---

*D*inner was, to put it simply, *perfect*. Mina's cooking was a beautiful mix between comfort food and gourmet. Mac and cheese served in small cast iron skillets and sprinkled with black truffle shavings. Perfectly cooked filet mignon topped with bubbling parmesan. A chocolate soufflé powdered with cayenne pepper.

But Mina—normally so loudspoken and grumpy—immediately recognized that a dinner with Drew was a different affair from a dinner with Zel's mother. She placed the plates on the table and faded away silently, giving them the illusion of being entirely alone.

Zel's hand lingered on the file folder. "Do you know what this is?" she asked Drew.

"I know enough. I snatched it back from the trash as soon as you left."

"Thank you," Zel whispered.

"And your mother wanted to give it back to you," Drew said. "That's why I turned away from you in the lobby. I wanted to give her a second chance."

Zel shut her eyes and visualized what had happened this morning in a different light. Drew had seen her and her mother, and he seized the chance to get on the elevator with Heather and give her the file to give back to her.

"You don't know my mom very well," Zel laughed. "I'm honestly surprised she didn't just throw away everything."

Drew bit his lip and focused on his food.

"Drew?" Zel asked, a laugh on her lips. "What did you do?"

"I might have mentioned my internet prowess," Drew said, grinning. "You know how, er, some people are when it comes to the internet."

"Did you threaten my mother with hacking?"

"I mean," Drew laughed, "it's not like I actually *could* hack anything, but I might have implied that if she didn't give you the file and her approval that I'd make sure you got both the file and all the other information you were looking for."

And suddenly it was all clear. Drew wanted to do more than get the information back to Zel, he wanted to give her mother a chance to not be the villain of the story. He wanted to let her be the hero, let her appear to choose the right path.

"Thank you," Zel said in a low voice. "My mother can be...difficult."

"Right," Mina said loudly from the kitchen. "We're leaving. You two stay as much as you want, but we're leaving." Mina's sous chef—a pretty girl with bright red hair—trailed behind her as she marched to the door. Zel glanced at her cell phone; it was already past ten. Where had the time gone?

Drew leaned back. "That meal was awesome," he said. "This place ain't too shabby," he added.

"Ain't too shabby?" Zel mocked his country accent.

"Yeah, it's nice." Drew grinned at her.

"It should be." The words were harsher than she intended.

"You've been working hard."

"It's a bit stressful," Zel admitted.

Drew stood up.

"What are you doing?" Zel asked.

"Helping you relax," Drew said, wrapping his hands over her shoulders. His thumbs dug into her tense muscles.

"More of your 'pressure points?'" Zel asked, thinking back to their meeting on the elevator.

Drew snorted. "Nah. I just happen to like having an excuse to touch you." His fingers rubbed her spine, and Zel arched her back, sighing happily.

"Just keep doing what you're doing," she moaned.

His hands went lower, just above her hips. "It seems like it may not have been an easy life, growing up with that mother of yours."

Zel sighed. No, Heather wasn't easy. But she was *her* mother. She started to try to explain, but Drew cut her off.

"I get it," he said. "I do. We can't help who we love."

"That is *really* good, by the way," she said as Drew's thumbs rubbed her spine.

"You have a complicated past," Drew said in a contemplative voice.

"You don't?"

"Oh, I do," he said. "But let's quit thinking about the past."

His hands dipped lower, his finger sliding beneath her blouse, over her clavicle, down to her breasts. He leaned closer, his face so close to her that she could smell the chocolate lingering on his breath. She tried to tilt her head towards him, but he evaded her. His lips claimed her ear, his tongue sliding down the edge and to her lobe. Zel gasped, her body going taut.

Drew wasn't the only one with sensitive ears.

His hands slipped under her bra, his fingers playing along the lace edging before dipping further in, brushing along her nipples. Zel threw his hands away from her, jerking around so she could face him, but as soon as she turned, he fisted his hand in her hair, pulling her lips to his and devouring her with a kiss that burned with passion and left her breathless.

He pulled her up, her body sizzling next to his as she stood. Drew's kiss deepened, and Zel's body arched against his, her butt pressed against the edge of the table. With a growl, Drew leaned over her and swept their dessert dishes to the floor. They clattered against the tile, but Zel didn't care as Drew hefted her up by the hips and placed her on the table. She braced her arms behind herself, using all her strength to match his passionate kiss.

His hands trailed down her body, and it felt as if her silk blouse was nothing but smoke, his touch burning through her. And then his hand slid down the tight pencil skirt, and Drew groaned with longing. He pushed the fabric up, bunching the material in his fist before letting go, before moving down, down, his hand on her knee, her thigh.

Zel was very, very glad that she hadn't bothered with hose. Drew's touch was hot and needy, sliding up and up. His kiss deepened, and Zel quit fighting gravity, letting her arms go slack. Drew's fingers pushed aside the thin material of her panties, stroking along the edge of her. She gasped, arching again, but his kiss shushed her, swallowing the sounds of her pleasure as his fingers pushed deeper, tantalizingly closer and closer. She was slick with desire.

One finger slid inside of her, then another. His thumb found her clitoris, rubbing gently, teasing.

Zel's hand flailed, connecting with his muscled arm, trailing to his hip, his pants, the hardness inside them.

She pushed him away, and he staggered back, his eyes dark and hooded with lust.

"More," she panted.

He stepped forward, eager.

She shook her head, sliding off the table. "Not here."

She grabbed his hand and pulled him to the door, to the hall, back to the penthouse suite.

rew went straight to the bed, shedding clothes as quickly as he could. But Zel lingered at the door, smiling at his eagerness.

"I've got to freshen up," she said coyly, turning to the bathroom.

When she closed the door, she leaned against the smooth, painted wood, her heart racing.

This is a bad *idea,* she reminded herself. She'd be leaving soon—a month at most. The closer the hotel came to completion, the sooner she'd be back in New York, on the other side of the country from Drew and his hard muscles and delicious lips and...

But just because she couldn't have something forever didn't mean she didn't want it *now.* This penthouse would be her ivory tower. Nothing could reach her here, not even time.

Zel went to the sink first, swishing mouthwash while she inspected her hair. She pulled the pins out and let her long, blonde tresses fall down her back. Then, in the mirrored reflection, she caught sight of the jacuzzi tub.

A wicked grin spread over her face.

She knew just how soundproof this room in particular was, so she knew Drew couldn't hear anything as she started running warm bathwater. She threw in some bubblebath and lit the candles along the corner. She threw her clothes off quickly, cracked open the door so Drew would know he could come in, and then turned to the tub, testing the water with her toes before sink under the pile of scented bubbles.

She sighed, leaning back, as the warm water enveloped her. It was bliss-ful...serene. And then her mind filled with Drew and what they were going to do in this tub, just as soon as he realized where she was...

"This is more 'freshening up' than I expected." Drew stood in the doorway, his eyes appreciative as he took in the scene.

Zel's eyes were appreciative too—Drew was entirely nude and fully erect.

She leaned up in the tub, just enough for her breasts to emerge from the water, bubbles clinging to them.

"Don't start without me," Drew said. His voice was low and gravelly, choked with desire. "Or...maybe do."

Zel cocked an eyebrow, and Drew met her lustful gaze. Fine. She could play this game. And she would drive him *wild*.

She leaned her head back, her blond hair floating past her neck. She languidly pulled it back, twisting it out of the way and then letting her hands trail down her body. She moved slowly, meandering over her curves. Zel cupped her breasts, and despite the warm bath water, her nipples were hard and firm. Zel brushed over the top of them, relishing in their sensi-tivity. She closed her eyes, imagining that it was Drew who touched her, not herself. She swirled her fingers over her nipples, then pinched them, the sensation both pleasing and painful at the same time. She gasped, and then smiled to herself when she heard Drew moan in response.

She peeked through lowered lashes at Drew. He gripped the doorframe with one hand, his eyes devouring her. His other hand stroked his condom-covered penis. It was so hard, she wondered if it hurt.

Zel leaned back more, exposing her long, white neck, arching her back so her breasts were prominent. Her hands dipped below the water, down her stomach, along her hips, down. She used one hand to steady herself on the bottom of the tub, and used the other tease her clitoris, one finger slipping inside. The warm water made her body relax, but the lust building inside of her coiled tight, tighter. She stroked herself with more urgency, her clit slick and smooth.

Zel moaned with pleasure, panting. Her eyes opened and connected with Drew. With a roar of desire, Drew strode across the bathroom, splashing water everywhere as he lunged for her. "God, I want you," he groaned, grabbing her hips under the water and pushing inside her of with one powerful thrust, roaring in triumph and satisfaction as he filled her.

His head bent down, kissing her neck voraciously. He kept one hand on the edge of the tub for leverage, but he bunched his other hand in her hair, protecting her head as he pulled out and thrust inside of her again. Zel panted his name, her clitoris so enlarged that it rubbed deliciously against his hard cock. The water sloshed in the tub with the rhythm of their bodies, the bubbles floating around them like stars.

She could feel that his need for her was so great he was about to burst already. Part of her wanted his eruption, wanted to see him explode with desire, wanted to push him over the edge, to fall with him.

But a greater part of her wanted this to last. She slithered out, pushing his chest with both her hands.

"Wha—?" Drew asked, lust making him slow.

"Shh," Zel whispered, smiling. She pushed him back, so that his head was resting on the edge of the tub. She swam over to him, floating above his penis, and understanding filled him. His hands went to her back, trailing up and down her spine, then they gripped her hips, driving her down. She splashed him, making him move his hands.

"Let me," she insisted.

Drew moaned, desire and need in his voice.

"Trust me," she said, using the water to support her as she slid up and down his cock, letting her body barely touch the head before slipping away.

He moaned louder, and Zel smiled as his fists clenched. She let her hips float above him, positioning the head of his penis at the entrance to her body. She gripped the side of the tub over his shoulders and sank down over him, engulfing him inside of her. She couldn't help the sound of deep satisfaction that erupted from her throat, and the sound made Drew lose control—he started to move his hands back to her hips, but she grabbed his arms, forcing his hands lower, to her thighs.

She undulated her hips, not quite letting him leave her as she moved up and down his shaft.

"Please," Drew begged.

Zel moved faster and faster. The water flew in waves around them, splattering across the marble floor, but she didn't care. She didn't care. Drew's grip on her thighs tightened, and then he let go, sliding his finger between their bodies, touching her clitoris.

Pleasure erupted inside of her with just that one touch. She slammed against Drew, her hands shifting from the tub to his body, clutching him as his finger slid up and down her clit, harder and faster. She matched his rhythm with her body. Her desire coiled tighter and tighter, and she clenched around him, waves of pleasure making her melt. Drew shouted, thrusting up inside of her, and then he, too, succumbed to his desire.

CHAPTER THIRTEEN

They ran more water in the tub so they wouldn't have to face the cold air outside it.

"We're going to get wrinkly," Zel laughed. Her head was snuggled into his chest, one arm draped over his body.

He kissed the top of her head. "I'll like you even then. Wrinkles are sexy."

"This is certainly wrinkly," she said, letting her hand drop to his groin.

Drew growled. "Keep that up and it won't be for long."

Zel chuckled, but moved her hand. "Your legs are so strong," she said, sliding her hand underwater over his firm thighs. "It must be all that bicycling you do."

"The cottage I'm renting while I do this job came with a bike, and I figured it was cheaper than using my own bike."

"Your own bike?" Zel twisted in the water to look up at him.

"A Harley. That's what I usually ride when I go to jobs."

"Jobs?" Zel had not been the one to hire Drew; Mr. Dickson had, stating he'd done excellent work at his LA hotel.

Drew nodded. "My work is really good, but kind of temporary. I've got a reputation as being the go-to guy for one-time jobs. Once the network is up and running, I'll work with the management Mr. Dickson hires to train them, and I'm gone."

"Gone," Zel repeated in a whisper.

"You're leaving too, though, right? Back to New York?"

Zel nodded, not looking at him. She didn't want to talk about that. She didn't want to think about what would happen when it was all over.

"I like the freedom of this work," Drew said. "I can go anywhere."

"I travel a lot," Zel said. "But I always end up back in New York." The Dickson headquarters were there. Richard Dickson's main office was in Manhattan, and even though some of his brothers had set up satellite offices across the nation to help oversee the development of the hotels, everything always came back to New York.

"I've been to New York. I helped set up the Garden Hotel."

Zel gasped. She worked on the Garden Hotel, a beautiful palatial property that bordered Central Park and was designed to look like a conservatory. It was her first project; one reason why Richard had wanted her to work on Hotel Ever After was so that she could oversee the design of the restaurant, one he wanted to emulate the Garden Hotel's.

"I met Richard in college," Drew continued. "He gave me my first big break, so whenever he needs a job, I go there."

"Shame there aren't any plans for more hotels in the city," Zel said. She knew Richard's development schedule better than she knew her own plans for the future, and this was the only hotel that had his attention at the moment.

Drew looked at her funny, no doubt catching the hint of remorse in her voice. "You know," he said, "I don't have to have a job to go to New York."

"What?" Zel twisted in the water so she could face him.

"Like I said, my job pays well. I'm due for a break. And my motorcycle is due for an adventure."

"I..."

"Don't say you can't. This hotel is almost done; there are only finishing touches. Richard can get one of his brothers to come up and oversee the rest. We could take the long way back to New York, maybe help you complete that file you've been working on the way."

Zel bit her lip, contemplating. "But..."

"You don't have to be alone," Drew said. "I could go with you. I have nothing here." He paused. "Nothing but you."

Zel thought about the hints he'd dropped about his past—a damaged father, a fear of heights, secrets left unsaid. She realized now that he hadn't been hiding them from her, he'd been waiting. Waiting to share his life with her.

Maybe not forever.

But definitely more than one more night.

"We could go together," Drew whispered into her hair. "See what happens next."

Zel's heart leapt with joy. "I would love nothing more."

"Nothing?" Drew said, twisting his hips so she could feel his hard cock pressing against her leg.

Zel's smile turned languid. "I can think of at least *something* else I might love to do right now..."

"Something," Drew choked out, smiling.

"Something," Zel repeated, twining her legs with his and floating over his body.

～

*W*hen they finally made their way to the bed, Drew proved one more time just how strong his legs were. *Bless that bicycle,* Zel thought, before she quit thinking entirely.

By the time they woke up the next morning, Zel's muscles screamed in protest at doing anything other than lay in bed. She was happy to oblige, snuggling into Drew's side.

Her phone, however, insisted on attention. It flashed and beeped with each new incoming message.

Are you okay? Aria texted. *There are some delivery men down here waiting for you.*

You can sign for me, Zel texted back.

Drew grunted and pulled Zel closer to him. He was half awake, but Zel could tell he was ignoring her phone, hoping to continue cat napping. Zel smiled and curled next to him, but kept her phone out. She had to send a message to her boss. Thankfully, she was pretty sure his blissful vacation in Paris would put him in a good mood to accept her proposal...

As soon as she hit send, another text flashed across her screen. She was worried Aria was having trouble with the front desk, but instead, the message was from her mother.

Thank that young man for me, she said. *He's got a good head on his shoulders.*

Zel glanced over at Drew. *I will,* she texted back.

I wanted to say goodbye, but I don't want to bother you. I'm heading home now.

Zel blinked at her screen. It was very unlike her mother to exit without a performance. *Really?*

Really. You need your privacy, and I don't want to be in the way.

Thanks, Zel texted.

After a few moments, her mother sent another message. *I'm sure that hacker already told you his scheme, but he was right. You have my blessing, for what it's worth.*

It means a lot, Zel typed quickly. And then she added, *Mom.*

Zel let her phone drop on the nightstand, then turned back to Drew and kissed him on the nose. It was time for them to wake up. They both had work to do.

Drew stirred, and the sheet fell away from his body, exposing a part of Drew's body that was already awake and *very* alert.

But first... Zel thought, lowering her head to kiss him.

CHAPTER FOURTEEN

"Already? You're leaving already?" Aria pulled out the chair across from Zel and plopped down, her eyes wide and sad.

"Yeah..." To be honest, Zel was sad to leave Hotel Ever After. It was her baby, the project she'd been overseeing for months... "But I talked to Mr. Dickson, and he agrees that everything is mostly done here. He's sending his brother, Eric, up from the LA hotel to wrap up the last hires and loose ends."

Eric had been at Hotel Ever After on and off again since Mr. Dickson left for Europe. Eric was ready now to stay on until the hotel's launch.

"I knew you would only be here for a while, but I think I forgot about how you'd be leaving." Aria fiddled with the end of her apron string. "It's been lonely here, with Bette galavanting through France. You've been a good friend."

Hearing Aria say it like that, to label her a friend and not just someone she knew, filled Zel with warmth. "Don't worry," she says, "I will definitely come back. It's not like Fairhaven doesn't have a hotel!" She laughed.

Aria smiled, but she reached across the table and grabbed Zel's hand. "Promise?" she said. "Promise you'll come back and visit sometime?"

"Absolutely," Zel said, and she meant it. New York would always be home, but Fairhaven would be her Narnia, the secret place where she found magic.

"A cross-country trip," Aria said dreamily. "With Drew." She shot Zel a significant look.

Truth be told, it was probably for the best that Eric Dickson was flying up to take over the early management of the hotel. Zel's mind—and usually her body as well—had been elsewhere, most often in the penthouse.

"I'm really looking forward to it," Zel said honestly. "I never thought I cared about seeing Yosemite or the Grand Canyon, but with Drew..."

"You, him, a motorcycle...it's going to be awesome. Camping under the stars?"

"Okay, calm down country girl," Zel said. "I may be roadtripping, but I'm still a New Yorker at heart. We're getting hotel rooms."

"Not as nice as this one."

"Never as good as this one. None of those other hotels have you."

She stood up and hugged Aria tightly, reminding herself that she would see her again.

Zel went back up to her room, now mostly empty. She'd packed one small case with a few changes of clothes—new, casual outfits she'd picked up at the local store. There was no need for her business suits and dresses on the road. She had one compact and an eyeshadow palette in her case as well—like she told Aria, she wasn't a savage—and her hair was bound up in a braid that was sure to come undone on the bike.

The file folder was in a special section of the bag. While not a hacker, Drew was good with a computer, and he'd been able to find her a few more details about her birth mother—including a picture. Her birth mother looked...kind. Gentle. Her hair was cut in a pixie style, but it was the same blonde as Zel's. Her eyes were pale blue, but they looked a little sad. Zel wondered if the sadness had anything to do with her.

Zel had no intentions of adding to that sadness. She didn't want to accuse her birth mother or blame her. She had had a happy—if somewhat dramatic—childhood, and she had a mother who loved her, deeply. She didn't need answers; she didn't even really have questions. It didn't matter to her why her mother gave her up for adoption. There were a myriad of reasons, each one perfectly valid. There was no room in Zel's mind or heart for anger at that.

Zel just wanted to know her. This woman was a part of her past, and she just wanted to look into eyes that were like her own and say hello. She wanted to hug the woman who had once, surely, hugged her as a baby. She wanted to tell her that even though she had been adopted, and she was wrapped up in her mother's love, there was still a string that led her back to her.

And she hoped that maybe meeting her would make the sadness in her eyes fade, at least a little.

The rest of Zel's belongings had been packed up in boxes and shipped back to her Manhattan apartment. They would be waiting for her—as would her job and her life—when she got there. For now, she and Drew had this magical in-between time to get to know each other, to decide on their future.

"Thank you," Zel whispered to her empty room, to the hotel, to Fairhaven.

And then she left.

~

Zel crept up behind Aria to give her one last parting hug. Aria was so intently reading something on her computer that she didn't even notice. Through the big glass lobby doors, Zel could see Drew on his Harley. He'd turned in the keys to the cottage he was renting, and with the network done, he had nothing keeping him in Fairhaven but her.

"Boo!" Zel said as she grabbed Aria. She was so startled that she actually screamed a little, then giggled nervously and tried to shut her laptop.

"What are you looking at?" Zel said, pushing the screen back up.

A Forbes article on the Dickson family of hoteliers filled the screen. The group picture of the entire family—Richard in front, his four brothers and one sister flanking him—was blown up, with the cursor blinking over Eric Dickson's face.

"I just wanted to see who was taking over the hotel after you," Aria said, and while it was a perfectly valid reason to be looking Eric up, huge red blotches stained Aria's fair skin.

Zel leaned back, examining the picture. "He *is* hot," she conceded.

"Who's hot?" Drew asked, taking Zel's bag from her and hefting it over his shoulder.

"Eric Dickson."

"Do I need to fight him for your attention?" Drew asked casually.

"Nah, not my type. Eric's like, model-hot. You know, sexy in an utterly gorgeous kind of way. I like the nerdy boys."

Drew stuck his tongue out at Zel. "Thanks for that," he said sarcastically.

Aria made a movement to close her laptop again, her cheeks still flushed.

"I think Eric may be Aria's type, though," Zel said in a sing-song voice.

"No!" Aria said quickly, the laptop finally slamming closed. "No! I mean, um."

"He's nice," Zel said. "I usually work with Richard on construction, but I've met Eric loads of times. He's *very* friendly." She winked at Aria. While she worked under Richard, Eric had known she was off-limits, but she'd witnessed first hand the number of women who'd fallen for his dark hair and blue eyes. "But be careful," she added, remembering the streams of different girls he'd invite to parties, "he's a bit of a player."

"I don't need...I mean..." Aria stuttered, struggling for words. "I'm sure he won't even notice me."

Zel swept her friend into a hug, then leaned back, brushing Aria's red hair from her shoulders. "I'm sure he will," she said. "So be careful. But if you want, go get 'em, tiger."

Drew shifted Zel's bag from one hand to the other. "Ready?" he asked.

"Absolutely."

Zel cast one last look around Hotel Ever After, and then followed Drew to his bike. When she was a kid, she used to imagine she was a princess being saved by a knight in shining armor. She never thought that the tower he rescued her from would be in a hotel like this, and she never pictured his white stallion as a silver Harley, but Zel had to admit: This was far, far better.

CHAPTER FIFTEEN

"You are a sad mopey bucket of *gloom,*" Ursula, Aria's roommate, said.

"Shut up." Aria threw a strawberry at her, and Ursula caught it and ate it, smacking her lips and somehow not even smearing her lipstick.

"Bette's gone," Ursula said, counting on her finger. "Your new bud Zel skipped town. But you still have me."

Aria tried to smile. She had known Ursula since high school. Of course, back then, they hadn't been friends. Ursula had been the school slut, and proud of it, and Aria had been the school nerd, and while she wasn't exactly proud of it, she didn't know how to be anything else.

Then both girls had gone to the same university, and Ursula had requested to be Aria's roommate. At first, Aria was nervous—what did Ursula want from her?

Turns out she wanted a friend. And one who had never looked down on her for her numerous boyfriends or promiscuous attitude. After they both graduated, Ursula decided to develop her photography career and wanted to move into a cottage by the sea. Aria was swept along with her, as usual, picking up a job at the Happily Ever After bookstore. She had been at Happily Ever After—and now the hotel café—for five years now, but Ursula's photography career had shifted first into being an author, then a singer, and was currently somewhere between model and actress, depending on who was asking.

"Fine," Ursula said in mock disapproval. "Fine, I'll do it."

"Do...what?" Aria asked.

"I'll go with you to your boring little café and bookshop. You're twisting my arm here."

Aria grinned at her friend. "Thanks, Sula." She shot her a Vulcan salute. Ever since finding out that the one nerdy thing Ursula indulged in was *Star Trek*, Aria loved using the nickname for her best friend that was almost the same as the lieutenant's on the show.

"Watch it, nerd girl," Ursula said, but she was smiling.

~

While just a little more than a week ago it seemed as if the hotel would never be complete, now there was nothing but minor details and finishings. The stream of deliveries had finally stopped, and the stream of job applicants had started.

"Is this where I leave this?" a young woman asked, handing Aria a resume and a printed job application bearing the logo of Hotel Ever After. Aria glanced at the name—Ella Barrymore—but handed the papers back to her.

"Sorry," she said, "the manager who's taking applications hasn't arrived yet."

Ursula slipped behind the café counter and started making herself an espresso. Technically, only staff were allowed back there, but Aria knew Bette wouldn't mind, and she also knew it was pointless telling Ursula that she couldn't do something. All that would do is make her want it more.

"Do you know when the manager will arrive?" Ella asked. She glanced at her watch.

"Sorry, no," Aria replied. "He's flying up from LA, but I'm not sure when."

"Hey," Ursula said as she dumped the sugar bowl into her espresso. "Don't you work at the grocery store?"

Ella nodded. "And I'm a waitress at Greta's."

"I thought you looked familiar," Ursula said.

"And you want a third job?" Aria asked, noting the dark circles under the girl's eyes.

Ella's smile tightened. "We need the money." She glanced at her watch again. "My next shift starts soon."

Aria took the papers back from her. "I'll give this to the manager when he arrives," she said. "I promise."

"Thank you," Ella said, bowing her head a little. "Really, thank you so much."

"No problem," Aria said, but Ella was already leaving.

"What job does she want?" Ursula asked, looking over Aria's shoulder at the resume. Ella had listed skills in waitressing, reception, and house-cleaning.

"All of them, I think," Aria muttered.

"Yeah, yeah, yeah, who cares?" Ursula's grip tightened on Aria's arm. "*Look.*"

The most gorgeous man Aria had ever seen walked through the door.

Easily six feet tall, with a sweep of black hair and icy blue eyes that seemed to take in everything, this man strode into the hotel as if he owned the place. Which, Aria realized with a start, he sort of did.

Eric Dickson, brother to Richard Dickson, the new chief manager of Hotel Ever After.

The light streaming through the glass doors in the lobby illuminated Eric's body, outlining the hard lines of his arms, down his chest and torso. He didn't look like a body builder, but he did look like the kind of man that could break up a bar fight without spilling his beer. The kind of man who could not be intimidated, the kind that looked at the world as if he were a giant among mere mortals.

"Pretty boy," Ursula scoffed under her breath. She had no use for men who did nothing but look good; that was her chief complaint among the male models she worked with. "They never have any common sense," she'd rage as she slammed pots and pans around, cooking dinner for the two of them. "If they didn't have nice asses, no one would listen to a damn thing they said!"

But despite Ursula's contempt now, she couldn't seem to muster the strength rip her eyes away from Eric Dickson. They both watched as he strode across the lobby and straight to the front desk. He picked up a binder from behind the counter and disappeared into the office for a moment, one hand pulling out his cell phone. Within a few minutes—before Ursula could finish another espresso—he came back out of the office. He handled the few people waiting for a manager's attention effi-ciently and quickly, sending the interior decorator back to the rooftop bar with clear instructions on how to arrange the tables, approving the new head chef's request for some specialized equipment, and accepting a stack of applications for new jobs from the housekeeper in just a few minutes.

"Ella's application!" Aria said, remembering. She grabbed the girl's application and resume and made her way from the café to the front desk. When Zel had managed the hotel, it hadn't seem like that big of a walk, but now it felt ominous and she felt timid, like a mouse purposefully approaching the very hungry cat.

"Yes?" Eric's voice was deep and melodic, and Aria trembled under the full intensity of his icy gaze.

"I have, um, an application for you."

Eric took the paper and added it to the stack he already had, but then turned his attention to Aria. "Ella, is it?" he asked, reading the resume.

"No!" Aria's voice was so vehement that Eric's look turned curious, amused. "No," she added in a softer tone. "I'm Aria. I work, um, over there." She pointed to the café that connected the old bookshop to the lobby of Hotel Ever After.

Eric's eyes returned to the resume in his hand.

"A, um, girl dropped that off earlier," Aria said, explaining. "I said I'd give it to you, Mr. Dickson."

A hint of a smile crept up his face, but it didn't reach his eyes. "So you know who I am."

"I was friends with Zel before she left."

His eyebrow quirked up.

"Um, can I get you anything?" Aria added.

His other eyebrow jumped up.

"I mean, um, from the café?" Aria mentally slapped herself. How obtuse could she be?!

"No," Eric said, straightening the stack of applications and turning away. "I don't want any coffee."

And it was clear from his tone that he didn't want any more of her, either.

Aria slunk back across the lobby. Ursula, who had been watching the exchange but couldn't hear anything, gripped Aria's arm as soon as she got close enough.

"Well?" she asked, eyes gleaming.

"I don't think he likes me very much," Aria said.

"Oh, good." Ursula grinned. "In that case, I call dibs."

Well, that does it, Aria thought. Ursula always got what she wanted.

ARIA & THE SEA

CHAPTER ONE

"*H*ave you heard about the pre-launch party?" Ursula strode straight behind the counter of the café, sliding an espresso cup under the machine.

"I *just* cleaned that," Aria groaned. She didn't bother mentioning that Ursula wasn't supposed to go behind the counter—employees only. Stopping Ursula was like trying to stop the wind.

"Sorry." Ursula shot her a sympathetic look, but it was too late—the espresso machine was already churning out hot liquid for Ursula's.

Aria scowled, but couldn't truly stay mad at her roommate and friend. She continued wiping down the cafe counter. It had been a long day. "And yes," she added, "I've heard of the pre-launch party. How could I not?" That party was the biggest reason why it had been such a long day—Eric Dickson had hired all the best party planners and decorators and DJs and who knew what else from LA, and they all liked to chug coffee and comment on how "quaint" the attached bookstore was before tapping on their smartphones and dashing off, leaving dirty mugs and coffee rings over all the tables.

"It's going to be *epic*," Ursula said. She leaned over the counter, watching as Aria stacked chairs on top of the round café tables and start sweeping.

"You could help." Aria swept a lock of red hair off her sweaty forehead.

The summer was still warm, despite the approaching fall, and the espresso machines ran hot.

Ursula waggled her tiny espresso cup and made a half-hearted attempt to wipe down the machine she'd just dirtied.

"Finally," Ursula said, with an exaggerated smile. "Finally something awesome is happening in Fairhaven."

Awesome was a relative term. Aria understood why the party was happening. To drum up a more elite clientele, the Dickson Hotel Corporation was hosting a massive pre-launch party. Top celebrities from around the nation (and perhaps the world) would be flying in for the party and staying for the grand opening. It promised to be a spectacular affair.

Aria had watched from the sidelines. The café she ran stood between the old bookstore (which she also ran, using the same register to check out both coffee and books) and the lobby of the hotel, an innovative design by Richard Dickson as part of the negotiations with Aria's boss, Bette Franklin. She wasn't a hotel employee—not that employees were invited to the pre-launch party—but she had been a silent observer of the stream of party planners, the dozens of floral arrangements, the huge shipments of shrimp and lobster, paté and caviar.

"They've hired Rumpled Stetson to play at the party," Ursula said. "And have you seen the crates of champagne? It could fill the pool." She paused. "Maybe Eric *is* going to fill the pool with champagne. Holy shit, that'd be cool."

"They're not filling the pool with champagne," Aria said. But she wasn't actually so sure. If Zel, who had been preparing Hotel Ever After for opening, were still here, the party would have been a tasteful affair, something like a magical ball with fancy dresses and tuxedos.

But Eric Dickson, who'd taken over after Zel went back to New York, had a different style. Eric's pre-launch party was gearing up to be a wild, rhinestoned blow-out. There was a thin veneer of class—the champagne, the rich menu, the glittering Swarovski crystals—but after seeing the stream of preparations, Aria had no illusions about what the pre-launch party was going to actually be: a high-class kegger.

She wasn't sure how she felt about it. She wouldn't *mind* a huge, wild party, but at the same time, it felt like she—like all of Fairhaven—was being excluded. Because amongst the decorators and bartenders and other people Eric had shipped in from LA, there were also all the guests, staying in the newly completed hotel rooms. They wore clothes that probably cost more than Aria made in a year with jewelry sparkling so brightly she could see it from across the lobby. They looked down their noses and turned away from her as if she was a chimney sweep, not a barista/bookstore manager.

Aria leaned against her broom as Ursula made another espresso behind her, biting back a smile. She should know better than to try to close down the café before Ursula had had a chance for a caffeine hit. It didn't matter that it was seven o'clock at night; Ursula needed her espresso.

Aria's eyes drifted over the lobby. Eric Dickson was hunched over the front desk, taking notes with one ear pressed against the hotel phone, cradled in his shoulder. He may be planning a party that wasn't really Aria's style, but she had to admit that he was giving it his all. She didn't care about whatever fancy band he hired for the party, but she admired the way he spent every waking hour working to make the launch of Hotel Ever After a success.

And she admired the way his dark hair dripped down between his eyes, the way his back muscles pulled against his white shirt as he leaned over the desk, the way his fingers twirled his pen, the way his eyes sparkled so brightly they rivaled the jewels of the fancy hotel guests.

"Well, I guess I'm going," Ursula said in a bored voice.

"Going?" Aria said stupidly.

"To that pre-launch party thingie. I got an invite."

"You *did?*" Aria whirled around, her mouth opening in shock.

And then she realized just how Ursula had gotten an invite. Because while Eric was everything Aria wanted, he wasn't hers.

He was Ursula's.

"He just feels obligated to invite me," Ursula said casually. "Or maybe he just wants arm candy. I can be arm candy if free shrimp is involved."

Aria swallowed down the bitter jealousy rising in her throat. That was the worst of it—knowing how she felt about Eric, her attraction to him only rising as her esteem for him grew. Knowing how she felt, and knowing how Ursula felt. Because Ursula didn't think about Eric at night, no more than she thought of any other man. She didn't dream about what his lips tasted like or long to run her hands over his chest. He was just a toy to her, and a temporary one at that. Because after the grand opening of Hotel Ever After, Eric was leaving, back to LA and his real life, or perhaps to another hotel in the Dickson Corporation line. Either way, he'd be gone, and Ursula wouldn't really care.

But Aria would.

"You know," Ursula said, her eyes shrewd, "it's kind of boring with him, honestly. He's nice to look at, but his mind is always on work."

Part of Aria was glad. Ursula usually was quick with her men, and the thought of her best friend and roommate with the man she dreamed about...

"What is it about Dickson men that makes them so work-focused?" a familiar voice called from the bookstore side of the café.

Aria whirled around, squealing with delight. Bette strode forward, her cheeks flushed with sun, her lips parting in a huge smile. Aria ran up to her, wrapping her arms around Bette.

"How was Paris?" she asked breathlessly.

"*Wonderful*," Bette said. Her eyes gleamed. When Richard Dickson had come to buy out her bookstore, he hadn't bargained on Bette, who most definitely would never sell. And he certainly hadn't bargained on falling in love with her. As soon as the hotel plans were finalized, Richard swept Bette away to a dream vacation in Paris, the city Bette had most longed to visit.

"I got you something." Bette dug around in her turquoise leather bag and produced a small velvet box.

"I hope you're not proposing," Ursula said as she languidly strolled closer. "Aria's my roomie, and I'll fight to keep her."

Bette stuck her tongue out at Ursula. Aria opened the box.

"Oh," she breathed, "it's beautiful." A tiny ceramic seashell dangled from a gold chain. The shell was no bigger than her pinky nail, but exquisitely etched and dipped in gold. Aria immediately slipped the necklace on, fingering the chain as it nestled in her collar.

"It reminded me of you," Bette said, beaming. "I know you love the ocean."

Aria hugged her friend, grinning. "It's *perfect*," she said.

Ursula inspected the necklace and nodded in approval before giving Bette a brief hug. Ursula was like that; she showered people she didn't like very much with attention, but she was cat-like in the way she kept people she cared about at a distance.

"What's that?" Ursula said idly, and for the first time, Aria noticed the giant flashing diamond on Bette's finger. On Bette's left ring finger.

"You're engaged?!" she screamed loudly. She grabbed Bette's hand and inspected the ring closer. The *rings*. Plural—a thin band encrusted with pale blue topazes rested beneath the solitaire.

"We've not made an official announcement," Bette said, her eyes darting to the front desk at the lobby, where Eric had been moments before. "Richard's calling his family soon. Apparently, they're very big into weddings and events and things, but Richard and I..."

Aria smiled. It's what she loved best about Bette—how laid back she was. She couldn't imagine a big to-do wedding for her. A secret elopement made far more sense.

"Was it magical?" Aria asked, as Ursula rolled her eyes.

"Perfect," Bette breathed. "But later. I'll tell you all about it later. How are things here?" she asked, looking around. "The hotel looks amazing. And business is..." her voice trailed off. For all she had just complained about Richard and the other Dickson men loving their job, Bette's first thought was always on the bookstore.

"Business is fine," Aria assured her. "Up, even. Expanding the café and opening to the lobby has brought a lot of curious people through the doors."

"Good, good," Bette said, grinning. She turned to Ursula. "So, you're going to the pre-launch party?"

"Might as well," she said, shrugging, as if the most exclusive party of Fairhaven's history was just a casual night at the movies and not worth doing other than to stave off boredom.

"And you, too?" Bette asked, turning to Aria.

Aria felt her pale cheeks flush. "I'm not invited."

Bette laughed. "Of course you are! You can be my plus one."

"But—Richard?"

Bette grinned. "As if he couldn't go to his own pre-launch party. You're *going.*"

And that, apparently, was that. Bette regaled them with tales of Paris and everything she'd seen and done in Europe, steamrolling right past the sinking fear in Aria's stomach that she shouldn't attend the party at all. She wasn't really the party type of girl. Ursula would fit right in—Sula had never seen a party she didn't become the center of attention at—but Aria...

Even to see Eric, she didn't think it'd be worth it. She was awkward at best, embarrassing more usually. Being in situations where she had to be social made her clam up and sulk in a dark corner where the music was loud and she could use that as an excuse not to talk to anyone.

No, no. She shouldn't go. She *couldn't* go.

Her eyes flicked from Bette into the hotel lobby, to Eric.

What was the point of going to a party, knowing that he would be there and not even see her?

─────────
CHAPTER TWO
─────────

*B*ette slipped into work mode easily, helping Aria close the register and lock the doors to the bookstore. Ursula watched languidly, lounging on a sofa that was technically in the lobby but near the café.

As soon as they finished closing, Bette took a moment to examine the lobby. "It really is amazing," she said in a soft voice. "Just the thing Fairhaven needed."

Aria wasn't really sure that was true.

"So where's good old Dick?" Ursula said.

Bette smirked; Richard would surely hate to know that it was she who made his nickname popular among her friends. "The Dicksons are all work, no play. He stayed in New York when we changed planes from Europe; he's escorting a few top clients to the pre-launch party. And visiting his mother." She scrunched up her face.

"All work and no play?" Ursula said, cocking an eyebrow up. "Even in France?"

Bette's grin widened and a blush crept up her cheeks. "Well, not in France."

Ursula crowed with laughter, kicking her feet up on the velvety cushions of the lounger.

"Want to check out the hotel?" Ursula said.

"Sure," Bette said, but she looked a little confused.

As Ursula led them across the marbled floor to the gleaming elevator doors, Bette hung back. "Since when did Sula turn into a tour guide?"

Aria's eyes shot to Eric.

"Her...and him?"

"Yup," Ursula answered. She held the elevator door open her Bette and Aria. "It's nothing serious," she added, but she needn't have bothered. Nothing was ever serious with her.

The elevator opened up on the seventh floor. "All the rooms below this are just normal hotel rooms, boring," Ursula says. "Here's where it gets interesting."

"I *know*," Bette said, sticking out her tongue. "It was *my* idea."

"Well it was a good one," Ursula said. Guests weren't being admitted until the next day and maids were adding finishing touches to the suites—fresh flower bouquets on the tables, chocolates and champagne chilling in the refrigerators, lavender water spritzed on the linens.

One of the maids rushed past, her arms full of fluffy towels. She shot Aria a smile, and Aria realized she recognized her—Ella, the girl who had applied to work at the hotel a month ago.

"So each room is modeled after a room in literature," Ursula said, even though she didn't really need to explain. Aria had watched as the interior designers carted in the decorations; Bette had proposed the idea to Richard when the hotel was still just blueprints.

But, Aria had to admit, it was pretty magical to see it completed. The seventh floor was dedicated to the classics. The room Ursula showed them had been modeled after Jane Austen's works, a quill and ink standing beside a half-finished letter from Mr. Darcy. Next door was a Sherlock themed room. A deerstalker perched impertinantly on the bedpost; a violin leaned against the corner.

Each floor up got more and more whimsical. *The Wizard of Oz*'s room had prisms in the windows that cast the black-and-white decorations in rainbows. The Narnian room had a real lampost in the corner, and the wallpaper glittered like snow. There was, of course, a very ample wardrobe for adventurous guests. The suite based on Tolkein's works actually had a round door perfect for hobbits, but inside was more elegant than the finest elven palace.

"This is my favorite," Ursula said, leading Bette and Aria to the twelfth floor, the last floor with guest suites. Each one was dedicate to a different fairy tale, and each had a meticulous level of detail. Ticking clocks and a glass slipper on display in Cinderella's room; luxurious bedding and a spinning wheel for Sleeping Beauty's; a live apple tree and sparkling mirrors for Snow White's.

"It's better than I imagined," Bette said. "It's so perfect, linking the rooms to stories. If a hotel and a bookstore had a love child, this is it."

Aria smiled. Hotel Ever After pretty much was the love child of a hotel and a bookstore, and the love child of Richard and Bette.

Bette yawned hugely as they pushed open the stairwell doors and entered the top floor of the hotel. "Sorry," she said through the yawn. "Jet lag."

"Need a break?" Aria asked.

"Nah, I need to get back on a normal sleep schedule."

"Good, because this is the best." Ursula grabbed Bette's arm and dragged her to the rooftop restaurant. A sign spelled out the words *The Enchanted Forest* just above a small display of the menus.

And it was aptly named. The Enchanted Forest restaurant had real branches forming a canopy overhead, twinkling with fairy lights. Lit paper lanterns cast an ethereal glow. Aria knew that the tables were usually artfully arranged around the room to give the allusion of privacy, but instead, they'd been pushed up against the walls and in the corners of the room. The tile floor gleamed, and a temporary stage with musical instruments stood on the far wall.

"Really, it's going to be packed," Ursula said. "Eric's been worried about that. But the ballroom..."

"Isn't finished yet," Bette supplied. When Ursula looked surprised, she added, "Richard was raving about it. A delay with the tiler, I think?"

Ursula led Bette around the room, pointing out where the bar was going to be, exclaiming over the band that Eric had hired, confiding that the ice sculpture he'd commissioned was due to arrive tomorrow morning and was going to be in the shape of a unicorn with champagne flowing from its horn. Aria hung back. She was having a hard time imagining a thumping base and a hundred guests and the smell of alcohol in such a beautiful room.

"You're going to love this," Ursula said, startling Aria out of her reverie. "Have you seen the pool yet?"

Aria shook her head. She'd heard of it, but had spent most of her days at the hotel in the busy café and bookstore.

Ursula drug her to the opposite wall. What Aria had assumed were floor to ceiling windows were actually a wall of glass doors. Ursula pushed one open and the three women stepped onto a long, spacious balcony.

"Oh, it's lovely," Bette said, looking out over Fairhaven. Hotel Ever After was the tallest building in town, but that wasn't saying much. Fairhaven was a small town, and the heart of it was straight out of a picture book, with a charming little Main Street full of shops and restaurants, trees lining the sidewalks, and little courtyards hidden in alleys. From the balcony, they could see the mountains green and dark, looming in the fading light. And, glittering on the horizon, Aria could just make out the ocean. If she closed her eyes she imagined she could smell the salt.

"No, *look*," Ursula said, pulling Aria closer to the edge of the balcony. She pointed down the side, and Aria leaned over, her new necklace swinging out.

Water twinkled up at them.

The pool jutted out under the balcony, lit with underwater lights that made the water shine like a crystal. The design was breathtaking; the infinity pool extended out, giving the appearance of a floating expanse of water, waiting for them to jump in.

"How do you get there?" Bette asked. "I don't remember a pool in Richard's plans."

"There's a spiral staircase," Ursula said. "To the left of the restaurant. Want to see?"

"No, no," Bette laughed, yawning again. "I may have to call it a night soon." It was only seven, but she'd travelled halfway across the world to get here tonight.

"Was the flight very bad?" Aria asked, still looking down at the pool. Part of her wanted to jump over the balcony and dive into the water.

"Nah, not really." Bette yawned again. "Just long. Eight hours from Paris to New York, then another five to get here."

Aria shuddered. "I don't think I could be on a plane that long."

"Even for Paris?" Bette asked. Her eyes were on the horizon, looking at the ocean, but Aria could tell that she was really walking along the Champs-Élysées with Richard.

Ursula shrugged, turning her back to the view and leaning against the balcony. "I could care less about Paris. Everyone goes to Europe. I want to go somewhere new. Maybe Dubai."

"Dubai? That's random!" Bette laughed. "Everyone goes to Paris because Paris is magic. There's all the tourist stuff, sure, but the macaroons and the crépes and the steak frites and..."

"What about you?" Ursula asked Aria as Bette rambled about the food. "Paris or Dubai?"

Aria grinned ruefully. "I'm not getting on a plane for a day. Neither is worth it."

"You know, you could take a cruise," Bette pointed out. "Travel like the rich a hundred years ago."

Aria considered it. "That would be nice," she said. Days and days on a boat with nothing but the water surrounding her...that was far more pleasant than being cooped up in a metal can and thrown across the sky. "In that case," she said, "I would go to...Copenhagen."

"Copenhagen?!" Ursula laughed. "I didn't think you were the type." She mimed blowing smoke from a joint at Aria.

Aria waved the imaginary smoke away. "No, no, not for that," she laughed. "For the art. To bike along the waterways. And they have pancakes."

"We have pancakes."

"Theirs are better."

Bette laughed at their bickering, but the laugh turned into another yawn. "I better get home so I don't fall asleep at the wheel," she said. But instead of moving away from the balcony, she reached into her purse and withdrew a thick paper envelope. "For you." She handed Aria an official pre-launch party invitation. "And I've already had your name added to the list, so don't try to weasel out of this." She leaned in closer. "Leave your comfort zone, at least for a night. It could change everything."

"You would know," Aria said in a low voice.

"Exactly." Bette smiled.

"Okay, so, before you go, you *have* to see the penthouse suite," Ursula said, leading Bette back through the restaurant. "You get to it through a secret doorway, and it's like a room in a castle; it's gorgeous."

"I've been there," Bette said, both laughing and blushing at the same time. Ursula noticed immediately, and started to laugh at her.

A bitter taste filled Aria's mouth as the two of them turned away from the penthouse suite and moved toward the elevators instead. It was fun looking at the ways the different rooms in the hotel were decorated to look as if they came from books and fairy tales, but she didn't want a reminder of why Ursula knew so much about the hotel. And she didn't want to know why Ursula knew so much about the penthouse suite. She didn't want to imagine her best friend and roommate in that room with Eric Dickson.

Her heart couldn't take that.

The next morning, Aria woke with the dawn. Sunlight streamed into the thick glass windows of her little cottage, and she yawned and stretched, relishing the warmth. She supposed she should have thicker curtains hanging there, blocking out the light, but—unlike Ursula—Aria liked being awoken with the sun. It felt like a promise between her and the rest of the day.

When she made her way to the kitchen, she was surprised to see Ursula awake, sitting at the little round table covered with a blue gingham cloth. Ursula often complained about how "kitschy" the cottage was, but she never tried to change anything. Secretly, she liked it. The cottage had been Aria's grandmother's before she died, and it was a place both girls thought of as home long before they made it theirs.

"What are you doing up this early?" Aria asked, moving to the coffeemaker. There was already an old pot made, dark sludge on the bottom. "You haven't been to bed yet, have you?" she asked.

Ursula shook her coffee mug. "Guilty as charged."

"Your heart is going to just give out one of these days. You're going to chug another espresso, and your heart is literally just going to give up and move out."

Ursula pulled a face. "I don't think that's going to happen."

Aria dumped the old coffee out in the big farmhouse sink and started brewing another pot. "This isn't for you," she told Ursula. "At least not until after noon."

Ursula stretched. "I'm going to bed anyway. At least I won't be tired for the party tonight."

"I suppose not," Aria told the coffeemaker.

"Aria?" Ursula was always the first one to notice when Aria wasn't saying everything she meant to.

"I'm not going," Aria said. She thought about the invitation Bette had given her, the beautiful Enchanted Forest where the party was being held. "It's not really my scene, you know? That party is for important people from all over. I won't really know anyone."

"You'll know Bette," Ursula said. "And me."

And you'll be with Eric.

"It's not really my scene, you know?" Aria repeated.

Ursula snorted. "Anything outside of the bookstore isn't 'your scene.'"

"See?" Aria shrugged. "I shouldn't go to the party."

"No," Ursula said, her voice rising, "you *should*. It's *good* to do things that 'aren't your scene.' Ugh," she added. "You sound like Eric."

"Like—what?" Aria couldn't keep the surprise out of her voice.

"He's just like you. He thinks there's this distinction between stuff, like only certain people do this or that. It's annoying. You don't *have* to be one way or another. You can just, you know, have fun."

"The party doesn't really sound like that much fun," Aria said.

"Of *course* it's going to be fun," Ursula snapped. "Eric may be uptight and over-focused on work, but he knows how to throw a party."

"I have to go." She couldn't just stand there, listening to Ursula talk about Eric. She couldn't pretend like it didn't sting, to know how well Ursula knew him.

Rather than a witty comeback, Ursula clamped her lips shut, watching her roommate. It was so unusual that Aria cast a look behind her. Ursula leveled her with a contemplative stare, her eyes appraising her.

Aria left the cottage, the wooden door banging shut behind her.

~

The sea calmed her nerves, her thoughts, her heart. The sea always did that.

Aria's cottage was old and weatherworn and far too small for both Aria and Ursula. But it had no front yard—instead, it faced the beach, and it took just moments to leave the warm comfort of the old house and step into the sea, which provided a totally different kind of comfort.

Aria wrapped her arms around herself as she stared out at the crashing waves. It was getting late in the season, and there were no more tourists out.

The ocean was where Aria felt like home.

When she was younger, before her parents died and she moved in with her grandmother, Aria's family had taken a trip to Florida to take a cruise through the Bahamas. It had been wonderful and now held a sort of dreamlike idolization in Aria's memory, one of the last memories she had of her parents, and one of her favorite memories of falling in love with the ocean. Her childhood belonged to the Atlantic.

The Pacific was harder than the Atlantic, wilder, but she loved it all the same, and in some ways she loved it more. The Atlantic was a memory; the Pacific was reality. The Atlantic—at least the Atlantic she experienced—was always warm and serene, gently pushing her back to shore with soft waves. The Pacific was tempestuous and often cold and sometimes angry... but sometimes it was smooth and easy, like a caress. The Pacific changed in ways that her memory of the Atlantic couldn't, and Aria adored it because it changed, because it held secrets and depths she didn't know.

Because it reminded her of her.

Aria looked around now. Not only were the tourists gone, but so was everyone else. The beach was devoid of all people, and the ocean was empty. It felt like the end of the world, and she and the Pacific were the only survivors. It felt like the whole ocean was hers.

Moving quickly, Aria slipped the straps of her dress down and wiggled out of her clothes. She unhooked her bra and kicked out of her panties, storing her clothing under a black rock near the bank before racing into the cool waters of the sea, diving under the waves as soon as she could.

This was freedom.

About a quarter of a mile off shore, a monolith of black rock rose from the waves. Aria aimed for the rocks. In windier weather, it was dangerous to swim this close. Unlike Florida's sandy beaches, much of Fairhaven's coast was rocky, only a thin strip of sand and then sharp, jagged pebbles. The monolith towered above the sea, but boulders were hidden at its base, sometimes exposing craggy cavelike formations at low tide. When the weather was bad, the waves threw Aria against the rocks, threatening to drag her down.

But the weather was good today, far more peaceful and calm than her own mind. Aria swam until she started to feel the rough boulders under her feet, and then tread water carefully, maneuvering around the monolith.

The tide was a little low. Aria checked the shoreline—empty. Careful of the rough edges, she climbed up one of the boulders on the side of the monolith that faced the sea, hidden from shore if someone decided to take a morning stroll.

The sun beat down at her, and the waves lapped at her skin as she found the spot she was looking for—a rare smooth surface, worn away by the relentless ocean, that dipped and curved against her body as she lay down.

She let out a peaceful sigh. This was bliss. Warming under the sun with the water whispering in her ear.

This was all she needed.

CHAPTER FOUR

*A*ria started to drift off as her skin dried in the sun, salty and warm, her body lapping at the heat of the stone she lay upon. And—as had happened every night for the past two weeks—her dreams went straight to Eric Dickson's arms.

She wasn't quite fully asleep, but she was drowsy enough let her mind fill with possibilities. She envisioned the Enchanted Forest restaurant glittering with fairy lights and candle flames, soft music—not the pumping rock pop of the band that had been hired—and no one. No one but her and Eric. He'd sweep her in his arms to dance, his warmth seeping through the thin material of her dress as she breathed in his scent, something earthy and sensuous.

And then her mind drifted deeper. His hands sliding down the thin straps of her dress, exposing her neck and shoulders. His lips trailing fire along her skin, his hands eager yet tentative as they gripped her hips, pulling her against him.

Aria's own hand splayed across her flat stomach, then down, to the mound between her legs. She kept her eyes shut, her mind focused on Eric as she tentatively let her fingers delve lower...in. She toyed with herself, prolonging the pleasure, letting the anticipation build.

She was slick with saltwater, and her dream made her slick with essence, too. Her finger glided inside her, and her body clenched as she finally succumbed to the pleasure. She slid up, her clitoris already hard as her finger swirled around, increasing pressure. She gasped, letting her body arch into her hand as she sped up. The tension within her coiled tighter and tighter.

In her mind's eye, she saw Eric. She felt Eric. His breath on her bare skin, not the wind. His fingers, not hers. Silken bedsheets, not a smooth rock warmed by the sun. She imagined him, she imagined what he would feel like, and it was this thought that drove her to climax, and it was his name she whispered as she came.

~

*A*ria startled awake at the sound of a man's voice.

It took her several moments to orientate herself. She was lounging of the rocks of the monolith, a quarter mile out into the sea, and there was a man's voice...

And she was naked.

She popped her head over the edge of the rock and saw, to her very great surprise, a boat. Not a boat—that wasn't right. A *yacht*. Small, sure, but still—definitely a yacht. It was far enough away from the rocks to not be in danger of sinking, but close enough that Aria could hear the man on the deck. And see him.

Eric Dickson.

"Shit, shit, shit," Aria said, squashing her body against the rock, praying he didn't look her way. What were the chances?

Aria couldn't quite hear him—just the cadences of his voice. He seemed to be on his cell phone; a miracle in and of itself given how far he was from shore and Fairhaven's notoriously bad cell signal.

"Hey!" Eric's voice called in Aria's direction. "Is someone over there?"

Shit, shit, shit, Aria thought. She dared one more peek—Eric was peering over at the monolith, a hand shading his eyes, staring.

She was partially hidden, but her white skin had to be glaringly obvious against the black rock. She couldn't stay there. Not *naked*.

Why do I like to skinny dip? Aria groaned internally. Taking a deep breath and keeping very, very low, Aria slid away from the rock, away from Eric's eyes. Her hair was still wet and therefore darker than it's normal vivid red, so maybe, maybe, he wouldn't notice...would think it was his eyes playing tricks on him...

"Hello?" Eric shouted. "Is someone over there?"

Don't think, don't think, just do, Aria chanted in her mind as she let go of the rock and plunged into the water, careful to go over the side Eric couldn't see her. From his angle, thanks to the craggy rocks, he must have only caught a glimpse of her pale skin and red hair, nothing more. His voice sounded doubtful...and the sun was in his eyes. There's a chance he didn't see...

As soon as Aria plunged under water, she held her breath and kicked, hard, away from the monolith and behind the big rocks. Out of sight. She couldn't face Eric when she was clothed at the hotel, how could she face him naked in the ocean?

Eric tried one more time—"Hello?"—and then seemed to give up. Aria let just her face surface the water so she could breathe. Her heart was racing, pounding louder than the waves that beat against the rocks.

She'd almost been seen by Eric Freaking Dickson.

She was grateful the water was cool, soothing her face burning with embarrassment. How could she have been so stupid? It wasn't *that* early in the morning. Of course someone would be up.

She just never thought it would be Eric of all people who would almost catch her asleep, naked, on the rocks. At least he hadn't seen what she'd been doing *before* she dozed off...

After her heart quit threatening to rip from her chest, Aria dared to swim a little closer. She clung to the rocks, using them as cover. What was Eric Dickson doing out here anyway? He was *always* at the front desk of Hotel Ever After, giving orders, barking into the phone, setting up schedules and meetings. He didn't even take a break for coffee at the café while at work—what was he doing on a yacht on the day of the big reveal of the hotel at the pre-launch party?

When Aria finally got a good peek at him, she saw that he'd put up his cell phone. He wasn't scanning the monolithic rock for her, either. He stood on the deck of his small yacht, staring out at the horizon.

It was so...odd to see him quite like this. Eric Dickson was *not* quiet. And yet the way he stood there, just appreciating the peace and the calm and the ocean...it reminded Aria of herself.

Eric's boat drifted closer to the monolith, and Aria wondered what she would do if it got too close to the hidden boulders. Should she expose herself in an effort to save his boat?

Before she could decide, she heard the unmistakable sounds of a cell phone ringing.

Eric was close enough now that Aria could hear him from behind the rocks. She was about to dive beneath the surface and make her way back to shore—and her clothes—but then she caught a name she knew.

"Hey, Ursula," Eric said. His voice sounded sad.

Aria froze in the water.

"I just wanted to make sure we were clear about tonight," he said. "I mean, it's been fun, but I didn't want to lead you on..."

His voice trailed off as Ursula said something, but Aria didn't stick around to listen to more. Ursula had been treating her relationship with Eric as casual, but she knew her best friend, and she knew the longing look she got when she looked at him.

And she knew what it felt like to *not* be the one Eric Dickson wanted.

As soon as Aria's feet touched the rocky surface of the shore, she grabbed her sundress, threw it on, and headed straight back to her cottage.

She did not look at the yacht on the horizon.

When she burst into the cottage, Ursula was sitting at the table, coffee mug in front of her. Her phone sat by her hand.

"Sula," Aria said, breathless from her walk up from the beach.

"Ari? Is something wrong?" Ursula asked, jumping up.

"I—is everything okay?" Aria asked.

"Of course it is," Ursula said. "Are *you* okay?" She smoothed down Aria's wet hair, framing her face.

Aria nodded, but she couldn't help but examine her friend. Were Ursula's eyes red because she hadn't slept all night or because she was upset at Eric's casual dismissal of her?

But how could she ask? *Oh, I just overheard your boyfriend talking about you while I was swimming naked next to his yacht.* Yeah, that wouldn't go over well.

"I...um...." Aria started.

Ursula pulled her to a chair at the table. "Let's talk about tonight," she said.

"Yeah," Aria said slowly. "Tonight. Are you and Eric..."

Ursula waved her hand, dismissing Aria's words. "Unimportant. But what *is* important is: What are you going to wear?"

"No, Sula." Aria pressed her lips together, searching her friend's face. "This thing with you and Eric—are you going to get hurt?"

Ursula shrugged. "It's not serious, Aria. Jeez, everyone's asking about this today. *It's not serious.* This is just a fling. We're going to the party together for fun, and then we move on."

Aria worried her lip between her teeth. Ursula did care more about living in the moment than a serious relationship. Maybe she really didn't care about Eric beyond having a fun time.

"Wait a minute..." Ursula said slowly. A huge grin spread over her face. "I know what this is about."

"You do?"

"You...*you* like Eric!" Ursula crowed. "I had no idea! Okay, I had an idea, but this is more than just thinking he's hot, you *really* like him, don't you?"

Aria felt her cheeks growing warm.

Ursula howled with laugher. "Ari! Oh, you're adorable."

"I'm not adorable!" Aria protested, her embarrassment turning to anger.

Ursula sensed she'd gone over the line, and her laughter left her lips, but not her eyes. "So you don't want Eric?" Ursula challenged.

"I..." Aria's eye lost focus as she thought about the question. "I want adventure. Like the kind in books. I want a whole new world from this one. I'm not happy here. I mean, I love Fairhaven, and this cottage is my home, and you're my family, but..."

"You want more," Ursula said quietly.

Aria nodded.

"I just live every day the same. Go to work, come home, maybe go for a swim or read a book. Repeat. Repeat. Repeat. I want something more. I want *passion*."

Ursula leaned back. She was completely serious now, her eyes dark and watching. "If you want passion, you have to get it yourself," she said finally. "But remember, there's more to life and adventure than passion. Trust me. I can get 'passion' whenever I want it," she said sardonically. "But passion without purpose becomes kind of meaningless after awhile."

Aria reached for Ursula's hand, concern spread across her face. Ursula shot her a half-smile. "I like the chase," she said. "But when I get the guy, I never know what to do with him."

Hope flared in Aria's heart. Maybe Ursula really didn't care about Eric the same way he didn't care about her.

"Well," Aria said in what she hoped was a teasing tone, "maybe you can just give Eric to me for awhile then."

Ursula looked like the cat that got the cream. "I knew it," she said in a low voice. "I knew you really liked him." Before Aria could protest, Ursula continued. "If you want Eric, you're going to have to fight for him."

"What do you mean?" Aria couldn't keep the defensiveness from her voice.

"I want to have a good time tonight," Ursula said. She got up and took her coffee mug to the sink. "I don't care if it's with Eric or not. And if *you* entertain me, then I won't mind giving him to you."

"Let me say again: What do you mean?" Aria didn't even try to hide her wariness this time.

"I mean, if you want to have Eric to yourself tonight, you have to earn him. You want passion? You don't get it by sitting around, talking," she said, waving her hand in the direction of the kitchen table.

"What do you want me to say then?" Aria asked, totally lost.

Ursula yawned. "I don't want you to *say* anything." She stretched. "If you want Eric tonight, you have to seduce him. And you have to do it without speaking."

"Without speaking?" Aria said. Ursula started heading to her bedroom, yawning again, but Aria jumped up and followed her. "Sula, what do you mean?"

"Passion isn't about words. It's not talking. It's action. So you can't talk to Eric tonight. You have to get him with"—Ursula bumped her hip against Aria's—"body language. Clothes, dancing, actions. You do that, I will gladly give you to him."

"He's not a thing, you know," Aria grumbled. "You can't just 'give' him to me."

Ursula dismissed this with a laugh. Men were, to her, always just things. "You know what I mean," she said. "No hard feelings if you end up with Eric, not if you earn it."

"By amusing you."

"By stepping out of your comfort zone. You hide behind words, Ari, and you use them to build up excuses to not live. So no words. Not even to talk yourself out of this."

"But—"

Ursula smiled as she pressed a finger against Aria's lips. "No. Words."

She yawned hugely. "Now Mama needs some sleep," she said. "But after lunch, I'm getting up. We're going to start on your look."

"My look?"

Ursula looked Aria up and down with a critical eye. "Oh yes," she said. "If you can't speak, you've got to let this"—She waved her hands in Aria's direction—"do all the work. Girl, you need a shower. Use my expensive conditioner stuff. If you smell like salt when I wake up, I'm going to give you a bath myself."

Before Aria could protest, Ursula blew air kisses at her, stepped into her bedroom, and shut the door in her face.

CHAPTER SIX

*A*ria's hair wasn't quite done drying when Ursula burst into her bedroom. Although she'd only snatched a few hours of sleep, Ursula seemed perfectly ready to take on the night.

"Okay!" she said with the air of someone who's made a huge decision. "Time to get you ready. You first, then me."

"I can get myself ready," Aria pointed out. She shook her damp hair behind her.

"There are blow dryers, you know," Ursula said casually. "They are a thing that exist."

"Yes, but should they?" Aria had a bad relationship with hair dryers. It was almost impossible to get them to work on her long, thick hair that seemed to soak up water like a sponge. She'd overheated the motor out of more than one model before giving up on dyers entirely.

"Come, come," Ursula said, grabbing Aria's hand and dragging her to her bedroom.

Ursula's room looked more like a star's dressing room than a bedroom in a seaside cottage. Her bed was shunted to the corner and hidden by sheets hung like curtains in a makeshift canopy. Front and center was a huge vanity, complete with lightbulbs around the mirror, littered with makeup of every kind. This was something Sula took very seriously. Ursula treated makeup like armor, and her curling iron like a sword with which to slay the men who crossed her path.

"Sit, sit," Ursula said, pushing Aria into the chair in front of the mirror.

"First, hair," Ursula said, all business. Before Aria could protest, Ursula tackled her mess of red tangles with a brush. In less than fifteen minutes, Aria's hair was neatly smoothed with oil and then wound around huge curlers and stacked around her head.

"I look ridiculous," Aria said, staring in the mirror.

"Good thing you're not going to actually wear the curlers to the party." Ursula smirked. "Now strip."

"What?"

"Strip."

"No!"

"Yes. You're not getting makeup all over my clothes."

"I'm not wearing your clothes."

Ursula narrowed her eyes, examining the dress Aria was wearing. Cream colored with pink trim, it was one of the nicest things Aria owned.

"No," Ursula said simply.

"What's wrong with it?"

"You're cute," Ursula said.

"No, seriously!"

"No." Ursula turned back to her closet and emerged with a green bustier and a black leather skirt.

"No," Aria said, eyes widening.

"Strip."

"But—"

"You want Eric? Strip."

Aria opened her mouth to protest again, but she knew it would be no use. It wasn't just the bet; Aria knew that if she was going to win at the art of seduction, she needed black leather, not pink trim.

Careful of the curlers, Aria lifted her dress over her head. Ursula plunked her back down onto her vanity chair and started on her face.

"Fortunately," she said, "we've got the same coloring, mostly. And I've got a few things that were too light for me that will look perfect on you." She held a bottle of foundation against Aria's neck, examining the color, and then picking up a different one.

"Do we really need to do all this?" Aria asked.

"You can't speak tonight, remember? So everything else about you—including your clothes and makeup—has to speak for you."

Aria bit her lip.

Ursula crouched down so she looked Aria in the eyes. "What are you so scared of?" she asked.

Aria's drifted her discarded dress on Ursula's bed. "What if it's not enough?" she said in a low voice. When Ursula looked confused, she continued. "What if we do all this—the clothes, the hair, the makeup. What if I do it all, and he doesn't even notice me?"

A grin spread across Ursula's face. "Oh, trust me," she said. "He is going to notice you." She turned Aria around and started to pat moisturizer on her face. "And you already are more than good enough for him. He's not worthy of you, love, we're just going to make sure he realizes that."

~

*A*ria was glad that Ursula didn't go too heavy on the makeup. "All good makeup does is highlight who you are, not cover you up," she stated. That didn't make sense as Ursula was gripping Aria's chin and carefully lining her eyes, but when she finally saw herself in the mirror, she understood.

Aria had been most afraid that, by the time Ursula was done, she'd look like her roommate, not herself. The makeup was subtle, but it was designed to enhance the things Aria loved about herself the most. Her bright green eyes looked huge, her cheeks were illuminated with finely milled glitter, and her lips demanded attention.

And when Aria slipped the black skirt and green top on, she felt more comfortable than she expected she would. Not that the outfit was comfortable—it pinched at the top and forced her to walk more carefully than her flowy sundresses—but wearing these clothes felt like second nature. Aria smoothed down the front of her outfit, staring at herself in the mirror. She felt...braver. Powerful.

Is this what I want? Aria asked herself. *One night of seduction and passion?*

The answer was simple. Yes. She wanted one night to be the person she'd wanted to be—the one lusted for, the one wanted. She was tired of being invisible, of watching from afar.

She wanted her moment in the sun, even if it would burn her.

Because going after Eric had made Aria realize that she wanted to go after a lot more in life. She loved Fairhaven and it would always be home, but she wanted more. She felt like a goldfish that wanted to escape its bowl.

When Aria turned around, she saw that Ursula had already changed her outfit. She'd opted for a simple black dress and thrown her hair into a high bun. For most women, this would be a somewhat casual look. For Ursula, she needed only a cigarette holder to be Holly Golightly.

Ursula checked the time on her phone. "Eric's sending a car," she said. "Are you good on your own?"

"Yeah," Aria said.

"Really?"

Aria stood straighter, meeting Ursula's gaze. Ursula smiled. "Yeah," she said. "You're ready."

CHAPTER SEVEN

*I*f Aria had to describe the pre-launch party she would sum it up in one word: thumping.

The music was so loud that she could hear it while the elevator was still rising. She almost didn't get off at the top floor, but she was caught in the crowd behind her.

Fake it till you make it, Aria reminded herself, Ursula's favorite expression. *If you want passion, you have to take it.*

She strode into the transformed penthouse restaurant.

People whirled around her, and although she didn't recognize many of them, there were a few faces that popped out of the crowd. Several actors and models she recognized from magazines, a few groups she were sure were in some pop bands, and a couple people who were famous for being famous and had the wealth to prove it. Aria let out a shaky breath. She wasn't supposed to be here—but she *was,* and she was going to pretend like she belonged until she did.

She scanned the room, hoping to see a face of someone she knew as a friend rather than from a magazine.

"Shrimp?"

Aria turned as the sous chef of the restaurant offered her a plate of h'or d'vours. "Hey Ruby," Aria said.

"You nabbed an invite, nice," Ruby said, pausing to brushing hair off her face. "We had so many last minute cancellations that we've recruited every spare person we could find to help out tonight. It's been a mad house."

"What happened?" Aria gasped.

Ruby shrugged. "Flu maybe? Dunno. But more than half the staff called out."

"That sounds terrible! Do you need help?"

Ruby rocked back on her heels. "Girl, you're not here to work."

Aria looked down at her outfit. "I guess not, but..."

"Don't worry about," Ruby said, smiling sincerely. "We tapped the housekeeping staff—the hotel's only got a handful of guests now, just the people here." She nodded to one of the other waitresses, and Aria recognized Ella, a new maid.

"Well if you need me..."

"Go. Enjoy yourself. Go nab that bossy bastard you keep staring at all day."

Aria felt her blush creep up her cheeks, but she couldn't help but look around the room, wondering where Ursula—and Eric—were.

"Over there," Ruby said in her ear as she took her plate of shrimp and moved deeper into the crowd.

And there he was. Eric sat far away from the band, on one of the cushioned benches against the wall. Ursula was curled up next to him, playing on her phone. She looked up as if she could feel Aria's gaze, grinned at her, and gave a short jerky nod towards Eric.

And it all suddenly became clear to her. She had two choices. She could seize this opportunity and go out on a limb, doing what she could to go outside of her comfort zone and experience the things that she had been so afraid to try before. Or she could walk away. The bet with Ursula and the promise to Bette notwithstanding, there would be no shame in just leaving the party. She could go now.

It came down to one simple question. Who did she want to be? She could be who she had always been, or she could claim a different persona. She could be someone else.

She would take a chance on herself.

She chose change.

Taking a deep breath and straightening her spine, Aria strode forward, in the direction of Eric and Ursula. She caught Ursula's eye, and her friend gave her a small secret smile, a gleam of pride in her eye. Ursula knew her better than anyone else, and she knew that this wasn't about getting the guy—it was about getting *herself*.

The music that had once been intimidatingly loud, seemed to seep into Aria, the notes sparking fire in her skin, the rhythm soaking into her bones. She started to move with the sound of it, not consciously--she wasn't dancing, she was simply trying the music on, ss if it were a new pair of leggings. She rolled her hips as she walked forward, entering the crowd of dancers. She looked around. This is what dancing was, what it truly was. Being washed away in the music, forgetting yourself in the movements. The band—a led by a singer from Hollywood called Rumpled Stetson—set a fast pace, but Aria didn't try to keep up with it. She closed her eyes and swayed, her pace becoming more frenetic as the tempo increased.

As she danced, she thought about what her life was now, what she wanted it to be. In truth, she'd never really thought about *her* desires before now. When her parents died, she was still in high school, and she moved in with her grandmother, who was perfectly happy living in Fairhaven and doing nothing more. Aria let her grandmother's life become her life. She had taken no other choice simply because no other choice had presented itself, without realizing that she couldn't wait for the options to appear, she had to make them.

She was making them now.

Aria closed her eyes. There were easily more than a hundred people in the restaurant-turned-dance-club, but she felt alone. She felt the same way she did when she was sun bathing at the monoliths in the sea. The sea reminded her of Eric, and her hands slid over her body, thinking of the way she touched herself before, of the way she wanted him to touch her. Her hips undulated, relishing in the way her leather skirt felt against her skin. The silk bustier felt like water over her body.

Aria's eyes opened to slits so she could see the dizzying array of people around her, the glittering lights. Her body felt like it was on fire, and she lifted her heavy red hair in both her hands, swaying with the music and then letting it drop down her back.

The song ended, and Rumpled Stetson called for a ten minute break while the band imbibed in Eric's generous open bar. Most of the dance floor rushed to the stage, trying to get closer to the lead singer, but Aria stood there, just a few feet away from Eric.

As if pulled by magnets, her dancing had brought her closer to him. And his eyes raked over her body, open wanting vivid.

Aria's gaze flicked to Ursula's and she saw the pride surging in her face.

Ursula unwound herself from the bench seat and casually walked over to Aria.

Eric didn't notice.

"Now *that* is how you seduce a man without words," she whispered as she passed Aria. "Go get 'em, tiger."

*A*ria had danced her way across the restaurant and into Eric's view, but those last few steps as she went over to where he was sitting felt like they spanned a mile. She was acutely aware of the sweat that glistened on her face, the damp hair that clung to her neck.

But she drew closer anyway. She nodded to the place where Ursula had been moments before, asking if the seat was available without speaking.

Eric looked at the seat as if he were surprised to find it empty. He scanned the crowd, looking for Ursula, but when he didn't see her, he nodded for Aria to sit. "This is a side of you I haven't seen before," he said. His eyes were appraising, and for the first time, Aria felt like he had noticed her. But he knew her name. He knew her well enough to know that the dance was somewhat unusual. He hadn't been completely ignorant of her existence.

Aria opened her mouth to speak, but she remembered can her bet with Ursula. Not speaking had gotten her this far, and she wasn't sure she wanted to break the spell of silence. Instead, she turned her attention back to the dance floor. So many women had mobbed the band that she couldn't even see the infamous lead singer as he tried to push his way back through the crowd and reclaim his spot on stage.

"These parties..." Eric said, taking Aria's silence in stride. "They get old after a while. They all start to feel the same, no matter what I do. This hotel is the most unique property in my brother's business; hell, it's one of the most unique hotels in the world. And yet this party feels the same as the one I went to before it, and the one before that."

He shifted in his seat so he fully faced Aria, and he waited until she turned to him before he continued. "But you," he said, "are different."

Aria bit her lip, unable to keep the smile from her face.

"I like surprises," Eric said, moving closer.

So Aria surprised him again. Rather than lean in for the more intimate conversation he was obviously angling for, Aria jumped up. She headed to the big glass doors that led to the balcony, and she didn't look behind her to see if he followed. She went through the doors—it was mercifully empty here, despite the warmth from the dance floor inside—and let her hand trail on the banister as she meandered.

She heard the door open, and knew Eric had followed her.

Ursula was right—seduction was fun.

"I've been watching you," Eric said, catching up to her. "And I know you've been watching me."

Aria paused, but she didn't turn to him. She turned to the sea in the distance. Had he seen her then? Did she wish he had?

"You intrigue me, Aria," Eric said. "I thought perhaps your interest was in Ursula."

Aria cocked an eyebrow.

"I thought you were being protective of her," Eric said. "But we never did anything, really, and it was obvious that Ursula could take care of herself and that you knew that."

Aria smiled and nodded her head a little in acknowledgement. The day Ursula needed Aria to defend her was like the same day the world would turn upside down.

"But I felt your eyes on me," Eric said, his voice deepening. He raised his hand, hesitated, then touched the side of Aria's face, near her eye. "It was hard to catch you looking, but I felt it."

Aria let her head rest in his hand, let her eyes linger on his lips.

"I travel a lot. My brother builds hotels all around the world, but that's the only part he cares about—building them. But hotels aren't the field of dreams; you can't just build them and expect people to come. That's where I come in. I make the hotels cool. I bring them to life. I make people want to come here." Eric couldn't take his eyes off Aria. "I like my job," he continued. "My brother owns more than thirty hotels, and I'm the guy who goes in and makes them better. I fly from city to city and come up with ways to improve each location, to launch them or revitalize them. I spend every day working on making something good even better. It means I don't get to know many people. Relationships are hard. And it makes me a cynical bastard. I see the worst in everything—that's what my job is."

He sighed. "This job makes me judgmental. But it means I know exactly what I want." He searched Aria's eyes.

"Say something," Eric whispered. "Say you wanted to know me the way I wanted to know you."

But Aria wasn't going to ruin this moment with words. She leaned forward, letting Eric's hand on her face slide down her neck, and she pressed her lips against his.

She put everything she was feeling into the kiss, and she let her body— her whole body—continue to speak for her. She dared to let her tongue flick into his mouth, and he met her passion tenfold, deepening the kiss and drawing her body closer to him. She could feel him through the thin material of the silk bustier, his hands on fire, lighting up her skin. She pressed her hips against his and couldn't help but smile through the kiss.

Her hands crept up, her fingers winding through his hair, twisting through the strands. Eric's mouth slid down her neck, nibbling on the exposed skin, and Aria leaned up, sucking on his ear lobe. He gasped, then growled, clutching her tighter.

"I have to get you alone," Eric said, his voice deep and raspy, his eyes glazed with lust.

Aria smiled, nodding eagerly.

"We can go to the penthouse," Eric said. He pulled her down the length of the balcony, slipped through the side door to avoid the dance floor and leave the restaurant as quickly as possible. He started down the hallway toward the penthouse suite, but Aria stood where she was.

"Aria?" Eric said, and she couldn't help but feel a little pride in the way he doubted himself in that moment. She was fully in control, and she loved it.

In answer, Aria led Eric the opposite direction of the penthouse suite. Toward the door that led to the swimming pool.

The door opened to a small changing room and sauna, then a spiral staircase led them to the pool. It was a brilliant design, maximizing space, and meant that much of the pool was indoors, directly under the restaurant Eric and Aria had just left. About six or seven feet jutted out under the balcony, but the rest of the pool was hidden, a private cove where no one could see the people in the pool without actually being there themselves.

The music above them was so loud they could still feel it thudding through the roof, but the pool itself was quiet and cool.

"Aria?" Eric asked, and there was a question in his voice.

Fortunately, she knew the answer.

*A*ria reached around and let the zipper of the tight black leather skirt slide down. She shimmied out of the skirt, tossing it toward the lounge chairs that rested at the back of the wall. Eric moved to help her undress, but Aria stepped back, shaking her head. The bustier laced in the front, under her breasts, and she undid the stays slowly, watching as his eagerness and anticipation built and built.

The green silk bustier dropped away, exposing Aria's breasts. She wore only lace panties now.

Eric's eyes were wide and hungry. He looked like he wanted to carry her off, caveman style, right then, but Aria kept her lips pressed together, and, ignoring him completely, dipped a toe into the warm pool water. She walked sedately down the tiled steps, deeper into the water, kicking off and gliding across the pool, letting the water pull her long red hair behind her. A moment later, she heard a splash as Eric followed her, but she didn't look around. The water moved around her, and she could tell he was coming closer and closer, but she didn't turn until he reached her, tentatively wrapping his fingers around her wrist and pulling her to him.

She drank in the image of him, water dripping off his hair, desire written plainly on his face. She started to swim away, but he didn't relinquish his grip on her wrist, pulling her back to him through the water. She brushed against his hips, and realized he was completely bare.

And very, very hard.

"Aria," Eric breathed into her hair. Goosebumps erupted on her skin.

His hands went to her ass and clenched around the lacy panties she still wore. The material bunched in his hands, and she felt the delicate threads rip away. He splashed the ruined panties away, letting the black lace drift away from them.

There was nothing between them now but water.

She swirled her legs in the water, wrapping them around his waist. He growled in desire, surging up and claiming her lips as his own, devouring her in the kiss. Their bodies were slick with water, slick with desire. His hands roved up and down her back, sliding through the water, trailing over her skin. She arched into his touch, letting the water carry her as she leaned back. Eric took the opportunity let his touch shift, sliding over her front, twirling around her breasts. Aria's nipples were taut and hard, and Eric's touch made her whole body coil in desire.

She lifted up, the water dripping over her bare shoulders. She gripped Eric's shoulders, leveraging her body against him in the pool so her breasts were at his lips. He eagerly claimed a nipple, sucking the water from it, twirling his tongue over the taut surface. Aria's fingers clenched in Eric's hair, but she unraveled her legs from his waist, sliding her hands down his face, his chest, down, down, to his hard cock. Underwater, she wrapped her fingers around his shaft, squeezing playfully then letting her fingers trail up and down the long, hard length. Eric threw his head back and groaned, the sound ripping from him. She increased her pressure, moving up and down his cock, letting her thumb brush over his head.

With a feral growl, Eric threw Aria back, splashing the water. He grabbed her ankles, pulling her back to him, then lifting her ass and spreading her thighs to bury his face into the mound between her legs in one fluid motion. He wasn't gentle, but Aria didn't want gentle. The water was gentle. Eric was a storm, his tongue a hurricane as he flicked it over her clitoris, his moaning desire sending vibrations through her body.

His hands clutched her hips, keeping her floating on the water at his mouth. One hand let go, a finger stroking into her to match the rhythm of his tongue. Aria bit back the shout of pleasure that overwhelmed her, holding onto it, letting the desire grow and grow inside of her.

Dully, she was aware of the thumping music, the thumping bodies of the dancers in the floor above her. No one there knew she was climaxing in Eric Dickson's arms, that her body was shuddering with relief as she came apart, that the water wrapped around her, and his arms pulled her close, and there was nothing, nothing but this moment, this pleasure, this satisfaction.

Eric pulled her close. Her body felt like melted butter floating on the surface of the pool. "Not yet, darling," he whispered, his hand sliding from her breast back under the water, back to her slick mound. He teased the outside of her lips with his finger, gently stroking her clit. Aria's eyes widened and she gasped, the coil of desire within her snapping back.

"Are you sure you want this?" Eric said. "Say it. I need to hear you say it."

"Yes," Aria breathed, the first word she'd spoken to him that night. "I want this. I want you."

❧

*E*ric pulled Aria through the water to the side of the pool, where he'd left a condom. He hastily put it on, then turned to Aria.

Her breasts floated in the water, and she could feel the warmth between her legs mingling with the cool water. No more games. No more silence. This was happening, this, and she chose it. And she *wanted* it. She wanted him.

Eric moved slower now, as if he was afraid she was a water nymph and would disappear. When he touched her, his hand gripped hers, and she could feel the desperation, the need, through his grip. She let him pull her through the water, gently, closer.

Before, their actions were tempestuous and urgent. Now there was a deliberate nature to the way Eric held her. To the way his eyes sought hers. To the way his lips claimed hers. This wasn't lust; this was something more.

As their kiss grew stronger, Eric shifted their body, putting Aria's back against the smooth pool tiles. Her legs went instinctively around his waist, and she felt the hard shaft of his cock at the base of her being. Eric used one hand to support Aria, and the other to position himself against her opening. He broke the kiss, watching her intently as he entered her, his full length pushing into her.

Aria gasped, her body shuddering, clenching around his cock. Eric groaned and dropped his head against Aria's shoulder as he thrust up into her again, harder. The water gave them momentum, splashing up against the side of the pool as he pushed into her again and again. Aria gripped Eric's strong, hard back, biting into his back as she neared another orgasm. Eric hissed in pleasure at her bite, and turned his head to her neck, licking up her skin and twirling his tongue around the shell of her ear. "Not yet," he whispered, slowing down and withdrawing his cock.

Aria whimpered, but Eric shifted his hand from her hip to her crotch. He slid his cock back into her, but let his finger glide along the top of her clit. "Eric," she groaned.

He chuckled. She had made him chase her; now he would make her chase the orgasm he wanted to give her.

He matched his finger to his cock's sure strokes, thrusting into her with perfect rhythm as he pressed into her clit, not letting up, harder and harder. Aria gasped, choking on his name, unable to find the breath to scream in bliss the way she wanted to.

Eric turned his body, and, still inside Aria, he pushed the both of them through the water, close to the edge that looked over the side of the hotel.

"Someone will see," Aria whispered into his ear. The feeling of swimming together, still united, was surreal, maddening, sexy.

"Everyone's inside," Eric said, pumping into her. "But it's exciting, isn't it? The idea that someone *could* see."

It was, in a way that Aria had never really considered before. All it would take was one person walking out to the balcony, looking over the edge into the pool, and they would see the two of them, wrapped around each other, Eric thrusting into her, her breasts moving across the water's surface, her face gasping in ecstasy, his body so tight it seemed ready to burst.

And she loved the idea that it was possible. That someone may see. It was dangerous and sensuous and so, so hot. It was the same thrill she got when she stripped her clothes to skinny dip in the ocean; it was the same exhilaration she had felt when Eric had almost caught her this morning.

"It was you, wasn't it?" Eric said, thrusting into her again. They surged forward into the pool. Closer to the edge. Closer to being seen. "This morning. By the rocks. I thought I saw someone. I thought I heard someone. A little moan—" He pushed inside of her again, his finger flicking across her clitoris, and Aria moaned, her body clenching around his cock. "Yes," he groaned. "That was what I heard. I heard you."

His pace quickened, the water sloshing around them as he drove into her. "I was thinking of you," she confessed.

With a shout he couldn't contain, Eric's body arched as his hips slammed into hers, his cock filling her and pulsing as he came. Eric grabbed Aria, holding her against them as they swirled in the water, both shuddering with their climax.

CHAPTER TEN

They drifted to the edge of the pool. Aria looked up at the balcony—Eric was right, no one was there. She looked through the glass wall. The pool was designed to feel as if you were floating over nothing. It gave her a touch of vertigo, but she liked the swooping feeling in her stomach as she tread water and stared at the beautiful little town below.

"What brought around this change?" Eric asked, tucking a wet strand of her hair behind her ear. "You always seemed so...focused. A little shy? But you're not shy tonight."

Aria wanted to turn away from his intense gaze, but she didn't. "I just wanted passion," she said.

Eric barked in laughter. "You are *definitely* passionate." He swam closer to her, caging her against the wall with his arms. "And I find that fascinating. I've spent these past weeks watching you, wondering if I had a chance with the hot redhead at the café."

It was Aria's turn to laugh. "Oh, you had a chance!"

"You keep your feelings hidden well," Eric said. He nuzzled into her neck, kissing her collarbone delicately. "What will it take to make you open up?"

Aria let her body float up, her legs rubbing against Eric's. Her eyes drifted to the flashing lights and the loud music of the party above them. She wondered what she would do if someone came out on the balcony and looked down at her and Eric, nude, wrapped around each other. She was surprised to find out she didn't care.

"What if I gave you a little reward," Eric said, his hands gliding under water, grasping her hips. "A little something for every answer you tell me about yourself?"

Aria wiggled against him, rubbing her hips around his already hard cock. "That could be arranged," she said in a low voice.

Eric eyes darkened, and his hands squeezed involuntarily around her. "Why didn't you tell me sooner that you wanted me?" he asked first. His hand cupped her vagina, one finger teasing around the edge.

"You chose Ursula," Aria said simply.

Eric paused. "We were never a 'thing,' you know," he said seriously. "We both just wanted to hang out. We never did *this*."

"I know," Aria said, smiling. "I talked to her first."

"I'm an idiot," Eric added. "I figured I would only be here for a month or two at most; what was the point of getting really involved?"

"Is this really involved?" Aria asked, wiggling into his hand.

Eric flicked a finger inside her, making her gasp and giggle. "I'm the one asking questions."

"So ask another one," she said. The anticipation was killing her.

"What do you want more than anything else in the world?" Eric asked.

He teased her with his fingers, waiting for her to answer, and Aria was tempted to say that *this, this is what I want*. But while it is what she wanted right this moment, it wasn't her heart's desire. "I want adventure," she said. Eric thrust a finger inside of her, and she gasped.

"Continue," he said in a low voice, his eyes intense.

"I want to see things I've never seen before," Aria said. Eric's thumb found her clitoris, sliding across the hard nub. A second finger joined his first.

"I want to have at least one moment every day where my heart is racing," Aria said.

Eric drew her closer, wrapping one arm around her to keep her from floating away, using his other hand to bring her to the cusp of orgasming again. "That's beautiful," he whispered to her, his thumb stroking across her clit. "And is your heart racing now?"

She arched against him, pushing into his hand, her breasts bobbing over the water. Eric dropped his head down, sucking the wetness from her nipple, nibbling across her sensitive skin and pressing his ear against her chest. "Ah, yes," he said in a liquid voice. "Your heart is most definitely racing."

Aria gasped for breath. Her hand went down to his erect, hard cock, and she wrapped her fingers around it, stroking up and down with the same rhythm he used on her. He sucked in a breath, crushing her against his body and, somehow, his fingers moved even faster, harder than before. Aria almost let go of his cock, she was so overwhelmed by the sensation, but she wanted to torture him with the same touch he was torturing her.

"Hey!" a drunken voice called out above them! "Look you guys, a pool!"

Eric's eyes widened, and they both swam away from the edge, hoping to be blocked from view, and partygoers streamed out of the restaurant and onto the balcony.

"There's people in there!" someone else shouted, pointing down.

With a scream of glee, a woman jumped over the side of the balcony and into the deep end of the pool jutting out. She splashed into the water fully clothed, screeching with laughter. "Come on in; the water's great!" she shouted to the people above.

Then she turned. "Hey! It's Eric Dickson! Errrrric!" she slurred, swimming closer.

Aria's heart thudded in her chest. Before anyone could say anything else, she dove under, using the water to block out the sounds of the drunken woman, of Eric trying to explain what was happening, of more people shouting from the balcony. She surfaced near the steps. Almost a dozen people had jumped into the pool now, all drunk, all clothed...but that didn't seem like that would remain the case for long.

Perhaps it was cowardly to leave Eric with a pool full of drunken people, but it was his party, not hers. She jumped up the steps, grabbed a towel from one of the lounge chairs, and scooped her clothes up in one fluid motion. No panties, though. Those were...somewhere...ripped apart in the pool. Aria didn't want to think about it. She raced up the stairs, away from the party that had erupted into her perfect moment with Eric.

She thought she may have heard him call her name, but it was hard to hear anything over the din of the new arrivals.

CHAPTER ELEVEN

---

*A*ria decided to walk home. It was only a few miles from the hotel to the beach, and walking the trails that overlooked the ocean was a far more enjoyable way to spend her evening than naked in a pool full of drunk strangers.

But not more enjoyable than being with Eric...

She thought about what it had been like tonight. Not just being with him, but the steps she took for that to happen. She had been so scared, nervous. But when it came down to it, finding the courage to go after what she wanted was the most alive she'd felt in...well, in years. And when Eric asked her what she really wanted in life, her answer had been true. And a surprise. If Ursula or Bette had asked her what she wanted one afternoon at the bookstore, she would have said something glib. More books, more coffee. An afternoon off, to swim in the ocean. And sure, she liked those things.

But what she really wanted?

She wanted her heart thudding out of her chest. She wanted anticipation that felt like torture. She wanted to be surprised—by the world, by herself.

She wanted more of today.

More of Eric, yes, but more of the other bits of today, too. She even liked the embarrassing bits. Having sex in the pool, just under the balcony, had felt dangerous. She had known they could be caught. She had *liked* that they could be caught. And even though the end of the night was somewhat ruined by people jumping into the pool, it also made her happy.

"What a story," she said to the night. This was like the kind of stories that Ursula always had, and when she told them to Aria, this would be the ending that would make them both laugh with glee. In many ways the fact that tonight ended with the party joining her in the pool just made the story better.

Aria stopped when her toes hit sand. She looked out over the beach, to the moonlight glittering on the waves.

The thing was, she didn't want a story.

She wanted a *life*.

Aria walked right up to the sea, letting the cold water wash over her feet. She sank down to the sand, not caring that her skirt was getting damp. White foam crept over her skin, and Aria smiled. She loved the ocean, because the ocean covered the world, and touching its waters connected her to it. Being near the sea was like being near the whole world.

Aria leaned back, her knees still in the air but her head resting on the sand. The ocean at night was the best. The tide was rising, creeping up around her, and it felt like she could slip into it, live under the water like a mermaid. She opened her eyes, drinking in the eternal stars, the sky vaster than the sea.

"I thought I would find you here."

Aria squeaked in surprised and scooted up. Eric stood over her, looking down, his head blocking the moon.

"What are you doing here?" she asked as Eric sat down beside her.

"Did you really think I was going to stick around that party?" he said. "It was far too boring without you."

"No one in the history of ever has thought a party was boring without me," Aria laughed. "I'm usually the one who makes a party boring."

Eric leaned closer, wiping some sand off the side of Aria's face. "This party isn't boring," he said in a soft voice.

"Give me a moment." She said glumly.

"Hey, what happened?" Eric asked.

She shot him a smile, but she couldn't keep the sadness out of it.

"What is it?" Eric pressed.

"It's just..." She paused. "No matter how much I want to, I'm still here, aren't I? And I'm not going any where. This was the greatest adventure of my life." Aria's laugh was short and bitter. "And Ursula has these sorts of adventures every night. How pathetic is that?"

"Is something an adventure if it happens every night?" Eric mused. Aria shot him a look, but he continued. "No, seriously. Believe it or not, I don't go skinny-dipping and skip a huge launch party every night. Tonight was an adventure for me too." He tapped his hand on his knee. "I think adventure is a matter of perspective. It's not this big, grand thing. You don't have to have a private yacht and a passport to have adventure."

"It helps," Aria said.

Eric laughed. "I'll concede that point. But adventure happens when you do something different, something you'd never do otherwise. It's not the size of the adventure that matters, it's the size of your courage. If you're scared to do something and do it anyway, what does it matter if the fear you faced was flying across the world or walking across the room and introducing yourself to someone new?"

"Well," Aria said, "I'm glad I introduced myself to you."

"Me too." Eric smiled.

"Although," Aria said, her voice lowering, "I still feel as if I don't know you as well as I could."

"Oh?" There was an instant spark of desire in Eric's eyes.

"Mm-hmm," Aria said. She let one finger trail from his cheek, around his ear lobe, and to his chin. "Let's play that game again, shall we? Only this time, I'll ask the questions."

Eric growled and threw himself at her, a low chuckle reverberating through his chest as he pressed her into the sand, claiming her mouth with his. A wave washed over them, reaching to their knees, and Aria used her distraction to roll Eric over in the sand. She straddled his hips, looking down at him.

"I'm the one asking the questions," she reiterated, and she ground her hips against his, feeling his hard cock. Eric groaned, leaning his head back in the sand.

Aria picked up his hand and brushed the dirt from it. She kissed his palm. It tasted of salt. "Tell me what an adventure for you would be," she said. "If it's not private yachts and passports, what is it?"

"This," Eric said, his voice gravelly. "Now."

Aria paused, biting her lip as she looked at him. But he was telling the truth, she was almost certain of it. She rewarded him with a kiss in his palm, but then let her tongue slide up along his finger, pulling it closer and wrapping her lips on the tip of it. She slid his whole finger into her mouth, swirling her tongue against it, watching as he squirmed under her, wishing she was sucking on something else.

"Good," she said. She dropped down, her hands on either side of his head, her breasts rubbing against his chest, his cock hard under her hips, grinding into her through their clothing. Aria was distinctly aware that she no longer had any panties.

"If you don't like the parties, why do you do them?" she asked.

Eric blinked, and Aria could tell that he was really considering her question. "Who says I don't like the parties?"

Aria leaned back.

"I *do* like them," he said, his voice insistent. "It's just...they feel... I enjoyed them more before."

Aria dropped down again, licking the side of his chin up to his earlobe. She teased the tender flesh with her teeth for a moment, then whispered into his ear, "What changed? If you liked them before, why not now?"

Before he could answer, she bit his earlobe again, then licked up the shell of his ear, letting her warm breath tickle him. He groaned, but when Aria paused, he quickly answered.

"It feels hollow now," he said. "Parties for people I barely know, in hotels that haven't properly opened, in cities I only visit once."

Aria's kisses went down his neck, across his collarbone. She rested her lips against the little divot in his clavicle and said, "Why don't you quit then?" She pressed down her hips, feeling with relish how much he desired her.

But his answer was real. "I don't know," he said. "Jealousy? My brothers have their lives together, and I'm just the go-to party man. This is my way to prove I'm worth something." His hands snaked up, grabbing her hips and pushing her against his hard cock. He groaned, a low guttural sound of desire.

Aria licked him from his neck to his mouth, ending on his lips and kissing him so deeply that she forgot for a moment where she was. "What do you want, then?" she asked when she pulled away. "If your job is empty and your adventures hollow, what do you want?"

His eyes were dark with lust. Another wave crashed over them, higher now, but the cold water seemed to sizzle on their hot skin.

Eric's hands crept to Aria's waist, squeezing her, clutching at her. "What do I want?" He barked in laughter. "Aria, I want *you*."

CHAPTER TWELVE

*H*e twirled her around in the sand, his body hard and needy, his hands sliding over her damp skin. The ocean roared in her ears, and for a moment, she let herself be swept away by it all, by the sea, and desire, and *want*.

Eric's hand slipped down the top of her bustier, and he fondled her nipple, his mouth quirking up at the tiny gasps of pleasure that escaped her lips. She pushed herself up, claiming his mouth and pulling him under with her.

"You don't know what it's like," Eric said, weaving his hands into her hair, "to have everything and nothing at the same time."

The ocean faded away. The stars became blackness. Aria pushed Eric aside, slowly, regretfully.

"What?" he asked, disorientated from her change in mood.

"You're right," she said. "I don't know what it's like. My parents died. I've had to work since I was in high school to make sure I had enough to eat every day. I didn't have anyone to pay for my college, to give me a job throwing me parties."

"Aria, I didn't mean it like that—"

She raised a hand to stop his words. "You have a loving family. You have money, a ridiculous amount of money. You have opportunities. *Take them*. You're sitting here, telling me that your life is so empty, but it doesn't have to be."

"It wouldn't—you could come with me…" His voice trailed off as he saw her face.

Because Aria wanted her *own* adventure. She didn't want to be the source of someone else's. She knew he hadn't meant it to be this way, but she couldn't help but feel used. She had thought this fling was mutual, but he didn't see her as a person. He saw her as an escape.

She got up, her stomach churning. And the worst of it was knowing that Eric was the kind of man who didn't need to use someone else as an escape. He could escape whenever he wanted to.

"Aria, wait!" Eric called, but she turned and started walking away. Her cottage was nearby, just off the beach. Her home. It wasn't much. But it was hers. And it was a part of her adventure.

Part of her was very, very glad that Eric didn't chase after her.

Part of her was not.

~

The next morning, Ursula found Aria sitting at the kitchen table, a cold mug of coffee in her hands.

"What are you doing up this early?" she asked.

Aria lifted her mug in a salute. "Not been to bed yet."

"My," Ursula said, sitting down across from her, "how the tides have turned."

Aria nodded.

"So…" Ursula started. "How was the party?"

Aria looked up from the paper she had been studying. She tried to hide the smile creeping across her face, but couldn't. "Wonderful," she breathed.

"I told you you'd like Eric." Ursula paused, noting Aria's hesitation. "What happened? Did you not get along?"

"Oh, we did."

Ursula grinned. "I noticed that Eric was one of the first in the pool, and naked. One of the first to leave too. I wondered if perhaps he hadn't been alone, and didn't want to stay alone…"

Aria cocked an eyebrow but didn't say anything.

"So…what happened?" Ursula pressed.

"A lady never kisses and tells."

"This lady does all the time and that lady," she said, pointing at Aria, "listens. Every. Time."

Aria pressed her lips together and hummed a little tune.

"That good?" she asked.

"That good," Aria confirmed.

"So what are you doing here then? Shouldn't you be shagging him senseless on his yacht or something?"

This was clearly the wrong thing to say. Aria turned back to the papers in front of her.

Ursula bit her lip. Clearly something had happened between Aria and Eric—something good, and then something not as good. But Ursula was a good enough friend to not try to get Aria to speak when she wasn't ready.

"What are you doing?" she asked instead, indicating the papers.

"Going over finances," Aria said.

"...Finances."

"Mm-hmm," Aria muttered, tapping her pencil on the sheet.

"Are you in trouble?"

"What?" Aria asked, looking confused. "No," she laughed. "No, I just... I want to see the world."

"The world." Ursula felt very stupid repeating everything her roomie said, but she couldn't wrap her head around what was happening.

"Mmm, the world," Aria confirmed. "I'm not getting on a plane, though."

"No planes, got it," Ursula said, looking at Aria as if she were crazy.

"It'll take work."

"Oh, obviously."

Aria nodded absent-mindedly. When she didn't say anything else, Ursula wrapped her knuckles on the wooden table just in front of Aria's papers. "What will take work?" she asked, exasperated.

"They have these cruises," Aria said. "They go all around the world. I can get on the ship in Seattle. It'll take me five or so years, I think, to save up enough, but I'm going to go. I am going to see the world."

Ursula nodded her head appreciatively. "Ah," she said. "You've finally decided to have your adventure."

Aria met her gaze. "I really have," she said.

"Does this have something to do with a certain party-planner and hotel organizer?"

Aria allowed herself a smile. "Yeah," she conceded. "It does. He reminded me that we can take what we want."

"I like that," Ursula said. "Don't forget that. Don't ask for what you want. Take it."

"I should have learned that from you a long time ago," Aria said.

Ursula shook her head. "You learn that kind of lesson on your own. Eric didn't teach it to you. You taught yourself."

Aria smiled at her friend, and nodded a little, her gaze sliding over to the paper. Finances would be tight, but she knew she could do this. And for the first time, it felt like she had a purpose. She'd spent her life since her parents died focusing on what needed to be done immediately. How could she make one paycheck last until the other one. And that way of life hadn't been wrong. It'd been necessary. She had to survive.

But she was past the point of survival now. Only she'd let herself stay in that mode, that feeling of fear and need to push aside what she wanted.

No more. She knew what she wanted. And she'd take it.

Ursula started chatting about the party, laughing at the way everyone had jumped into the pool as she poured herself a cup of coffee. Aria let her mind drift to Eric.

She wanted him too. And she wanted him to want her.

Why did I walk away last night? she asked herself for the millionth time.

Because I had to, she answered herself.

She had thought she wanted a fling, the kind of one night stand Ursula was famous for. But hearing him talk about himself, really opening up... she knew she wanted more. And he did too. Staying with him would have ruined that. It would have satisfied their longing, yes, but Aria knew it would have made the hollowness inside them both grow. It was a temporary fix.

She wanted more. She wanted an adventure that would outlast the night.

CHAPTER THIRTEEN

*A*ria was almost asleep when she heard a knock on the door. She grunted and rolled over. Ursula could get it.

The knocking grew louder.

Aria stuffed her head under a pillow. Shoot. She'd forgotten that there was a reason Sula had been so early to wake up—she'd already left for work.

Whatever it was, it couldn't be important.

The knocking did. Not. Stop.

"What?!" Aria shouted, throwing back her covers. "What could possibly be so important?" She stomped down the hall and yanked the front door open.

Eric Dickson stood in front of her.

Eric Dickson. On her doorstep. Looking as if he'd not slept at all last night.

"Good," he said, "you're home."

"What do you want?" Aria growled at him.

He blinked, surprised. "You're chipper."

"I've not slept a wink."

"Neither have I." He stepped into the kitchen. "You were right," he said, turning to her quickly. She wondered just how much coffee he'd had. "You were right about it all."

"About what?" Aria yawned hugely.

"About having all these opportunities and never taking them. I've been so focused on work and trying to live up to my brothers' names, and I just...you were right," he finished lamely.

"Hooray," Aria said.

"I wanted to thank you." Eric voice was lower, less frantic.

Aria smiled at him. She was always grumpy when she didn't have enough sleep. "I'm glad, really," she said. "I'm just tired."

"God, me too."

"You were up all night?" she asked.

"All night."

"We're ridiculous."

"Totally."

"I thought..." Aria paused. "I thought you were going to be mad at me," she said. "For leaving last night."

His eyes didn't leave hers. "I understood. I mean, I was...in a bit of a bind. But I understood. You're not a one-night adventure, Aria. You're a lifetime adventure."

She wasn't entirely sure what he meant by that.

"So..." Eric said, drawing out the word. "It looks like we could both use a nap. And you could nap here, sure, but..." His lips twitched up in a mischievous smile.

"But?" Aria said, putting a hand on her hip.

"But you could also nap on my boat. It has a lovely deck, and I know you like the ocean..."

"Your 'boat,'" Aria mocked. "You mean your private yacht?"

"It's a nice boat," Eric conceded.

"You want to take me on your private yacht for a *nap*."

"There are worse ways to spend the morning."

And Aria had to admit he was right on that front.

~

*A*ria changed into a bikini and a sundress, and Eric whisked her out to his yacht, driving it up the shoreline until they were near her favorite rock jutting up from the water. He spread massive, thick towels out on the deck and, after slathering herself with sunblock, Aria lay down. The warm sun was still gentle in the morning light, and the waves splashing against the boat were more soothing than any music.

Aria half thought that Eric would use this as an opportunity to continue what she'd stopped last night, but even as she started to peek at him, she heard his soft snoring. She smiled, closed her eyes, and let herself dream into the adventure.

~

When she awoke, Aria found Eric leaning over the railing of the boat, looking out to sea. She stood up and moved over to him.

"You were right about everything," Eric said, not looking away from the sea. "I've already contacted my family. I'm taking a break from the hotels for awhile. I have some exploring to do."

"That's—that's great," Aria said, and she really meant it.

"But I was right, too." Eric turned to her. "About how lonely it can be. How hollow it is to have adventures without anyone by your side."

Aria bit her lip, searching his eyes.

"Will you come with me? I know you care about your job, and it wouldn't be forever, but we could have some fun. We could find our adventure."

"Are you asking me to drop everything and sail away with you?" Aria asked.

Eric smiled sadly. "I knew it was mad. I couldn't expect—"

"I would *love* to go away with you," she said. "I was up all night trying to figure out how I could do just this."

"How you could sail away with me on my yacht?"

Aria laughed. "No, stupid. How I could leave everything and have my adventure. And here you come in, a prince charming on a boat—"

"A yacht."

"—And offer me exactly what I wanted?"

Eric smiled at her. "Well, you have something I want too." He bent closer, playing with the ends of her hair.

Aria slid her hands over his hard chest. "Likewise," she said.

"Shall we take this below deck?" Eric asked.

Aria's eyebrows shot up. She thought about how sexy it had been last night, in the pool, when there was every chance someone would catch them. She stepped away from Eric, and shimmied out of her sundress. The sun was warmer now, and she relished in the feeling as she unhooked the front of her bikini top and let her breasts fall free from it.

Eric's eyes widened. He looked around, as if to ask *here?* But it was just them and the sea. And the chance. The chance that someone would walk close enough on the shore to see them, or another boat would drift by. There was the chance, and the chance was *exciting*.

Eric lunged at Aria, and she laughed as she tugged his shirt off. He grabbed a condom out of his pocket before yanking his pants off. Aria stepped back, sliding her bikini bottom down her legs, and Eric growled with desire, lifting her up and carrying her to thick, sun-warmed towels on the deck.

Aria slid her hand over the hard expanse of Eric's cock, playing with the head. He bent his neck back, groaning as she stroked him gently, gently, her fingertips barely brushing his sensitive skin. Aria leaned up and took the condom from Eric's hand, ripping it open with her teeth and positioning it over the head of his penis. Instead of rolling it down with her hands, though, she pressed her lips against the tip and used her mouth to push the condom onto his member. Eric's hand clenched in Aria's hair, and she could feel his restraint vibrating through his muscles.

He pushed Aria gently against the towels, and when she was laying there, naked, warmed only by the sunbeams pouring through the bright blue sky, he took a moment to admire her. Aria's first instinct was to hide, but no—this was part of her adventure. She lay there, relishing in his gaze, his obvious appreciation of her body. Eric reached out with one hand, almost hesitant, and allowed himself to stroke the side of her face, down her chin, across her chest, cupping her breast.

Carefully, as if he were afraid this moment would break, Eric positioned himself between Aria's legs. He let his hands move from her breasts down her side, his fingers splayed across her stomach, then down further, wrapping his hands around her hips, wiggling her slightly so that he was just at the entrance.

His hands moved down, one hand sliding between them. He let a finger flick inside her, and his eyes closed in bliss. "So wet," he said in a low voice. "You're so wet. You're ready for me."

In answer, Aria lifted her hips, and Eric's cock slid a few inches into her.

One hand gripped her hip, and Aria could see the restraint on his face, the need to surge into her, but the control it took to wait. "Not yet," he ground.

He slid his finger along her clitoris, teasing the hard nub, rubbing it gently then sliding down, rubbing his cock against her entrance. Aria moaned, throwing her hands to the side and gripping the soft fuzziness of the towels. Eric made a pleased noise deep in his throat and moved his finger up again, swirling around her clit. She was slick with desire, and she could feel Eric's cock just at the edge, throbbing.

She bucked her hips, eager for him to feel her. Eric tsked, grinning. "Not yet," he teased again.

"Now," Aria begged. He flicked her clit with his finger, and she moaned, loud.

The sound seemed to crash against Eric's restraint, and with a growl, he gripped her hips and drove into her, gasping as the full, hard length of his cock filled her. Aria shuddered in delight, clenching around him, and Eric groaned. He cupped her ass, his thumbs against her hipbones, and withdrew slightly before plunging into her again.

"Eric," Aria moaned.

He slid one hand between them again, teasing her hard, tight clit with one finger as he matched the rhythm with his thrusts.

Aria peeked her eyes open. The world was all around them, the ship on the water under the vast, eternal sky. And they were naked and making love for all the world to see.

She thrust her hips up, her body rolling in waves of pleasure. She swatted Eric's hand away, and he surged into her, harder and harder, faster and faster. She screamed, not hiding the sound, letting the whole world hear her taking her pleasure.

CHAPTER FOURTEEN

"So...you're going?" Bette asked, leaning over the counter at the cafe.

"I don't expect you to hold my job for me. I have no idea how long I'll be gone or when I'll be back, and..."

Bette smiled. "I completely understand. Take your time. And when you *do* come back, know that the job is yours. Although I wouldn't be surprised if you'd moved on to better things. You were always too good to be a bookstore-manager-slash-barista."

"But I've always loved it here," Aria said in a lower voice.

Bette smiled. "Me too. And you'll be impossible to replace."

She moved around the counter and wrapped Aria in a hug. "I'm so happy for you," she said.

Aria couldn't help but blink tears out of her eyes. She had told Ursula that evening that her five-year-plan to escape and see the world had been turned into a one-week-plan. Ursula played it off as if she were happy to have the cottage to herself. "And don't think I'm paying rent—this is me house sitting for you now; you should be paying *me*," she said, joking, but Aria knew that no one would miss her as much as Sula.

Except, perhaps, Bette. She hadn't expected to be so emotional when she turned her notice into Bette, but now her eyes were burning, and she half wanted to take it all back and promise Bette she'd work at Happily Ever After forever.

"None of that!" Bette said, reading Aria's doubt on her face. "This is your adventure!"

Aria sniffled. "I'll write all the time," she said.

"No you won't, and that's okay," Bette said. "I'd rather you be off having a grand time than waste your time writing. Where are you going?"

Aria's face lit up. "No idea! Eric said north first, to Seattle or Portland. And then...I don't know! Maybe Alaska? Or all the way across the sea to Japan or Australia? I don't know!"

Bette smirked. "That's the advantage of having a Dickson boy," she said. "They can take you anywhere."

"Where are you going next?" Aria asked.

Bette smiled and busied herself with something at the register. "I think we'll be here for a bit," she said, her eyes not meeting Aria's. "But meanwhile, I have to find a replacement. There's a girl who's applied here every week for a month—"

"Ella Barrymore?" Aria said.

Bette nodded. "She seems eager?"

"She was nice when I spoke to her," Aria said. "I think she got a job as a maid, though."

"I talked to Richard today. Apparently, the maid job is part time, and she wants to pick up hours here too."

"Hard worker."

"Tell me about it."

Bette leaned back. "But you're going to be okay?"

"Better than okay."

Bette pulled Aria into another hug, then shooed her off before they both started crying.

Eric was waiting for her just outside the hotel. "I don't know why you didn't come in with me," she said.

"Big Brother's not too pleased with me taking time off," Eric said. When Aria raised her eyebrows, he waved his hand dismissing her worry. "It'll blow over. It helps that Hotel Ever After has now successfully launched, and there are no new hotels in our immediate future."

"You're sure?"

Eric tucked Aria's arm into the crook in his elbow and started walking through the cobblestoned streets of Fairhaven down toward the marina.

Aria silently said goodbye to all her favorite places. The ice cream shop. The library. The restaurant where she always celebrated her birthday. The bar where she celebrated Ursula's.

"We'll be back," Eric whispered in her ear. His breath caused a shiver of delight to spread down her back, warm and liquid like honey.

"I know," Aria said. Besides, it wasn't much of an adventure if there wasn't a home to return to.

When they got to the marina, Eric helped her up the gangway. She checked below deck—although the boat was huge, it was far smaller than her cottage, and she had had to pick out the things she brought with her carefully. A few books. Her parents' photo. Sundresses for when they went south; a puffy coat for when they went north.

Eric had moved his things over to make room for hers. She'd only slept in this bed once, after she'd brought over the boxes, but it already felt just as much like home as her room in the cottage did.

Her fingers lingered on the shell necklace on the dresser, the one Bette had given her before the party. The shell curled around, circling out in a spiral, and her finger traced it, starting in the center, then wider and wider, up and out until she was twirling her arm away, her whole body, she was spinning and spinning, and laughing.

Beneath her feet, the engines of the yacht purred to life. Aria raced to the stairs and burst out on deck.

"Ready?" Eric asked, his hands on the wheel.

Aria scooted beneath his arms and knocked his hands away, gripping it herself. "Ready," she said, looking out to the horizon.

———————

CHAPTER FIFTEEN

———————

*E*lla Barrymore was still wearing her maid outfit when she stepped into the café at Hotel Ever After.

"You're going to have to change before you start work," Bette said, not unkindly.

"Oh! Yes! I'm sorry!" Ella's cheeks flushed. She turned to go—the staff dressing room and lockers were beneath the lobby.

Bette grabbed her wrist, holding her back. "I have to confess," she said, looking grim, "I have my concerns. It can't be easy, pulling back to back shifts, not even going a few steps from one job to the other."

Ella's heart sank. "I *promise*," she said, "I can do this. I have to do this. Please—I won't forget to change uniforms again."

Bette smiled. "I understand. Just let me know if the pressure it too much, okay?"

Ella nodded, but she was more than eager to scurry off. She didn't bother with the elevator, ducking into the employee's stairs and bounding down to the locker room.

Stupid, stupid, stupid. She'd known she would have to change from the silly maid uniform into her normal clothes for her shift at the café. What had she been thinking? She barged into the locker room, already pulling the blouse out of her skirt's waist band and crumpling the material in her hand.

That was the problem. She hadn't been thinking. She was too tired to think.

I can do this, she thought to herself. *I have to.*

The words had become her mantra, ever since her stepmother first got sick. Insurance only covered so much, and while Lynn had other daughters from her first marriage, they didn't live with her like Ella did. They didn't see what she went through, how bad it got.

How much she needed help.

I can do this. I have to.

Ella tugged her t-shirt over her bra and traded her skirt for jeans. At least this job didn't require ridiculous clothing. She slammed her locker shut, then glanced at her ancient cell phone. Fifteen minutes. First day at the new job, and she was already fifteen minutes late because she forgot about stupid clothes.

It wasn't until she was plodding back up the stairs that she realized she'd forgotten to trade the heavy black service shoes for her regular sneakers. *Oh well,* she thought, *this will have to do.*

Bette was busy with customers in the bookshop by the time Ella returned, so she started clearing away a plate and a few mugs from the tables that created a fuzzy barrier between the hotel lobby and the attached bookstore. She wasn't entirely sure what to do with the dishes once she had them stacked up in her hands, but she figured clearing them was a good step.

"Excuse me?" a man asked.

Ella's head shot up, panic gripping her heart. Bette was still busy in the bookstore, but this man was tapping his foot impatiently.

"Be right with you!" Ella called, dumping the dishes into a plastic bin near the trashcan and hoping that was the right place for them. "What can I get for you?" she asked.

Please don't want coffee, please don't want coffee, she chanted in her head. She could pour from a pot, but this place had a fancy espresso machine that was two feet long and wider than her suitcase. She had no idea how to operate it.

"Dirty chai soy latte, low foam, with an extra shot," the man said in a rush. "Venti."

"Venti?"

He rolled his eyes. "Right. You're not Starbucks. Large. Whatever."

Ella's eyes flicked from the cups to the register to the man. "Uh," she said. "For here?"

"To go." The man glanced at his phone. When Ella didn't move, he shot her a look. "I'm in a hurry," he added.

"Right. Right. Okay." Deep breath. Ella would worry about charging him after. First she had to figure out what a dirty chai soy latte, low foam, extra shot even *was*. Whenever she indulged in a fancy coffee, she only ever got a latte. Sometimes, on extra fancy days, a vanilla latte.

Chai was tea, right? She scanned the boxes of herbed tea that lined the front of the counter, but didn't see any there.

She needed time. She needed Bette. She needed a rescue.

The man across the counter looked at her curiously. "It's probably in the fridge," he said. His tone was less impatient, more curious.

"Sorry—what?" Ella asked.

He smiled. His urgent attitude had faded entirely. "The chai. It's probably in the fridge." He nodded to the small black unit against the wall.

Ella tugged the door open and found a box labeled "chai." She pulled it out and put it on the counter.

"Milk was in there, too," the man said, smiling.

She shot him a relieved look. Latte—milk. She knew that. She reached for a gallon of red-capped milk, then paused, her hand sliding over to the carton of soy.

Now there was a carton of chai and a carton of soy on the counter.

She stared at them.

She closed her eyes and wished this was all over.

She opened them.

The soy milk seemed to be mocking her.

The man reached across the counter and plucked a paper cup from a stack. "Here," he said. "First the shots. Two of them."

Ella eyed the espresso machine as if it was a mortal enemy.

The man leaned one hip on the counter. "This isn't that different from the one I have at home," he said. "Okay, first you need the beans." He pointed, and when Ella touched a button, fine black powder burst into the little metal scoop attached. She jumped back, surprised, and the man laughed. When it was done, she pulled out the metal cup.

"Tamp it down," the man said, and Ella noticed the little metal lid. She pushed it into the cup, pressing the grounds together. The man pointed to another fitting, and Ella attached it, then pushed a button, and thick, dark espresso poured out into the paper cup.

"Froth the milk next," the man said. Ella shot him a look. He seemed amused by her ignorance, but she didn't want to press her luck. She poured soy milk into the paper cup.

"No, here," the man said, reaching around the counter and handing her a cup-sized metal pitcher. Ella dumped the milk from the cup into the pitcher, then pushed it into the frother. The man pointed at the right button, and she flicked it on for a moment, then added chai, mixing it with the espresso in the cup.

She slid the concoction over to the man with a heavy sigh, her shoulders slumping as if she'd just raced a marathon.

"First day?" the man asked, blowing on the hot liquid.

Ella nodded. "I have no idea what I'm doing," she said. "Thank you," she added, "for being so nice."

"That's me," the guy said, "I'm a regular prince charming."

ELLA & THE BALL

*R*outine, Ella thought, *was the key.*

When she first started working two jobs with more hours than she had thought possible, she'd wanted to quit after the first week. Heck, after the first day. But she needed the money, her family needed the money.

And family was everything.

She was in a comfortable routine now. Up at dawn for a jog and a few minutes to herself. She treasured this time, even if it meant getting up that much earlier. Then a shower and her maid's uniform. An eight-hour shift at Hotel Ever After, cleaning rooms as guests checked out. A quick change in the locker room, then a four or five hour shift at the bookstore/café that was attached to the hotel lobby.

Then home. To her family. What was left of it.

Ella touched the necklace she always wore, a small silver charm of a tree, its branches forming a circle. Daddy had given it to Momma when she first got sick. The cancer had worked quickly, and Ella could still remember her mother giving the necklace to her, her fingers clutching the chain.

When Daddy had remarried a few years later, Ella was glad of it. The house had felt lonely with just her and Daddy. Her stepmother, Lynn, brought two daughters to the marriage, twins, Dru and Stacy.

It...hadn't been the family she was hoping for. Dry and Stacy were sullen and angry that they had to leave their old high school to move with their mother to Fairhaven. Ella had been in middle school then, and, she supposed, annoying to her new sisters, who largely tried to ignore her. But still, it had been family, and family was important.

When Daddy died of a heart attack a few years after that, while Ella was still in high school and the twins had started college, she felt this even more. Suddenly their family of five was down to two.

But we're still a family, Ella thought savagely. And when Lynn started to get sick—too sick to work—Ella had dropped out of college and started picking up as many jobs as she could. First there was only the menial work —stocking shelves at the grocery, waitressing. But she'd worked her way up to the significantly better jobs of housekeeping at Hotel Ever After, which paid very well, especially now that they'd bumped up her hours, and barista at the café.

She was grateful, at least, that her two back-to-back jobs were in the same building. And she was grateful that her second job was primarily in the café part of the bookstore, enabling her to chug as much coffee to stay alert as she needed to.

"Evening, Ella," a man's voice said as he crossed the hotel lobby and wove through the café tables to the counter.

"Hello, Mr. Dickson," Ella said. She straightened up. The owner of Hotel Ever After was often in the café to visit his wife, Bette, who ran the bookstore, but he rarely ordered a drink.

"Dirty chai latte, with an extra shot," Mr. Dickson said.

Ella whirled around to start the drink order, but she couldn't help smiling. That was the very first order for a drink she'd ever gotten, over four months ago. She had started working in the café without really knowing what she was doing, and when a man approached her with almost that exact order, she hadn't even known what a chai latte was!

Fortunately, he'd walked her through the process and been more than kind.

If only he could see me now, Ella thought, flicking the espresso machine's knobs and expertly pulling the shot.

"Oh, wait," Mr. Dickson said. "He told me to get soy."

Now the order was exactly the same as her mysterious first customer. She'd never seen him after that first day. She'd wanted to. She'd wanted to thank him for being patient and kind when she didn't really know what she was doing. She'd had enough horrible customers since then to truly appreciate the good ones. But he'd never returned to the café. She didn't even know his name.

As Ella pulled out the carton of soy milk, she wondered if perhaps the person Mr. Dickson was getting this latte for was her prince charming of the café. She scanned the lobby, but there was no one there.

"Anything for you, sir?" Ella asked as she sprinkled the top of the cup with cinnamon.

"No, thank you," he said. "And I've told you before; you can call me Richard." His eyes weren't on her though; they were on his wife, Bette.

"Hello, darling," he said warmly, dropping a kiss on her head. She moved closer to him, and Mr. Dickson's hand lingered on his wife's slightly rounding belly. They hadn't officially announced yet, but Ella knew they could expect a new little Dickson by spring.

"Can you stay?" Bette asked.

Mr. Dickson shook his head. "Meeting with the events planner for the Christmas ball."

Ella slid the warm cup of chai across the counter toward Mr. Dickson, and he lifted it in a salute before kissing Bette one last time and then crossing the lobby to the elevators.

"I love that man," Bette said, staring at him appreciatively until the elevator doors closed.

She turned back to Ella. "And speaking of Christmas coming up, we're doing some special coffees." She started going over the new additions—gingerbread flavored lattes, candy cane mochas, a winter spice tea, and mulled apple cider.

Before she finished, Bette gagged. She covered her mouth, her eyes widening. "I'm sor—" she started.

"Go! Go!" Ella said, moving aside so Bette could escape to the employee restroom behind the counter. She made it to the sink before losing the contents of her stomach.

Bette returned a moment later, looking green. "They call it morning sickness," she said weakly, with a smile. "But this is hitting me worse in the evenings."

"You're exhausted. Go home. I've got this."

Bette hesitated. "Are you sure?" she asked.

"Positive," Ella said confidently. "It's a Wednesday night, one of our slowest days. I can cover the café and the bookstore."

Bette lingered, but Ella could tell she wasn't well enough to continue. "I'll be fine," she reiterated. "Go."

Bette finally acquiesced, heading to the door. She waved at Ella as she left.

∽

*E*lla had been right; today was a slow day. A few teens went into the bookstore to pick up the latest fantasy novel from a popular author, and a book group leader at the local church browsed the religious section but didn't pick anything up. The café was busier, but as she was closing up, Mr. Dickson and another man got off the elevator. They shook hands, and the man headed off in the other direction.

"Mr. Dickson!" Ella called.

He headed her way.

"Did Bette tell you that she went home early?" she asked.

Mr. Dickson's eyes widened. "Is everything okay?" he asked, panic pitching his voice.

"It's fine. She wasn't well to her stomach, but she went home."

Mr. Dickson had his phone out and was flicking through his messages. "Reception is terrible on the top floor," he muttered. "Ah, yes. She's texted a couple of times. Apparently copious amounts of ice cream is going to help this problem." A relieved smile crossed his face. "At least she doesn't want pickles with it."

"Who was that?" Ella asked, watching the back of the other man as he turned down the hall and out of sight.

"Our events manager," Mr. Dickson said. "Why?"

Ella shook herself. She was imaging things, especially since she knew this man's drink order was the same as her prince charming's so many months ago. "Nothing," she muttered. "He just looked familiar."

Mr. Dickson headed out, calling his wife to confirm she didn't need anything else. Ella closed the shops, grabbing an extra muffin for her stepmother before locking up. She made herself a dirty chai, soy, extra shot to go.

CHAPTER TWO

*I*f there was one thing to be grateful for, it was that Ella's house was only a few blocks from the bus stop.

As she trudged from the stop up to the small white house on the corner—one of a dozen or more houses built exactly the same, left over from lumber mill days—Ella saw a sleek silver Mercedes parked in front of the porch.

Ella picked up the two boxes waiting on the steps; her mother always forgot to check for packages. From the labels on the side, she could tell that one was from Amazon and the other from a home shopping network.

"You've got to stop this, Mom!" Dru's voice rang throughout the house, and Ella sighed as she dropped the packages on the cluttered kitchen table. Dru meant well, she supposed, but she didn't live with her mother any more, and she always seemed to sweep in, cause chaos and hurt feelings, and then leave before she had to deal with any of the aftermath.

Ella was fairly sure this was either about Lynn's spending habits or hoarding. She had heard this argument a million times since her father died, and a million more every time Dru decided to stop by. It wasn't something Ella really felt needed to be rehashed.

Ella lingered by the table, out of sight but easily within earshot of the living room, where her stepmother Lynn spent most of her time.

Dru's voice carried easily. "Mom, where are you getting the money for this? Did you get a job?"

Ah, Ella thought, *so today's argument is about spending.*

Lynn muttered something she couldn't hear, but Ella could easily guess it was along the lines of, "You don't understand."

Dru made a disgusted noise. "You don't *need* more stuff," she said. "You need to get out of the house. Get a job."

Lynn's voice was meek and low. Ella's shoulders sagged. She knew her stepmother was reiterating how painful her chronic illness was to her stepdaughter. Dru never understood Lynn's illness. It had flare ups where it was difficult for Lynn to manage the pain; some days were fine, but the stress of a regular, daily job was almost impossible.

This time, though, Ella heard something else in her words. She moved closer to the door.

"It's not for me," Lynn pleaded. "It's for Christmas. I want to get you something. I have to spoil my grandkids."

"My girls don't need more junk," Dru said.

Ella winced. Lynn never thought the things she bought were junk, even if they weren't always to Ella's taste.

"I may not have much time left," Lynn said, her voice dangerously close to tears. "I have to take joy where I can, and I get joy from giving things to others! Is that so wrong?"

"*Yes,*" Dru spat. "Because you don't care about the gift, you just want to shop. Why else would you send a first grader this?"

Ella's curiosity got the better of her. She snuck around the doorframe and peered into the living room.

Dru had two daughters—a four-year-old and a seven-year-old. She'd divorced amicably from her husband, and they lived about an hour away, in a little house that was twice as big as this one, in a suburb that was twice as nice as this one. Dru's first grader, Becky, was obsessed with all things Disney. Which is why Ella was somewhat surprised to see her stepsister thrusting a brand new iPad at Lynn, not a Disney princess costume or a doll.

"She didn't like it?" Lynn asked.

"Mom!" Dru threw her hands in the air, exasperated. "She likes Lego's and princesses. She has no need for an iPad. This is way over the top for a kid!"

Ella stared at the iPad. She'd been wanting one for ages, ever since her old laptop finally gave up the ghost. She'd been checking her email on her phone for months now, and sliding tips into a special envelope in her sock drawer. She knew exactly how many shifts she had to work in order to pay for an iPad.

And she knew, without a doubt, that Lynn had bought that iPad for her seven-year-old niece with *her* money.

And what was worse? She was willing to bet that Lynn got the idea to buy an iPad from her. She remembered a few months ago talking about how she was saving for one. Lynn hadn't really been interested, but it was around the time of Becky's birthday.

And she remembered when Lynn had asked for $600. She remembered it very well. It was when she started picking up a Saturday shift to her work week. Because Lynn had needed the extra money for physical therapy. Or so she said.

Anger burned in Ella's stomach. She was breaking her back every day, saving money in her sock drawer and taking the bus rather than waste gas in her car, and this is how her stepmother repaid her? By throwing extravagant gifts at Dru's kids that they didn't even need.

The sound of sobbing brought Ella out of her anger. She crept forward. Dru looked exasperated, but Lynn looked utterly broken.

"I want to be the special grandma," Lynn sobbed. "I couldn't provide the good things for you and Stacy and Ella; I wanted to make up for it with Becky. I'm so-sorry," she said, her voice breaking. "I just wanted them to be happy."

Ella's heart started to melt. She was still mad about the wasted money, but she knew Lynn and Dru had a complicated relationship, and it tore Lynn up inside.

"Take this back to the Apple store," Dru said, dropping the iPad box on the table. "If you want to make the girls happy, spend some time with them instead of money on them."

Ella shook her head. That was the thing Dru never seemed able to understand. Lynn was an invalid. She couldn't bear the drive north, even if it was just an hour.

Dru looked up then and saw Ella. "She's getting it from you, isn't she?" she demanded.

"Getting what?" Ella asked. She wished she'd stayed in the kitchen.

"Money."

Ella shrugged.

"Mom, you should be ashamed," she said. "You're stealing from your stepdaughter."

"Not stealing!" Lynn said. "I get a prepaid credit card; I never go over my limit."

"Because your credit is so bad you can't get anything but a prepaid one!" Dru growled in frustration. "No more extravagant gifts," she said, picking up her Kate Spade purse and turning to go.

Lynn muttered something almost indistinguishable, although the words, "but Christmas!" were loud and clear.

"Not even for Christmas!" Dru said, and she strode toward the door without pausing again, despite Lynn's feeble cries.

She didn't leave, though. Ella watched her with her hand on the door. She turned around. "Ella?" she said in a softer voice.

Ella joined her in the kitchen.

"We've never really gotten along," Dru said.

Ella couldn't deny it. Her stepsister was a few years older than her, and even as kids, she never spoke to her all that much. Dru's twin, Stacy, had married someone important and moved to Tokyo, and rather than turn to the sister she had left, Dru had retreated into her own life, ignoring both Ella and Lynn.

Now, though, there was something vulnerable in Dru's look. "Maybe it's because I was so jealous of you when we were younger," she said finally.

Jealous? Her? Of me?

"Anyway," Dru continued, "please help Mom. She's spending far too much money. Look around."

Ella did. And she tried to see the kitchen as Dru did. Dishes everywhere—Ella was too tired after work most days to clean up, and she did it all in one sweep on Sundays when she had a day off. Trash was piled up by the door, with broken down boxes leaning against a cabinet. Even Ella had to admit it was a lot of cardboard, but Lynn had to order online; she was too ill to go shopping.

As if reading her mind, Dru said, "Mom's not sick, Ella."

Ella shook her head. She had seen Lynn's collapses. She'd helped her up from the floor when she'd fallen. She'd seen her too ill to eat, too ill to get out of bed for days at a time.

"Well," Dru conceded, "Mom *is* sick. But not in the way she thinks. She's a hypochondriac."

"You don't understand," Ella said softly.

"And she's a hoarder," Dru continued as if Ella hadn't spoken. "She does need help. But she doesn't need you to load up prepaid credit cards to enable her."

Ella opened her mouth, but couldn't think of the words before Dru spoke again. "Seriously, Ella. I've tried for years to talk to Mom, and it's not worked, so I'm extending a damn olive branch to you. You can't see the forest for the trees, but please trust me when I say you're not helping Mom. She needs professional help, but first she needs to realize that she needs it. And she can't do that as long as you're her back up plan for everything.

"Besides," she added in a sad voice, "you're worth more than being someone else's back up plan."

Ella was so surprised by these words that she could think of nothing to say, not even when Dru strode out the door and pulled it shut behind her.

Before Ella left for work the next morning, Lynn called for her to come into the living room. She noticed the iPad box on the table, and hope surged through her.

"Dru is so mean," Lynn said, and Ella couldn't help but note the childish undertones of the words.

"She wants to help," Ella said.

Lynn waved her hand, dismissing this. "She doesn't help, though, not like you." She motioned for Ella to come closer, and half-hugged her from the arm chair.

"Is your back bad today?" Ella said softly.

"It's always something." Lynn sounded tired, defeated. Then she took a deep breath, as if steeling herself, and picked up the iPad box. "Can you be a dear and take this back to the Apple store for me?" she said. "You can just get me a store card if they don't give you cash. I can buy the girls something else there."

"I'll do it before I go grocery shopping on Sunday," Ella said, putting the iPad back down on the table. "If I can get cash back, I can use it to—"

"No, no!" Lynn shot back quickly. "I need the money."

Ella's hands curled into fists, and she stuck them behind her back. "We need groceries."

"Oh, my dear, you *have* money for groceries. You're getting paid this week. Just use that. I need the money. For *Christmas.*" Lynn's eyes darted around Ella, focusing on the television screen behind her, and the home shopping channel.

She thought about what Dru had said. "When's your next doctor's appointment? We should save for that." Lynn's insurance covered her general practitioner, but much of her therapy was done out of network, and Lynn liked using alternative medicine, like acupuncture and massage therapy, to relieve her pain.

"I was going to talk to you about that, too," Lynn said. She slid a hand behind her and rubbed her back. "I think I'll need to go in next week for a massage."

There goes another hundred, Ella thought bitterly. But then Lynn winced in pain, pushing up against the armchair and twisting. These spasms seemed to strike sporadically.

"I'll get your ice pack," Ella said, heading to the kitchen. When she returned, a Visa card was sitting on top of the iPad box—the prepaid card that Ella re-loaded with money at every pay check. She picked it up silently.

She paused in the kitchen on her way to the back door. The two packages that had arrived yesterday were still on the table, unopened. Ella slid a knife through the paper tape. The box from the home shopping network held three blouses and a dress in Lynn's size. Lynn rarely wore dresses, but she said shopping for clothes helped her feel normal through her illness. Ella glanced at the packing receipt and winced at the price. She opened the box from Amazon next; toys for Dru's girls, a gold bracelet that was probably a gift for Dru, and a DVD box set of Lynn's favorite TV show. All together, it was clear where Lynn's last set of funds from her prepaid credit card had gone.

～

*B*elinda, the head housekeeper, liked to start the cleaning staff's shift with a pep talk. Today, however, was all business.

"As some of you know, Mr. Dickson is hosting a Christmas ball this year," she said in clipped tones. "We had a good launch earlier this year, and he wants to keep the momentum going."

Ella remembered how busy those first months at the hotel had been. The pre-launch party had been a wild success, thanks to Mr. Dickson's younger brother and his connections, and the clean up afterward had taken the full staff working tirelessly an entire weekend. People had even moved the party from the Enchanted Forest restaurant on the top floor to the pool below it, bringing with them copious amounts of alcohol and food. Afterwards, the hotel was booked out for the entire season, but things had slowed to a more normal pace by fall, the rainy season in Fairhaven.

"We need to make Hotel Ever After a *destination*," Belinda continued, pacing in front of the maids like a drill sergeant. "Our draw will be the Christmas ball, an elegant affair that the elite will travel north from LA and south from Seattle for. We've already had a few high profile reservations, and I'd like to remind everyone of the discretion policy."

There was a slight murmuring through the crowd as people tried to guess who would be in attendance. At the pre-launch party, Mr. Dickson had been able to snag Rumpled Stetson, *the* hottest pop star of the year.

"There will be three major events, culminating with the Christmas Ball," Belinda continued. "Two in the Enchanted Forest restaurant. The ball itself will be held in the ballroom."

Members of the staff nodded appreciatively. The ballroom was the last room in the new hotel to be constructed, and it had never been used before. Many of them hadn't even seen it. Ella hadn't; she'd passed the beautifully carved mahogany doors several times, and barely resisted the urge to peek inside the finally completely room.

"Because this is so important, I'm shifting some work schedules around." Belinda started to call names, assigning the cleaning staff to different locations.

"Benjamin, Danielle, Christy, and Ella," she concluded. Ella sat up straighter. "You four are going to be relocated to the penthouse floor to help with preparations for the parties before the ball. Report directly there for the next few days."

With orders given, Ella stood and moved to the door where the two other girls and Benjamin were already clustered together. "This is the best," Ben said, high-fiving Christy. "No toilet scrubbing for a week."

Ella laughed, but it wasn't that bad. Hotel Ever After was definitely the nicest hotel in a hundred mile radius; it was rare that anything was too awful when she cleaned rooms. Not that she didn't have stories. She'd helped clean up after Rumpled Stetson had stayed at the pre-launch party, and his room had been so trashed they'd had to reorder a new bed for it.

The five of them took the service elevator up to the top floor, where, behind the scenes, everything was already in motion for parties that wouldn't take place for another week.

"You assigned to me?" Chef Mina's voice was low and authoritative, her eyes piercing. Everyone knew that Mina Grimes was in charge of anything that happened at the Enchanted Forest restaurant.

"Yes, ma'am," Ella said immediately.

Chef Mina's wrinkled face broke out into a smile. "I like that. 'Ma'am.' Nice. Right then. We've got work to do."

Ella and the others joined the restaurant workers that were already rearranging the tables and chairs. Chef Mina explained that the parties leading up to the ball were centered on art—an open gallery one night, and then a closed auction for the pieces of art the following night. The ball would be on the last night, on Christmas Eve.

Chef Mina disappeared into the kitchens as Ella and the rest loaded the chairs up onto huge wheeled carts that were then pushed onto the elevator and to the storage area of the basement. It took three trips to clear everything out, including a few larger presentation pieces.

The restaurant felt far larger now, without the tables and only a few chairs scattered on the edges. Ruby, the sous chef of the restaurant and Chef Mina's second in command (and her granddaughter), clapped her hands for everyone's attention.

"No matter what department you're usually assigned to at the hotel, for the next week and a half, we're all working on one thing—the parties."

"Even on Christmas Eve?" Benjamin whispered to Christy.

Ruby heard him. "Even on Christmas Eve," she said. "The final ball takes place then. You're going to be there. And you're going to help with the clean up the next day."

"Grinch," Ben said, sticking out his tongue.

Ruby rolled with it. "I didn't set the rules. And you were all chosen for this because you said you didn't mind working through the holiday."

"Yeah, for pay and a half," Christy said. The others laughed; it was a lot of work, but the pay rise would be worth it.

"Yes, for overtime," Ruby said with a laugh. "I've talked to your managers already about your reassignment."

Ella tentatively raised her hand. "I have a second job," she said. "I can't—"

Ruby cut her off. "I've talked to Bette; she's fine with it."

Ella frowned, not sure of the situation. She remembered how sick

Bette had been before, and how she really didn't need to be pushing herself.

"In addition to overtime pay, you'll be receiving a bonus for your extra work," Ruby said, and that caused a ripple of excitement through the crowd. "So don't screw this up," Ruby added.

CHAPTER FOUR

*E*lla was a little disappointed when she wasn't assigned to the ballroom—she was still dying to see what it was like inside. But decorating the restaurant-turned-art gallery was actually kind of fun. Benjamin and Christy were old friends who turned everything into a competition, and Danielle was quiet but had a sly sense of humor that would send their group into giggle fits at the most inopportune times. Chef Mina frowned at them more than once—a scowl dark enough to sober them immediately—but as they never stopped working and were actually pretty good at helping out, it wasn't a problem.

At least not until Ella's prince charming strode through the door.

Ella was holding white tulle while Benjamin stood on a stepladder, stringing the garland through the chandeliers. Christy and Danielle were working on fairy lights, wrapping it around the tulle.

Ella spotted him when the door flung open. He was exactly as she remembered—tall, broad shoulders, a square chin and flashing eyes. His gaze skimmed over the room quickly, sharply, like a predator looking for weak prey. He stood silhouetted in the door by the light from the room for several long moments, judging the ordered chaos unfolding around him.

And then he started striding through the room. He spoke in a low voice, so low that Ella couldn't hear him, but the moment he opened his mouth, whoever was nearby froze to listen and then scuttled off to do his bidding. He left a flurry of movement in his wake.

When he reached Ella and her friends, he paused. He cast a long, slow look from the tulle in Ella's hands all the way up to Benjamin on the ladder.

"No," he said.

"No?" Benjamin replied.

"This is all wrong." He took the tulle from Ella's hands, then grabbed the string of fairy lights, unwinding it from around the cloth. Christy cried out in dismay as all their work came unravelled, but he ignored her. Spreading the tulle out, he nestled the fairy lights inside, giving it an ethereal look.

"Like this," he said, shoving the garland back into Ella's hands before turning on his heel and striding toward the kitchens.

"Who is that jerk?" Danielle said.

Benjamin rolled his eyes. "Ramsey Cordon," he said. "The big shot events coordinator they hired."

Ella's gaze followed Ramsey as Chef Mina and Ruby approached him with a platter of hors d'ouevre.

"I have to admit, this *does* look better," Danielle said, holding up the garland Ramsey had made.

"Yeah, but he doesn't have to be so rude about it," Christy grumbled as she started redoing the rest of the decorations. Ella's eyes were glued to Ramsey as he took a sample from the chef and nibbled. How could she have ever thought this man was a prince charming?

"He's just specific," Danielle said. "Besides, it's gotta be stressful to be hired to do one event and suddenly it's three. Between the ball, the art exhibit, and the auction..."

Ella didn't listen to the rest. She was thrown off by the abrupt, gruff way Ramsey gave directions—to say nothing of the disappointment that he didn't recognize her—but she couldn't help but remember the kind way he'd helped her on the first day at her job. Danielle was right; he was under an enormous amount of pressure with the additions to the parties.

"None of this is acceptable!" Ramsey's voice carried across the restaurant.

"Like hell it's not," Ruby shouted back, just as loudly.

Quiet descended over the restaurant.

Chef Mina—Ruby's grandmother and boss—put a gentle hand on her arm. Ruby shook it off.

"You have to give me chance," she insisted to Chef Mina, then turned to Ramsey. "I *know* I can make this work for the party."

"We don't have time for something so fussy," Ramsey said in a tone that indicated there was no room for discussion on this.

"You control this," Ruby said, indicating the room. "I control the kitchens."

"No," Chef Mina's voice cut across the room. "I do. And Ramsey's right."

Ruby threw her tray of hors d'ouevre on the table, and tiny little confections skittered across the tablecloth. "One day you're going to have to let me do *something*," she growled.

"Not today," Ramsey said. The back of his neck was red; he was holding in his temper. "And if you show me that level of disrespect again, you can consider yourself fired."

Ruby leaned into his face. "I'd like to see you try."

"There's no 'try,' about it," Ramsey said. "You're fired."

He left Ruby sputtering as he stormed into the kitchens.

"He can't do that!" Ruby wailed.

Her grandmother tried to comfort her, but it was clear that, yes, actually, Ramsey could do exactly what he just had.

"Be right back," Ella said to Benjamin. She stuffed the tulle into his hands and dashed toward the kitchen, ignoring the startled questions from her friends.

Ramsey was pacing back and forth in the kitchen, his fists balled. He was used to people taking his orders and doing them, that was clear. More prince than charming. He glanced at Ella, and there was fire in his eyes. He was itching for another fight, a chance to blow off steam.

Ella ignored him completely.

She walked past the fryers and grills toward the espresso machine by the kitchen door. Ramsey, curious, stopped pacing and watched as Ella started steaming soy milk and pulling an espresso. This machine was exactly like the one in the café in the lobby; it was an old friend to her by now. Within moments she'd whipped up a dirty chai, soy milk, extra shot. She slid it over the steel counter toward Ramsey.

He accepted the drink and took an appreciative sip. "Thanks," he said. "Do I—do I know you? How'd you know this was my favorite?"

Part of Ella's heart sank; he *still* didn't recognize her.

"Lucky guess," she said.

He raised the mug in her direction and took a deep sip.

"The thing is," Ella said, "Ruby has good ideas. She just gets, er, passionate about them." She turned to clean the espresso machine; she didn't think she could talk to him face-to-face.

"Dickson's worried about the image of this hotel," Ramsey said gruffly. "If we want to make this place a destination, we have to offer our guests something special. Which is what the Christmas Ball was supposed to be. Instead, now it's *three* events, not one, and we don't have time to do fussy hors d'oeuvre that will take too long to make!" His voice rose, his anger resurging, as he continued talking. Ella let the espresso machine hiss with steam to cut him off.

She turned around and shrugged as if she had no connection with any of this, as if Ruby wasn't one of the few people who'd been kind to her when she started working overtime here. "Maybe some could be made ahead? Or maybe you could ask Ruby for ideas for things that could be made more quickly?" *Or just cool it and not think you have to control every single thing...*

The big steel double doors burst open, and Ruby strode inside. Her face was paler than normal, and her eyes were red-rimmed, but she was maintaining her composure. "I'll just get my knives," she said, and even though Ella knew that, as a chef, Ruby kept her own knife set in the kitchen, it still felt like a mild threat.

Ramsey put down his empty mug. "Hold on," he said, his tone much more even now. "I think we can work this out. I maybe came on too strong."

"Maybe?" Ruby snorted, but as Ella slipped, unnoticed, out of the kitchen, she couldn't help but feel as if things were going to get better now.

After work, Ella stopped by the café and made herself a peppermint latte. She took it to go, but didn't have the energy to carry it out to the bus stop with her. Instead, she collapsed into one of the lounge chairs and sipped the warm coffee, relishing the way everyone else in the lobby was rushing around but she, for once, was still.

"Ella?" a male voice asked behind her.

Ella started, nearly spilling her latte, and turned to see the hotel owner. "Hi, Mr. Dickson," she said. "How's Bette?" Ursula, a friend of Bette's, was filling in at the bookstore and café.

"Please," he said, smiling, "call me Richard. And Bette's doing much better. Her doctor's given her a different anti-nausea medicine that seems to be helping."

"That's good," Ella said. She wasn't sure how to make small talk, especially with someone like the hotel owner, and she couldn't help but feel panic welling inside her when Richard took the seat across from her and leaned in closer, intent on a conversation.

"Ella," he said, his tone shifting to one of concern, "I've noticed that you're taking on more and more hours here. Is everything okay? Or are you just saving for Christmas gifts?"

Ella glanced down at her latte, her fingers tightening around the cup. "My stepmother...she's sick."

"I'm so sorry," Richard said immediately, a furrow creasing his brow.

I'm not sure I am... Ella pushed the dark thought away. Despite what Dru had said, Ella knew Lynn was sick. Maybe she was also a little wasteful in her spending habits, but that didn't detract from her actual illnesses.

"I'm just trying to help out the only way I can," Ella said. She sat her empty cup down on the little table.

Across the room, the elevator doors dinged. The bronzed metal doors slid open, and Ramsey stepped out. He kept his head down as he started toward the door, but he glanced up as he neared them.

Ella's heart surged.

Ramsey caught Richard's eye and nodded at him, smiling. His gaze slid to Ella. She saw the faint confusion on his face, and she saw the exact instance when he decided he didn't know her and he turned away without a second glance at her.

All she'd done was change out of her maid uniform. Was she that much a chameleon that he didn't recognize her in different clothes?

"I'm not supposed to tell anyone this," Richard said, resuming their conversation, "but you do know that we're giving out a Christmas bonus at the end of the month, right? You don't have to work so many shifts; you should take some time off. You need to think about your health, too..."

Richard's voice trailed off as Ella stood up. "Thank you, Mr. Dickson," she said. "Really. But I need more work, not less."

Richard's frown deepened. "Bette told me you'd say that," he replied. He took a deep sigh. "If you really mean it, we're looking for more people to waitress at the art gallery we're setting up in the penthouse. If you'd like—"

"Yes," Ella said immediately. "I'd love to. Thank you Mr. Dickson!"

Richard seemed to have given up getting Ella to call him by his given name. "In that case, I'll alert the management that you'll be available, and my assistant will get the details to you."

"Thank you!" Ella said again. She glanced at her watch—she needed to get to the bus. Richard, sensing Ella's worry about time, said a quick goodbye and waved her on.

As Ella boarded the bus, greeting the driver and taking her usual seat near the front, she smiled at Richard's concern for her well-being. Most people completely ignored the people who served them. They saw the uniform, not the person. By this point, Ella was fairly certain she'd been called "maid" more than her own name in the hotel. And more often than not, no one called her anything at the café, despite the fact that she wore a name badge. She may as well have been a coffee-producing robot rather than a human to most of her customers.

It's not that bad, she told herself as the bus lurched around a corner, and she reached for a bar to hold onto.

But sometimes it was. With people like Ramsey. She didn't really expect him to remember her from that first day of work at the café. It would have been nice, sure, but he wouldn't remember her after that. His kindness had meant something to her, not him.

Now? She wasn't so sure he was kind at all. He never seemed to notice *anyone*. How could he have shouted at Ruby like that? How could he have been so oblivious to her, even after they spoke again?

The bus pulled up at the stop on her street with a rattle and a hiss, and Ella made her way down the stairs, waving at the driver. With a shock, she realized that she saw this driver nearly every day, but she wasn't sure of his name. Just before the doors slid closed, Ella turned and popped her head back into the bus.

"What's your name?" she asked.

The driver grinned, his teeth stained but the smile sincere. "Edward," he said. His voice was gravelly, like a smoker's.

"I hope you have a wonderful night, Edward," Ella said.

Edward pretended to doff a hat he wasn't wearing. His smile was so wide that Ella could still see it even when he turned the corner and continued his route north.

*E*lla pulled open the fridge door. The extra shifts were starting to take their toll. The restaurant was now finally decorated, the art installations were up, the menu was decided, and she'd had a few quick sessions with Ruby to train her on proper waitressing etiquette. "You'll be fine," Ruby had assured her, but Ella was more worried about falling asleep on her feet than making a faux pas to one of the prestigious guests.

To help make the days easier, Ella had spent all Sunday preparing breakfasts and lunches ahead of time, taking out one pre-made egg sandwich and one Mason jar salad out each morning. It'd worked well for several days, but today...

Nothing.

There should be three more sandwiches and salads in the fridge, waiting for her.

"Lynn?" Ella asked, peeking into the living room. Lynn was busy wrapping boxes—Christmas was a few weeks away, but she loved the festiveness of wrapped presents, even if they didn't have a tree to put them under. Ella wanted a tree...there was just no room for it. She frowned at the living room, crowded with boxes, bags, and *stuff.* Dry was right. Part of Lynn's problem was hoarding.

"Mmm?" Lynn asked, not looking up from the roll of wrapping paper. She shifted the bright red foil to cover up some of the boxes. Ella thought at first she was hiding a present for her, but she recognized the name of a very expensive children's clothing boutique. More gifts for Dru's girls.

"Where has my premade food gone?" Ella asked. She glanced at her watch. She wanted to go for a run in the forest before coming back and heading to work.

"Those sandwiches?" Lynn asked, still not looking up.

"And the salads."

"Both of them were yours?" Lynn paused.

"Yes. They're my breakfasts and lunches for the rest of the week."

"The rest of the week?" Lynn's voice was pitched a little too high. "Really? You eat like a bird, one salad for lunch? That's hardly filling."

"It's all I have time for...Lynn, where did they go?"

"I didn't know," Lynn started, her voice whining.

Ella's heart sank. "You ate them."

"I didn't know they were yours!"

"They literally had my name on them," Ella said. Not because she'd thought Lynn would eat them, but because she stored them in the staff fridge.

"I was hungry, and I needed something quick!" Lynn said. "Besides, you were holding out on me." Her voice turned accusatory. "That was a fancy salad, El. We can't afford that name-brand stuff."

Ella swept aside the wrapping paper—not the cheap kind, but the thick, foiled kind that only came in sheets, not rolls. "But we can afford this?" she asked, looking down at the box of expensive clothing.

"It's for *Christmas,*" Lynn sniffed. "You can be a Grinch if you want to be, but *Christmas* is *important.*"

Ella knew her window for a morning run was rapidly closing, but she sighed and sat down beside her step mother. "Lynn," she said, "Christmas isn't about the gifts."

"I know *you* feel that way, dear," Lynn said. "That's why you're so easy to buy for."

At the dollar store, Ella thought.

"But the children—the children need happy memories."

"Memories aren't something that can be bought and wrapped in shiny paper." Ella fingered the stiff foil.

"You've forgotten what it's like to be a kid. You should take some time off, dear." Lynn paused. "After Christmas, and the bills, of course."

Ella took a deep breath and tried one more time. "Lynn, we have to pay your medical bills. And Dru said that the girls don't need extravagant gifts. They'd rather have *you* instead of a present."

"They can have both!" Lynn said, throwing her hands up, a huge grin lighting up her face.

"Lynn...I think Dru is right. I think you have a problem. And buying more stuff isn't helping it."

Lynn's face immediately soured. "How can you do this," she whispered, her voice edged with tears. "*You* know how much pain I'm in. I thought *you* understood. I thought you cared..."

"I do!" Ella said immediately.

"Let me have this," Lynn whimpered. "Please, Ella. Let me have Christmas."

It was such a pitiful plea, and it pierced Ella straight in the heart.

But Ella also knew their bank account. "We're bleeding money, Lynn," she said. "I'm working twice as much as before, but we can barely pay our bills as it is."

"It just Christmas," Lynn said in a wistful voice. "It may...it may be my last one..."

"None of your doctors think your back injury is life threatening." Ella forced her voice to be strong.

Lynn coughed. "You know it's more than just my back." Her tone shifted. "I'm sorry, Ella, I am. I just...this is the only source of joy."

Christmas or shopping, Ella thought, casting her gaze around the crowded room, the boxes on top of boxes. Any stranger would think she and Lynn had just moved into the house. *Or that we're hoarders*, she thought bitterly.

It'd never really occurred to Ella before that Lynn was a hoarder. Not until Dru pointed it out. Cluttered, yes. In need of a yard sale. Lynn was a shopaholic. But Ella was starting to think that Dru was right. Lynn was a hoarder. Not just someone who collected things; she had a serious, psychiatric problem, and Ella wasn't sure she could help her.

A stone sank in Ella's stomach. It was bad enough to pay medical bills for a hurt back that seemed to never be unhurt and migraines that had no discernible cure, but add therapy for hoarding...

"Where are you going?" Lynn asked as Ella turned and headed back to her room.

"To work," Ella snapped. She kicked off her neon pink running shoes with a dejected sigh and reached for her uniform. Maybe she could clock in early today.

CHAPTER SEVEN

*R*uby cast an appraising eye at Ella. "You ready?" she asked.

"Sure." Ella ran over Ruby's training in her mind. "I'm just mingling around and taking any empty glasses away. I have waitressed before, you know." The more experienced servers were in charge of serving drinks and food; Ella was merely collecting dirty dishes, a glorified busboy.

"Not like this."

Ella knew Ruby was right. The diner down the street was nothing like the fancy cocktail party tonight.

Her uniform was bland, made to fade into the background. A knee-length black skirt, white shirt, black vest. Ella had pulled her hair up into a bun, and wore only silver studs in her ears.

Although Ella had helped with the decorations and set up of the displays, even she felt her breath catch in her throat when she stepped out of the kitchens and into the main area of the Enchanted Forest restaurant. The ethereal fairy lights made the place look as if the roof faded into stars, and the art displays were carefully arranged into a natural flow.

Beyond all that, though, it was the guests who made the area look magical. The men were dressed in tuxedos with floral boutonnieres, but the women's gowns were breathtaking. Ella noticed some people from the tabloids Lynn loved—an actress in a gown made of gold lamé, a singer in emerald silk that flowed like water from her hips. She smoothed down her own black skirt.

I am nothing but the background, Ella thought, stepping out onto the main floor, tray held aloft in one hand.

It helped that everyone seemed to agree with her sentiment. No one gave her a second glance as she picked up empty champagne flutes or the tiny cutlery used for the hors d'ouvre.

Invisible.

But even invisible people see things. Like the way no one was really looking at the art. They were too busy looking at each other.

Which was a shame, really. There was beauty here, in the canvases tucked into the alcoves, the sculptures resplendent on the tables. Ella scanned the cards by the art pieces as quickly as she could while she did her job, noting the artists's names. Some of them had little quotes beside each piece from the artist, explaining the inspiration behind the work.

She stopped by one particular painting. It was dark—one of the darkest pieces there. A forest at night, the moon slicing like a curved blade through the bare branches. A long red carpet was the only bright spot on the canvas, extending into the shadows cast by trees, inviting the observer into the darkness.

Ella read the little placard beside the painting, memorizing the details so she could look up more work by the artist later.

Artist: Alice Sun

Title: Come Into the Darkness

Background: This painting is part of a series titled "On the Other Side of the Mirror." The only part of the series available for sale to the public, Sun typically reserves her works for specific people. Known for being blunt, of this piece, she said, "If you can't tell what I'm painting, you need new eyes."

"I love her work," a voice said behind Ella. She started and moved quickly to the side. The woman who'd spoken didn't notice her at all, even as Ella reached out and took her empty glass from her.

"I can't stand her as a person, though," the man said. "So pretentious."

"But her background," the woman continued. "So tragic..."

The man made a dismissive noise, then steered his date toward another art piece. They spent several long moments staring at the flowers painted on the canvas. Ella frowned. They were really well done flowers, true, but they were just...flowers. This painting by Alice Sun, it was intriguing. It made her think. It made her feel. She liked it because it was far more than just flowers.

"I can't imagine this hanging on my wall."

Ella froze. She was supposed to be mingling around the room, but Ramsey Cordon had just seen her being still for nearly ten minutes.

He looked at her. "Can you?"

"Um." Ella wasn't sure if she was supposed to speak. Ramsey was, technically, a guest but also her employer. "No, sir," she said finally. "I wouldn't want to hang this up in my house."

Ramsey nodded; she had given the answer he expected.

"But," she couldn't help but add, "that doesn't mean it's not a beautiful work of art. The value of a painting doesn't lie in whether or not it'll look pretty on the wall."

A woman nearby snorted in appreciation at Ella's words. Ella caught just a glimpse of surprise in Ramsey's eyes before she plucked his empty glass from his hand and hurried back to the kitchen. Her heart beat rapidly. She'd said nothing so wrong that he'd fire her, but there was something about Ramsey Cordon that put her on distinct edge.

From the kitchen doorway, she cast a glance back at him. Maybe it was the way he so perfectly filled that tux that made her heart race. He wasn't a bulked out man—he was shorter and less broad that Richard Dickson, for example—but there was an elegance to him, a finesse that she couldn't quite define. It was no wonder she originally called him a prince charming.

Ella glanced down at her own uniform, no longer crisp and smelling of fresh linen, and stained in one corner with a splash of some cocktail after a slightly drunk lady waved her hand a bit too exuberantly in Ella's direction.

Too bad she would never be a princess to match.

*D*espite working until past midnight, Ella woke early the next day, determined to get her run in. Her running outfit was worn and drab, but the moment she put on her neon pink running shoes, she felt instantly better.

She left without bothering to say good morning to Lynn. Lynn was on the recliner in front of the television, watching the home shopping network, but Ella wasn't sure if she'd fallen asleep watching or had turned it on the moment she woke up.

The good thing about living in Fairhaven was that, as long as you weren't near the highway, it was never too long to reach the forest. Ella jogged the two miles through the suburbs to the large forest, picking up her pace as the redwoods came into view. It always felt a bit magical to go into the forest that surrounded Fairhaven on three sides. The trees towered over them, their trunks sturdy, their broad branches blocking out the sun. It was the perfect place to run; even if it started raining or the sun was especially hot, the trees provided cover.

There were a few regulars on her morning run—an older man who helped run the bakery, a ginger boy who always outpaced her—but aside from them, Ella was pretty confident that she'd have the forest mostly to herself. The advantage of working shifts instead of a nine-to-five was being able to avoid places when they were at their busiest.

But maybe a half mile in the distance, there was a man running. He kept a pretty even pace, but Ella was slowly gaining on him, even as she recognized his outline.

It can't be, she thought, but there was no denying it. She'd studied his form far too often to not recognize Ramsey Cordon's backside.

"On your left," she said as she passed him on the forest trail. She was pushing herself harder than usual to pass him, but she didn't want to linger.

Out of the corner of her eye, she noticed that Ramsey cocked a smile and started moving faster too. Ella picked up her pace, just enough to make Ramsey work for it. He caught up with her, but it was clearly not that easy, and after awhile, Ella had mercy on him, slowing down just enough that she was sure he could keep up.

Ella's watch buzzed on her wrist; time for her to turn around if she didn't want to be late. She aimed for a large redwood a few meters off, then slapped the trunk when she reached it. A minute later, Ramsey did the same.

He bent over his knees, panting. "You win," he said.

Ella smiled. "I wasn't racing."

Ramsey barked in laughter. "Still, good race."

She smiled at him.

Ramsey wiped the sweat off his hand and then held it out toward her. "I'm Ramsey, by the way."

Ella blinked at him a few times, a little surprised. Still—even now, he didn't recognize her.

"Oh, shit, have we met? Were you at last night's art gallery?"

"Yes," Ella said simply.

"Blue dress?" She shook her head. "Pink?"

"No," Ella said. "Black and white." It was a safe answer, and she knew it —there were at least a dozen ladies dressed in simple black and white at the art gallery.

"Ah, damn," Ramsey said, sinking to the ground, leaning against the tree trunk. "I'm sorry. I'm shit with names and faces."

Ella cocked an eyebrow. "I can tell." She hoped he didn't see just how much it disappointed her that he *still* didn't recognize her.

"No, really," he said, throwing up his hands. "It's not just you! My therapist says I'm so focused on the task at hand that I forget about the people around me."

Ella was a little surprised at how easily he mentioned his therapist; it reminded her of the matter-of-fact way her father had treated life.

"You live around here, yeah?" Ramsey asked.

Ella nodded. "About two miles away."

"I'm only here temporarily," he said, "but I can see why people love this area. Why Richard built a hotel here. It's beautiful." He tilted his head back, staring up into the thick cover of foliage above them.

He turned back to Ella. "If you were showing a friend around town, what would you show him?" he asked. "I'm always so damned focused on work...I've hardly left the hotel. I don't know what made me come out today, but I'm glad I did," he added impishly.

"Probably my favorite place in town is the bookstore," Ella started.

Ramsey waved his hand. "Nah, I've been there. Great dirty chais there."

"Great books, too."

"I'm not much of a reader," he said.

"Maybe you should try different books," Ella smiled sardonically, "I hear they help people improve their memory."

Ramsey laughed. "Are you sure we met yesterday?" he said. "I can't imagine forgetting you."

"I'm not really that memorable," Ella replied. *Apparently,* she added silently.

"Where else should I go in Fairhaven?" Ramsey asked.

"Everyone goes to the beach. It's not much compared to southern California, but it's nice."

"I want to know what *you* like. I want to see town from your eyes, not as a tourist."

"Well," Ella said, "if you want to know my favorite thing in Fairhaven, I'm looking right at it."

Ramsey pointed a finger at himself, eyebrow cocked.

"No, you tool, the forest!" Ella laughed.

Ramsey stood up again, turning in a slow circle. "Yeah, it's pretty great."

"There's a little house just on the edge of the forest," Ella continues. "The backyard gives way to trees. I used to live there when I was a little girl."

It was back on the market now. Ella had noticed the For Sale sign on one of her runs earlier in the month. She had allowed herself to day dream the entire run of buying the house back.

And then she had come home to Lynn, and bills, and real life.

"This would be a nice place to grow up," Ramsey said.

Ella shrugged. It was...but it could also be difficult. Ella had enough work to make ends meet, but many of Lynn's appointments meant driving to the city, and Ella wondered sometimes if they should move there, be closer to the doctors, in an apartment instead of a house, with a variety of jobs available. She was so reluctant to leave Fairhaven though, the last connection she had with her father and her mother.

"You just look so damn familiar," Ramsey said. "I promise I'll recognize you in a moment."

Ella started out of her day dream. She suddenly very much did *not* want Ramsey to recognize her.

But he kept staring at her with those contemplative eyes.

So she did the only thing she could think to distract him.

She kissed him.

CHAPTER NINE

Ramsey's sound of surprise was muffled by Ella's kiss, but he quickly acclimated to the new situation. He wrapped his arms around her, pulling her closer, then cupped the back of her head with one hand as he deepened the kiss in a way that took Ella's breath away.

His tongue dipped past her lips, touching her gently—a question. She answered him in kind, noting the sweet-sharp taste of chai in his mouth.

Her hands slid down his back. He growled low in his throat, his muscles tensing under her touch. He ran his fingers along Ella's scalp, shaking loose her ponytail.

It didn't matter that they were both sweaty from the run, that Ella's watch was buzzing, telling her that time was up and she needed to get to work, that they were still practically strangers. What mattered was this moment, right here, right now, in the forest Ella always half thought was magical.

What mattered was that right now, she was *definitely* noticed.

Ella pulled away from Ramsey's greedy lips, sliding her tongue down his chin, nibbling at his neck. He tasted salty and earthy. Raw. She arched her hips against his as Ramsey's hand slid under the hem of her shirt, his big palms sliding over her smooth, flat belly.

Through the thin material of her running pants, Ella could feel Ramsey growing hard with desire for her. It made her feel wicked; it made her feel very, very good. She slid her hands lower down his back, toying with the waistband of his running shorts.

Ramsey's hands slid up her shirt, cupping her breast, teasing her nipple. Ella gasped with pleasure and desire.

She let herself have one moment to daydream.

She closed her eyes as Ramsey clutched at her, lust overwhelming everything else. She imagined him pulling her shirt off.

His smooth hands running down her sides, clutching her hips, pulling her close to him. And she wouldn't be afraid. She'd lean forward, wriggling out of her exercise bra.

He kissed her from her lips down her neck, to her breast. He sucked on her nipple, teasing the sensitive flesh with playful nips that promised at the intensity to come.

Ramsey pulled back, ripping off his shirt and spreading it on the forest floor in a show of the best chivalry he had to offer. Ella leaned back on the shirt, smelling the fresh earth of the forest all around them.

There was no one to see but the trees, and they would never tell their secrets.

Ramsey shimmied out of his shorts, then divested Ella of hers. His movements were sure as he slowly pulled her panties down.

"You've wanted this since the first time you saw me," he said.

Ella could not deny it.

"I can tell," he added, sliding a finger on the inside of her panties, feeling just how wet with desire she was. Ella moaned in anticipation, and the sound seemed to break any resolve Ramsey had been using to keep himself in check.

With a growl, he ripped away the thin material covering her, exposing her bare body to the open air. He took a moment to appreciate her, to memorize her every feature. His hands reached for her, starting at her shoulders, sliding down over her breasts, over her stomach, stopping at her hips. His grip tightened, almost painfully, as he looked at her with such longing. His eyes sought hers, his expression unreadable.

One hand trailed from her hips to the mound between her legs. Ella's breath caught in her throat, her pulse a rapid beat.

Ramsey didn't break eye contact as he slid one finger into her, gently, questioningly. He watched as she sighed with pleasure as he entered her, and a slow smile spread across his lips.

He used his thumb to gently tease her clitoris. Ella could feel the pressure mounting both painfully and pleasurably; she could feel herself grow slick and eager, feel the desire coiling deep inside her. Her back arched as she pressed into his hand, begging for more, wanting more, more, more.

"Naughty," Ramsey said in a deep voice. "Greedy."

"More," Ella gasped.

He did not oblige. Instead, his thumb quickened in pace, drawing her tantalizingly closer to the edge. Ella's hands flailed, gripping the dirt, and her breath came out in short, staccato bursts.

And then he withdrew.

"Not yet," Ramsey promised. He knelt up, nudging her knees apart as he positioned himself at her entrance.

"Are you sure you want this?" he asked.

In answer, Ella arched against him, pressing herself against his hard cock.

With a groan, Ramsey pushed inside her. She saw stars as desire burst within her, her body clutching around his cock, her back arching as she sought to pull him deeper in.

With careful, steady motion, Ramsey found a rhythm. It eased the tension that had coiled so tightly within Ella, almost soothing as he rocked into her, out, in, out. But then he grinned down at her, a wicked smile across his face, and he slipped his hand between them.

She was so sensitive there that she gasped at his mere touch; when he slowly started to stroke her clitoris with his fingertip, she could barely catch her breath to moan with pleasure. Seeing her reaction seemed to drive Ramsey wild; he intensified the touch, stroking harder in perfect rhythm with his hips.

He pounded into her, hard, faster, the rhythm overriding all her senses. Ella took in a deep breath as the tension coiled inside her tightened and tightened and then—

*E*lla's wrist buzzed as a second alarm warned her of just how late she was going to be to work.

She pulled back from the kiss—for that was all it had been. A kiss, and a daydream of something more. No matter how much she wanted this—no matter how much she wanted Ramsey to *really* see her, to know her in a way no man had ever known her—she knew she couldn't do that.

She had work to do and bills to pay.

"I have to go," Ella said, stepping away from Ramsey.

He shifted; his erection was vivid and seemed to cause him some discomfort. "I understand," he said, even though his eyes belied the statement.

"I'm sorry, I..." Ella's voice trailed off.

"Will I see you tonight?" Ramsey asked.

Ella blinked at him.

"At the art auction. Will you be there tonight."

"Yeah," Ella said, her heart sinking. Would he want to see her in a server's uniform? "Yeah, I'll be there."

And then she turned and ran back down the path without saying another word, her neon pink sneakers flashing through the forest.

"The point of art," Alice Sun said from the podium in the front of the room, "is not to be *pretty*." She said the last word with an obvious sneer, and half the guests at the art auction looked a little uncomfortable with the artist's abrasiveness. The other half nodded along, but Ella wasn't sure if they actually got what Alice was saying or if they were just pretending to.

While the gallery last night had been invitation-only, the art auction tonight was even more exclusive. There were only about fifty people here, each hand selected by Mr. Dickson or Ramsey. A dozen or so servers, including Ella, mingled among the guests, hidden shadows in black aprons.

Ella knew she should be working, but she was in awe of the woman standing in front of the room. She hadn't realized it, but it was the same woman who had snorted at her comments to Ramsey at the gallery showing yesterday. She felt honored that the prestigious artist was echoing her own sentiments.

"The point of art," Alice continued, "is to be *noticed*. It demands your attention. It cannot be denied."

Ella hefted the tray of dirty dishes on her shoulder and headed toward the kitchen.

"Most of you are too stupid to realize this," Alice continued. Ella froze, her eyes widening as the murmurs from the guests grew and people started to shift angrily. "You'll bid on silly little decorations to adorn your silly little mansions without thinking of what art truly is. But a few of you actually care about art, and that's why I'm here." She looked out at the audience. "Like her," she said, pointing right at Ella. "She understands art. But I doubt any of you even noticed her."

Ella stood like a deer in headlights as the guests turned to stare at the server Alice pointed at. The tray trembled in her grip.

Across the room, Ella saw Ramsey standing straight, straining to see who was the subject of everyone's attention. Ella blanched. She knew she would see Ramsey in her server's uniform, knew eventually even he would notice that the girl in the forest who'd kissed him wasn't a glamorous socialite but a lowly waitress.

She just couldn't bear for that moment to be *now*.

Ella dropped the tray, clattering silver and smashing champagne flutes. The guests gasped. At the podium, Alice Sun chuckled. "See? True art demands to be noticed."

For one moment, Ella gaped at the artist. Was she trying to say that *Ella* was art? She wasn't. This wasn't. It was a disaster.

Ella turned and fled into the kitchen, barreling through the big metal doors and crashing into Ruby.

"Ella?" Ruby asked. "What's happened?" She took in Ella's lack of a tray, the splattered remains of champagne and food on her shoes. "You dropped a tray," Ruby said in a horrified voice. "Tell me you didn't drop a tray. Chad Wolfson, the top food critic in California, is out there." Ruby groaned.

But then she looked into Ella's face and saw just how distressed she was. "Are you okay?" she said gently.

"No," Ella gasped. "Oh god. Everyone saw."

"It's embarrassing, but we've all done it," Ruby said in a kind voice.

But it wasn't just that she dropped the tray. It was that Ramsey had almost seen her, seen her for who—and what—she truly was.

"I can't do this," Ella said, her eyes wild.

"What?" Ruby asked. She pulled Ella away from the main kitchen area, into a small alcove, hidden from the main door.

"I can't do this. I want to help, I need the work, but Ruby—"

Ella's voice was cut off by the sound of Ramsey Cordon pushing through the big double doors of the kitchen. "Where is she?" he asked in his gruff voice. Ella couldn't tell if he was angry or shocked or anything else. She cringed against the wall, hiding her face.

"What do you want?" Ruby asked in a low voice.

The words hit Ella like a slap in the face, and she realized that for a very, very long time—maybe since her father died—no one had asked Ella what *she* wanted. She had fallen into the roll of provider and worker and door mat. And she was done.

"I want to quit."

"You're sure?" Ruby asked.

Ella nodded mutely.

Ruby pushed off from alcove, stepping into Ramsey's sight. "She quit," she said. When Ramsey tried to step past her, Ruby added, "She's already gone."

"Gone? But—" Ramsey sputtered.

"Maybe if you weren't such a tyrannical monster, she wouldn't have felt the need to quit over one tiny mistake!" Ruby shouted back. She definitely still had a chip on her shoulder over being fired, despite being rehired.

"It's not like that—" Ramsey started. He made a move toward the alcove where Ella was hiding, but Ruby cut him off.

"Out of my kitchen!" she shouted. "You've terrorized enough of my staff. Go back out there with the guests and let us handle this!"

Ella waited until the footsteps disappeared. Ramsey was back out at the art auction, and Ella was safe in the kitchen.

"He's gone," Ruby said, pulling Ella out of the alcove.

"I'm such a coward," she said mournfully. "I just couldn't face him." But it was more than that. She couldn't face the idea of working night and day for Lynn any more either. She was *done*.

"You're not a coward," Ruby said. She wrapped her arms around Ella in a ferocious hug. "You're *human*. And you don't need this job anyway. You don't have to deal with that jerk. You can just go back to your regular work."

Regular work...eight hour shifts cleaning rooms followed by five hours shifts making coffee... The mere thought of it exhausted Ella. She wanted to go back into that alcove and hide from her own life.

"You're worth more than ten Ramsey Cordons," Ruby whispered before she let Ella go from her hug. The words sank into Ella. This wasn't the first time someone had told her she was worthwhile, but for some reason—maybe because she was so tired, maybe because Alice Sun had noticed her when Ramsey hadn't, maybe because she was finally ready to claim herself for her own—for some reason she was *done* with sacrificing herself for other people.

"Ella?" Ruby asked.

Ella rolled her shoulders back. "I know what I need to do," she said. And it started with going home.

CHAPTER ELEVEN

*E*lla let the front door slam closed behind her.

"Ella?" Lynn called from the front room.

Ella stomped into the room. Lynn was exactly as she had left her earlier that morning—sitting in her recliner, still wearing the t-shirt she'd slept in the night before, the home shopping network blaring on the television.

This is my life, Ella thought, watching her stepmother watch the television. *I have worked my fingers to the bone every day, and I tell myself it's because Lynn's family, but...*

But she doesn't treat me like family. She treated Ella like a servant.

Art demands to be noticed, Ella said. *And so do I.*

Ella recalled the way Dru warned her that Lynn was sick, but not physically. She forced herself to look around the house the way it really was, not the way she thought of it. The mounds of clothes and toys and just *stuff*. Lynn was a hoarder, and her "illnesses" were nothing more than an excuse to avoid work and continue with her hoarding.

Ella stomped across the room and stood in front of Lynn.

"Could you skootch just a touch to the left, dear?" Lynn said, leaning to continue watching the television.

"No," Ella said.

The strong word was so out of place that Lynn actually blinked at Ella owlishly without saying anything in return.

Ella turned and shut the television off. "We need to talk."

"Now?" Lynn asked. She glanced at her watch. "Aren't you still supposed to be at work?"

"I quit," Ella said.

Lynn's eyes widened. "You quit? What? We need your paycheck!"

"No *we* don't," Ella said. "I still have my jobs; I just quit working the extra parties."

"Oh, that's good," Lynn said. "And didn't you mention you were getting a Christmas bonus? We can just use that."

"No, *we* won't," Ella said again, emphasizing the pronoun even more this time. "*I* will get a Christmas bonus, and *I* will use it as I see fit."

"Oh, of course," Lynn said, clutching her chest as if Ella's words had wounded her heart. "I just assumed you'd want to...with the bills...but of course, we'll make ends meet..."

"You're not understanding what I'm saying," Ella said, glaring down at her stepmother. "I mean that I'm done. With this. All of this. I'm done."

Lynn shook her head. "You're right...I don't understand. What happened at work? Why did you quit?"

"I quit because I realized I was done being used. I'm used in every aspect of my life, and I. Am. *Done.*"

"You're not used!" Lynn started to protest, but Ella slashed her arm at her.

"You use me as your own personal servant and bill payer."

"I don't mean to!" Lynn said, her voice a pathetic bleat. "I would work if I could! Ella, I'm sick, you know that..."

"I do know it," she said. "But you're sick in a way I can't fix. In a way the doctors can't fix. You need a psychiatrist and therapy."

Lynn's face turned red. "How *dare* you imply—"

"I've implied nothing. I'm stating it outright. You are sick in the head. You do need help. But I can't give it to you."

Lynn stood up—without the need of a back brace or a crutch, Ella noticed. "Out!" Lynn pointed to the door. "If you're not going to respect me, you can get out of my house!"

This cut Ella far deeper than she cared to show. She forced her face to remain impassive as she took a few deep breaths. This house wasn't supposed to be Lynn's. Her father had left the house in Ella's name before he passed away; it was Lynn who convinced her to sign it over to her for "tax reasons."

"I have spent the better part of my life waiting for you to see me as someone worthwhile," Ella said in a low voice. "I have tried in every way I know how to prove my worth to you. I have given you time, money, and love, and you..." She sighed. "You barely know who I am."

She turned with resignation and headed back to the door. Lynn turned the television up to full blast, staring at the screen with such intensity that it was clear she wanted nothing more than to pretend like none of this was happening.

Ella ran upstairs and hurriedly packed a bag with a few essentials, a photo of her parents, and a handful of things she didn't want to be without. She was leaving behind far more than she could carry, and she hoped Lynn would let her come back for more when she found a place to stay. Dru would probably help her. Maybe.

Ella thumped her bag on the floor. She wasn't sure Lynn would hear it over the blaring television, but Ella could see the way her spine stiffened and how she very pointedly didn't turn her back.

"We're not related by blood," Ella said, not sure Lynn could hear, "but I considered you a second mother. Why do you think I stayed with you? Why do you think I tried so hard to help you? But a mother wouldn't treat her daughter like you treat me. I know. Because you don't treat Dru the way you treat me."

Lynn didn't turn from the television, but she tilted her face toward Ella. She was listening.

"For the first time in my life," Ella said, "I'm going to do what's best for *me*. I don't know if you care or not, but I hope you can understand."

At this, Lynn turned. Tears were streaming down her face. "I understand that you're being selfish!" she hissed, barely audible over the loud commercials blaring through the room. "I hope you feel good about leaving me, sick and penniless!"

"I don't," Ella said, honestly. "But you're drowning, and I'm not going to let you hold me under any longer."

Lynn screamed obscenities at Ella, but Ella just picked up her bag and left. This house was messy and broken, but Ella needed to leave it. Ella felt the truth of it in her bones. Dru had been right; Ella's money had only been enabling Lynn to mire herself in her hoarding habits. She was as bad for Lynn as Lynn was bad for Ella; the best thing they could do was separate.

When Ella stepped out the door, the television was still so loud that she could hear it through the outer walls of the house. She leaned against the siding and a sob escaped her lips. Right or wrong, she was *free*.

And so, so alone.

CHAPTER TWELVE

"You sure you okay, honey?" Edward the bus driver asked.

No, Ella wanted to say. *I've just been kicked out of my own home and I have nowhere to go.*

"Fine," Ella said.

Edward frowned in the mirror, his lips pressed together in worry, but he didn't press the matter. Ella had gotten on the bus and ridden the entire route around Fairhaven three times now, and she was no sooner to figuring out what she needed to do tonight than before.

"It's just..." Edward paused. "You know the busses shut down at midnight, right?" he asked.

Ella bit back the cry of dismay rising in her throat.

"You got somewhere to go tonight, honey?" Edward asked.

Ella forced herself to look up, out the big bus window. They were downtown now, the Christmas lights criss-crossing the street, making everything look shinier than it really was.

"Here," she said impulsively as the bus pulled up to a stop at the bookstore. "Here is fine."

"Here?" Edward looked doubtful.

"Thank you," Ella said, grabbing her bag and jumping off the bus. It would be expensive—Ella didn't want to think about just how expensive it would be—but she'd spend the night at the very hotel she worked at. *Used to work at,* Ella reminded herself as she stepped into the grand lobby.

Her phone buzzed as she crossed toward the front desk. She paused, half hoping Lynn was inviting her back home, but it was Bette's number that flashed across the screen.

"Hello?" Ella answered the phone, her eyes scanning the lobby to the café, where a very nervous-looking Bette stood.

"Ella, are you okay? Ruby just told me you quit working for Ramsey, and—"

Ella changed directions, heading toward the café. Before Bette had even finished speaking, she waved her down. "I'm fine," she said, turning her phone off.

Bette rushed around the counter, wrapping her in a hug. "What happened?"

"I just...I couldn't stand working for Ramsey Cordon any more," Ella said.

Bette frowned. "He must have been a monster to make you quit."

"No." Ella shook her head. "I think I was more mad at the situation? A lot of little things. I was just so frustrated...he never really noticed me. I don't think he even knows my name." It sounded so stupid to say it out loud now, but it also felt good.

"I know how that is," a voice said from behind the counter. Ella turned to see Ursula, a friend of Bette's, stepping out with a small espresso in her hand. Ella had never understood people who caffeinated this late at night, but who was she to judge? The smell of the coffee right now was perfect.

"Nothing's worse than feeling like you're ignored," Ursula continued. She shook her long, dark hair behind her, and Ella couldn't help but feel a pang of jealousy. Who had ever ignored beautiful, stunning Ursula?

Bette nodded sympathetically. "Makes you feel like your worthless." She hugged Ella's shoulder's again. "And you're *not*."

Ella forced a smile. "Thanks."

"Right." Bette clapped her hands together as if she'd made a decision. "I can talk to Richard; I can get you working at the Christmas ball again. If you want to?"

Ella shook her head. "No," she said. "I don't want it. Not any more."

Bette narrowed her eyes, contemplating Ella. "Something else happened," she said slowly.

Ella nodded, tears welling in her eyes. Before she knew what was happening, Bette and Ursula had swept her to a table in the back of the café, where it was most private, and Ella spilled out all her secrets—the way Lynn had used her for so many years, the dreams she'd put on hold for

Lynn's illnesses, the way her paychecks were frittered away with a compulsive need to shop that went way beyond "shopaholic," the house filled to the brim with stuff, the empty way Ella felt every time Lynn slighted or ignored her again—all of it came out in a long rush.

"Damn," Ursula said slowly, appraising Ella. "That's rough."

"I had no idea," Bette said. One hand covered her mouth, as if she were shocked. "I knew you were working for your family, but I had no idea that your situation was this bad…"

Ella twisted a paper napkin in her hand. "Part of me feels like I should go home and apologize," she confessed in a small voice. "Lynn's not sick like I'd been thinking—she needs a psychiatrist, not a medical doctor. But she's still sick, in a way. She needs help."

"Doesn't mean you have to give it to her," Ursula said immediately.

"I understand the feeling," Bette added. "We all want to help the people we love. I've let my father talk me into things that weren't really in my best interest, that's for sure. But if there's one thing I know, it's this— you can't give up your own life for someone else."

"Especially if that someone else isn't even trying," Ursula added. "It's like an addict—she won't get help unless she sees she has a problem and understands she needs help. Sounds like as long as she has you as a crutch and a money supply, she'll never change."

Ella cast her eyes to the table. "I can't go back there," she said in a soft voice. She knew it. She'd known it the moment Lynn told her to get out. But even with her packed bag at her feet, she wasn't sure what to do next.

"Where are you going to go?" Ursula asked.

Ella looked behind her, at the hotel. "I was thinking of spending the night here," she said.

Bette nodded eagerly. "Excellent idea. I'll talk to the front desk."

Before Ella could respond, Bette had jumped to her feet and crossed the lobby toward the front desk. She leaned over it, talking to the clerk.

"I didn't mean—I have money," Ella started, obviously much too late. She started to get up, but Ursula grabbed her wrist and kept her at the table.

"So tell me about why you quit," she said. "I only picked up bits and pieces, but I take it this Ramsey Cordon guy is a dick?"

Ella shook her head. "No—yes—maybe? I don't know. He seems nice. He's been nice to me. But he just…he never noticed me." Her cheeks flushed.

Ursula leaned back, a smile spreading across her face. "Ah, I see," she said, and Ella was suddenly very, very afraid that she did actually see, far more than she let on.

"One problem solved," Bette announced, handing Ella a key card envelope.

"And another one, I think," Ursula said. "You want your boss to notice you?"

"Former boss, now," Ella said.

When she looked up at Ursula, there was a positively hungry look in her eyes. "You need to go to that ball."

"But I quit—" Ella started.

"*Not* as a waitress or a maid or whatever," Ursula said. "You need to go as a guest. As the star of the night."

Ella glanced from Ursula's toothy grin to Bette, who was nodding slowly. "You can't be serious," she said.

"You do know the girl who's sleeping with the hotel owner," Bette said.

"And carrying his baby," Ursula reminded her.

Bette patted her stomach. "I can definitely get you an invite."

"But I have nothing to wear!" Ella protested, fully aware of how silly that sounded.

"Consider me your fairy godmother," Ursula said.

CHAPTER THIRTEEN

*B*ette hadn't just gotten Ella a room at Hotel Ever After.

She'd gotten her the *penthouse*.

And not for a night. An entire week. Free of charge. Including room service.

When Bette had escorted Ella up to the room, Ella's mouth had dropped. "I can't," she started.

"You can, and you will," she said.

Ella had tried to protest, but Bette would hear none of it. "You deserve this," she said softly. "You have sacrificed so much of your life for everyone else around you. You deserve to have something nice for yourself. You deserve to be the princess at the top of the tower."

Ella knew that she should have spent the night luxuriating in the silky sheets or soaking in the jacuzzi tub. Instead, she used the suite's computer to look up her bank information. She'd always kept her account separated from Lynn's, but she made sure to change all her passwords to everything, just in case. She analyzed her income and savings, trying to figure out what she could do when the week was over and she could no longer be in the penthouse of Fairhaven's fanciest hotel.

All fairy tales, she knew, must come to an end. How'd the old one go? At midnight, the carriage turned back into a pumpkin. And it felt like a quarter past eleven already.

Ella woke the next day with her face on the keyboard. Someone was knocking on the door. She blearily opened it and found Ursula on the other side.

"It's..." Ella checked her watch. "Oh my goodness, I'm late to work!"

"You quit, remember?" Ursula said, pushing her way inside.

Ella's brain scrambled to catch up with the reality of her situation.

"Did you even take a shower last night?" Ursula asked. She stared at Ella. "You're wearing the same clothes you were wearing before."

"I don't want to—"

"What, be clean? Ridiculous."

"No, it's just—"

Ursula pushed Ella to the bathroom. "Take a bath. With bubbles."

"I don't have time!" Ella erupted, pushing Ursula's hands away. "I have to figure out where I'm going to live—"

"With me," Ursula said.

"With..."

"Me," she said again. "I'm in a little cottage by the sea. My best friend moved out to traipse around the world like a waif. On a yacht, though, so not exactly waif-like. Anyway, her room's up for grabs. Not forever, mind, but you're the kind of girl who just needs a place while she gets back on her feet, right?" She narrowed her eyes. "I'm guessing you already have an idea of what you want."

"There's this house, by the forest..."

"Right, so, then it's settled," Ursula said. "You're moving in with me while you save up for that house you want. And I'm betting, with the way you work and the ridiculous low rent I'm going to charge you, you'll be moved in within half a year."

Ella couldn't help but stand there and blink.

"Now go take a bath. We've got a lot to do to get ready."

"The Christmas ball doesn't even start until seven tonight!" Ella protested.

"And that's *barely* enough time as it is!" Ursula stood up and pushed Ella into the bathroom. "Bath! Now!"

〜

*I*t took far longer for Ella to get ready than she would have guessed. After her bath, Ursula did some sort of smoothing treatment on her hair, then forced her to sit at the vanity while she applied her makeup. The end result was nice—a sleek updo with a pearly headband, a pale pink flush on her cheeks, and a hint of sparkle on her lips.

"No need to do much to the eyes," Ursula mumbled to herself. She lined them in kohl and flicked a mascara wand through Ella's lashes.

From the neck up, Ella was actually presentable.

"But I have nothing to wear," she said, not for the first time.

There were several black garment bags strewn across the chair by the door. Ursula grabbed them all and rifled through the hangers, finally pulling one out. She unzipped the bag and withdrew a silky, pale blue gown with cream accents.

Ella's eyes widened. It was the most beautiful dress she'd ever seen.

"Everyone's going to be in bold colors today, mark my words," Ursula said. "This will make you stand out."

Ella was already wearing nothing more than a bra and panties—so as not to mess up her hair, Ursula had said. She stepped into the silk gown carefully, aware of how it clung to her every curve.

Ursula narrowed her eyes, evaluating. "No underwear," she said.

"Pardon?" Ella twirled in front of the long mirror by the bathroom.

"No underwear."

Ella squinted at her reflection. Sure enough, she could see the outline of her panties and her bra straps. The dress was utterly unforgiving. She shimmied out of her panties and unclasped her bra. It felt odd to have the luxurious silk chiffon against her bare body, but it was a nice sensation.

She blinked back tears as she looked into the mirror.

"What's wrong?" Ursula asked.

"Yesterday, I thought my life was kind of over," Ella said. "I rode the bus for hours. I thought I was alone."

"You're not," Ursula said, squeezing Ella's shoulders.

Ella nodded, her eyes alight. Then Ursula lifted a silver eye mask up.

"What's that?" Ella asked.

"It's a masquerade ball," Ursula said. She fit the eye mask over Ella's face.

"The only thing we need now is shoes," Ursula said. "But your feet are much smaller than mine. Do you have anything that would work? The dress is long enough to hide your shoes if not."

The floor-length gown would indeed cover everything. Ella smiled. "I have exactly the thing," she said.

Ella's bright, neon pink running shoes did *not* match her silky blue dress, but it didn't matter. No one could see her feet under the layers of cloth. And Ella needed her comfortable shoes. She intended to dance all night.

Her stomach twisted in knots as the elevator brought her down from the penthouse suite to the third floor of the hotel, where the ballroom was. Built overtop of Bette's bookstore, the ballroom had been the last room in the hotel to be completed. Ella had never even seen it before, and she wasn't sure what she expected.

It definitely wasn't a winter wonderland.

The huge mahogany doors to the ballroom were flung wide open, revealing the glittering ballroom sparkling with glass icicles and snowflakes. Ella handed her invitation to an attendant by the door and swept into the ballroom, her pink sneakers silent on the marble tile. Her eyes drifted up to the ceiling. An enormous crystal chandelier hung in the center, with gold-infused twirls of glass swirling down between the glittering bulbs that flickered like candles. The ceiling itself was painted in blue and silver to emulate the night sky. Thin lines illustrated the constellations, and the major stars of the sky were made of shining crystals illuminated in the ceiling.

"Reminds me of Grand Central Station," a woman said, passing Ella.

She wore a black mask over her eyes, giving her the appearance of a bandit.

Ella had never been to New York, but she had seen pictures of the ceiling of the station. This was far better.

A full string orchestra played on one side of the room, the notes of "Greensleeves" rising above the chatter. A few people started to dance elegantly, the ladies' skirts spinning around them like flower petals.

Ella was very happy to have the silver eye mask on. It made her feel like she belonged.

"Would you care to dance?" a man asked. Ella turned to see a familiar face—even with a mask on, she could tell this was Richard Dickson.

"Oh, um, thank you, but...I don't know how," she said. Her plans of dancing all night evaporated before her eyes. Why hadn't she thought of that earlier?

Richard gave her a half bow and returned to his wife. Bette gave Ella a little wave, and she grinned. She knew Bette had sent her husband over to help her break the ice, and she was grateful, but also perfectly happy to stick to the sidelines.

She had never seen such a beautiful room—the glass icicles and snow were matched by the towering Christmas trees decorated with silver garland and cranberries, live flowers and elegant accents. The people filling the ballroom were even more gorgeous, each lady in bold reds and greens to match the festive theme. Ursula had been right—Ella stood out in pale blue. *And neon pink*, she thought, wiggling her toes.

Ella drifted over to the side of the ballroom, where an elaborate buffet had been set up. She eagerly selected a cream puff.

"My compliments to the chef," she said, nodding at Ruby as she replenished the punch.

"Thank you," Ruby said formerly.

Ella tipped her mask up. "Ruby!" she said. "It's me!"

Ruby did a double take. "Damn, girl," she said, "you clean up good."

And then Ella saw him. Ramsey Cordon stood off to the side, beside a beautiful Christmas tree that had been decorated with strands of gold beads and live poinsettia blossoms.

Ruby nudged her toward him. "Yeah, I figured it out," she said after Ella cast a glance back at her. "And even if he's a colossal jerk, I think maybe he deserves a second chance."

Ella questioned Ruby with her eyes. "We had a talk after you quit," Ruby confided. "Maybe I was too quick to judge him."

Ella steeled her nerves and approached Ramsey. Before she could reach him, though, another gentleman touched her elbow. "Care to dance?" he asked, offering a gloved hand.

"Oh—um, no. Thank you? I'm sorry," Ella stuttered, already turning back to where Ramsey had been.

He was gone.

~

*E*lla lingered at the edge of the ball, reveling in the music, memorizing the scent of the dozens of Christmas trees, the view of the fluttering dresses. She hadn't had a chance to find Ramsey, but she relished in the freedom that being here, tonight brought. Her life wasn't an endless cycle of funding Lynn's hoarding. She was free.

"I was hoping I'd find you here."

A chill went up Ella's spine. But she suppressed the flush rising up her cheeks as she turned to him. Ramsey was dressed in an immaculate, close-fitting black tuxedo, but he didn't wear a mask, despite the theme of the ball. His only nod to Christmas was a sprig of holly as a boutonniere.

Ramsey pointed above Ella's head. Without meaning to, she'd stopped under the miseltoe.

"This seems a little coincidental," Ella said aloud.

Ramsey smiled. "I may or may not have been waiting for you walk this way," he said slyly.

"Me?" Ella asked.

"The beautiful girl in the blue dress."

Her heart sank. Even now, he didn't recognize her.

Before she could say anything, Ramsey pulled Ella forward into a kiss.

And that kiss—it was everything she'd hoped for. He tilted her head back, his hands gentle even as his lips ravaged hers. His tongue ran along her lips, and when she parted her mouth, he deepened the kiss, claiming her as his. She gasped, and he swallowed the tiny noise, wrapping his arms around her and pulling her even closer to him. The thin material of her dress felt like nothing; his hands seemed to burn through the material. She was deeply, deeply aware of how she wore nothing at all under the silk, and she wondered if Ramsey could tell. He shifted, and her hip brushed against the hard length of him.

When he finally relinquished her from the kiss, his hands slid around her shoulders, down her arms, erupting her skin in flame. He held her hand, his rough finger brushing over her knuckle. It was that small touch, such a simple, true gesture, that brought Ella back into reality. The world faded back into her senses, and she was dimly aware that the orchestra had struck up a new song.

Ramsey tugged on Ella's hand, spinning her into a dance. Ella wasn't the kind of girl who knew how to waltz, but Ramsey's sure steps guided her around the marble dance floor. Ella felt as if she were in a dream as he spun her out, her neon pink sneakers flashing from under the hem of the silky blue dress.

Ramsey pulled Ella close again, and she was reminded once more how thin the material of her gown actually was. His hand at her waist slid lower, just over the curve of her hip. A seductive smile spread over his face, and Ella knew that he could tell she was wearing nothing beneath the silk of the gown.

But something nagged in the back of Ella's mind. Ramsey had called her the girl in blue...but hadn't used her name.

"You know who I am, right?" she asked tentatively.

He dipped Ella low, and she suddenly felt all eyes on them. The dance floor had cleared. Everyone was watching just them.

"Of course I know who you are," Ramsey said. "You're the girl of my dreams."

Ella's heart sank as Ramsey pulled her up. Even now...he didn't know her. The silver mask she wore wasn't enough to truly hide her identity. Her friends had recognized her. Ramsey had kissed her, and he still didn't know her name.

She had never felt more worthless.

As he spun her out at the crescendo of the music, Ella let her hand slip from his. Rather than spin back into his arms, she broke through the small crowd that had gathered around them. Her steps broke into a run, and she didn't care at all that her garish pink sneakers were on display as she picked up the hem of her dress and raced to the exit.

As soon as the brass doors to the elevator opened, Ella dashed inside, her heart racing. She leaned against the cool metal and tilted her head up, looking at the mirrored ceiling of the elevator.

"I see you," she told her reflection. No one else may ever notice her, but *she* cared about herself. That would have to be enough.

The doors slid closed.

Almost.

An arm encased in a black tuxedo jacket sleeve jutted through the closing doors. The brass slid back open, and Ramsey stepped inside.

Ella's jaw tightened. She crossed her arms.

"Are you sure you want to ride in an elevator with a stranger?" she asked as the doors slid fully shut. Ramsey pressed a number on the elevator and it started ascending.

"I know who you are," Ramsey said. His voice was low, feral. He took a step closer to her, and Ella was suddenly deeply aware of how she was backed against the metal wall. The elevator rose, and her stomach dropped.

"You," Ramsey continued, a hairsbreadth away from Ella, "are Ella Barrymore. You're the most dedicated worker in this entire building, you're beautiful, everyone who knows you considers you a friend, and you *are* the girl of my dreams."

Ella's eyes were wide as Ramsey slipped the mask off her face.

"I hate that I didn't recognize you in the forest. When I saw you again at the art auction, I didn't mean to terrify you. I wasn't going to fire you or anything. I just wanted..." His gaze dipped lower. "I wanted to know you."

"I've felt that way since we first met," Ella said in a small voice.

The elevator doors slid open, and Ella stepped out onto the hallway. Ramsey stood in the elevator doors, his brow furrowing. "Dirty chai," he said in a soft voice.

"What?" Ella asked.

"You were the barista in the café the first time I came to this hotel for my interview with Richard. You were the girl who didn't know how to make a dirty chai."

Ella's heart sang. He *did* remember her—even their first meeting.

"I wanted nothing more than to leap over the counter and kiss you right then," Ramsey said, stepping out of the elevator and joining Ella in the hallway. "I thought about you for weeks. I took the job here over another one because I'd hoped to meet you again."

"I was right here," Ella said softly.

"Right in front of me..." Ramsey stepped closer. Ella's heart thudded in her chest. "I have been such an idiot. I get so wrapped up in work, I couldn't see the thing I wanted was right in front of me."

The elevator doors slid shut. Ella looked around—she recognized the twelfth floor of the hotel. Her room was one floor up.

"Don't you need to go back to the ball?" Ella asked.

Ramsey pulled his cell phone out of his pocket to check the time. Midnight exactly. "I'm officially off the clock now," he said, turning his phone off. "Whatever happens in the ballroom now isn't my problem." He laughed then.

"What?" Ella asked.

"If you saw my room, you'd know why this is kind of funny."

His eyes grew serious and flicked to Ella's, a question there.

"I wouldn't mind seeing your room," she said softly.

His lips quirked up into a smile. Ramsey offered Ella his arm and led her down the hall, pausing at room number 1212. He tapped the key card against the lock and pushed the door open for Ella to enter first.

She couldn't bite back her laugh of delight. Ramsey was in the Cinderella room, a giant clock across from the bed with two gold hands pointing to midnight. "Shouldn't something be turning into a pumpkin about now?" she asked as Ramsey closed the door behind him.

"Oh, there's a pumpkin," Ramsey said, nodding to an orange crystal pumpkin on a shelf surrounded by a half dozen small iron mice. "Richard has an eye for detail," he added, snorting.

"Well, I definitely didn't lose a shoe," Ella said, sticking a leg out from under the hem of her dress, exposing her neon pink sneaker.

"But it is how I first recognized you," Ramsey said. "I spent the whole ball going from lady to lady, trying to find you. Then I saw a flash of pink as you crossed the room and knew it was the girl who kissed me in the forest."

"Ha!" Ella said. "Well, if I'm Cinderella, and it's midnight...I guess the magic is over."

"Well," Ramsey said, contemplating. "Personally, I think magic's a matter of perspective. For example, in the story, midnight is when the fancy dress disappears."

He stepped closer, running his hand over the thin material of the dress, tugging at the shoulder strap. Ella couldn't rip her eyes away from his.

"Maybe midnight is when the magic just gets started," she whispered, kicking off her pink sneakers. Her stomach clenched with anxiety and fear and hope and desire as she reached behind her, sliding the zipper of the gown down, down. The silky material fell from her body easily.

Ramsey's eyes darkened as they drank in the full image of Ella, nude, in front of him, inviting. "Midnight's always been a magical time for me," he said, ripping his tuxedo jacket off. He yanked his bow tie away, then pulled his shirt so rapidly that buttons went flying.

"Shh," Ella said, stepping forward. Her movement seemed to paralyze him. He stood there, frozen, as Ella slid the thin white shirt off his shoulders, running her fingers down his back, over his chest. She could feel his heartbeat thrumming wildly under her touch, and it thrilled her to know that she was eliciting this reaction from him just by being here, just by standing in front of him, just by being *seen*.

Her hands dipped lower. She tugged at his belt, unbuttoned his pants. He was already erect, his hard cock straining against his boxers.

"Ella," he sighed as she reached for him, wrapping her hand around his shaft.

She pushed him backwards toward the bed, gently, but he stumbled as his legs hit the mattress, and she used the momentum to push him all the way down.

"Do you have a...?" she started. He leaned up, fishing in the nightstand for a condom, and quickly put it on.

Ramsey tried to sit up, kissing Ella and pressing her against the mattress. But she wriggled free, pushing him against the pillows. She got up on her knees, looking down at Ramsey's body. His legs were tight and muscled—all that running. A wicked smile crept over Ella's face as she threw a leg over Ramsey and straddled his thighs.

"You want this," she said, running her fingers along his cock.

Ramsey reached up, letting one of his fingers slide into Ella. He grinned as he felt just how eager and ready she was, wet with desire.

"You want *me*," Ella whispered, sliding her body against Ramsey's, her legs pressing against his hips.

"I want you," Ramsey said. Ella leaned up, positioning his cock above her entrance. "I want *you*, Ella Barrymore," he said again. He looked her right in the eyes as she lowered herself over his shaft, taking the full length of him in one long, fluid motion. Ramsey's breath rattled in his chest as he shuddered with pleasure. His fingers gripped Ella's hips, holding her down over him. She clenched against his shaft, and Ramsey's breath hitched.

His body shook with desire as Ella lifted up again, sinking back down. She loved watching him, loved seeing the way she was driving him wild. She rode him gently, relishing in every movement, the feel of him inside her, so thick and long but fitting so perfectly.

"Ella," Ramsey moaned, and the sound of her name on his lips made her clench again, her body rippling with pleasure.

Ella rode him languidly, arching her back up, her breasts taut and her nipples pointed as the coil of desire in her center tightened. Her hips found the rhthym of their bodies, and Ella leaned back, loving the feel of her body and his, united as one.

Ramsey reached up, his hand shaking, and ran his hand from her waist to her breast. His rough fingers slid over her smooth skin, cupping her breast, his thumb rubbing across her nipple. Ella gasped with pleasure, and Ramsey pinched the nub of her nipple between his fingers, gently, just right, just enough to set Ella's senses on fire. She rode him harder, leaning up and plunging down, relishing in the satisfying way she took all of him in, all the way to the hilt.

Ramsey growled, letting his hand drift behind her back and then pushing her down, bending his head so he could nibble at her breast, his tongue swirling over her nipple. Ella panted, moving her body against his, focused on the dual pleasure of his dick and his tongue.

And then his hand slipped between them, and he slid a finger up, just touching her sensitive clit. Ella sucked in her breath, stars flashing in her vision. Ramsey made a sound of pleasure deep in his throat, the vibrations skittering across her nipple. He applied more pressure to her clit, finding the same rhythm as he stroked against the center of her aching desire.

Ella couldn't help it; she bit the side of Ramsey's neck, moaning through his skin with pleasure as he increased his strokes. His tongue flicked across her nipple, his finger danced over her clit, and his cock filled her, slamming up into her.

"I—I—!" Ella gasped.

Ramsey roared in triumph, and in one smooth motion flipped Ella down on the bed so that she was under him as he drove into her, his need overwhelming his senses. He looked her right in the eyes as they both came together, each falling apart in a simultaneous orgasm that rattled the stars.

____

CHAPTER SIXTEEN

____

ONE WEEK LATER

*E*lla turned in her keycard to the penthouse somewhat reluctantly. Nothing would ever replace the magical week she had spent at Hotel Ever After. Especially since, for the entirety of that week, she hadn't left the hotel once.

She crossed the lobby to the café, where Ursula was waiting for her. "Quit looking so grim," Ursula said. "My cottage may not be a luxury hotel, but it's not half bad."

Ella grinned at her. "Sorry!" she said. "I really am grateful."

"No worries." Ursula whistled sharply. "Hey, Tom!" she called behind her, into the bookshop.

A man Ella recognized as Bette's father came out from the back office. He shook Ella's hand. "So you're the young woman interested in the house by the forest," he said.

"Tom's in real estate," Ursula supplied.

"I love that house," Ella said, "but I can't afford it right now."

"Not to worry, not to worry," Tom said waving his hand. "Bette talked me into investing in the property. I'll be renting it for a bit, and you'll be first on the buyer's list."

Ella's heart surged. "Really?" she gasped.

"Really." Tom looked past Ella and nodded his head toward Ramsey as he approached. "And here comes my first renter."

"You?" Ella exclaimed.

Ramsey grinned. "Richard indicated that there was a bit of a market here for an events planner. I've got a year-long contract, and I needed a place to stay…"

Ella squealed and wrapped him in a hug.

"I've got a feeling you won't be using my spare bedroom for long," Ursula said, grinning. She wolf-whistled as Ramsey didn't release Ella, tilting her head into a long kiss.

Ella finally batted Ramsey away as her phone started ringing. "Excuse me," she said, stepping to the side.

"Dru?" Ella asked in her phone. "Is everything okay?"

"Mom came to stay with me for Christmas," Dru said. "She drove herself. It was…a surprise."

"Oh!" Ella's heart jumped. "I'm so sorry. I should have called."

"She drove herself," Dru repeated.

The words finally sank in. Lynn, who constantly said she was too ill to be in a car for that long, drove herself to Dru's house.

"Your timing was a bit abrupt," Dru continued, "but I think this is a good sign. I think she's on the way to being healthier. She's going to move up here, at least temporarily. On the condition that she seek therapy."

"I'm glad," Ella said sincerely.

"Hey—thanks." Dru sounded like she wasn't sure how to really talk to Ella. "I know the past few years have been rough as Mom got worse. Thanks for being there. And thanks for helping her to let go."

"Special delivery!" Ruby called across the lobby as she approached the café. When she noticed Ella was on the phone, she covered her mouth and whispered, "sorry."

"I've got to go," Ella started.

"If you have some time off," Dru said, "you should come up here."

"That sounds nice," Ella said. She shot Ramsey a smile when he questioned her with his eyes. "I'd love to. I'll call you later?"

Dru rang off, promising to call that evening to arrange a family New Years dinner, just like their parents used to do when the girls were younger.

"Sorry!" Ruby said as Ella rejoined the group.

"What's all this?"

Ruby held up a large basket. "We're doing box lunches!" she said proudly. "Just talked Gran into it. Delivery downtown courtesy of yours truly. We're doing samples today."

Ruby passed out boxes of lunches, and they spread out the meals on the café tables. Ruby lingered, eager to see what everyone thought of the contents. Ella discovered five large, handmade crackers wrapped in paper, a small tub of tapenade, and an apple salad made with crisp diced apples, a soft goat cheese, and walnuts.

"Delicious!" she cried, eagerly digging in.

Ruby beamed at them, then her eyes grew wide with an expression that Ella couldn't tell was excitement or fear.

"What's wrong?" she asked.

"That's...*him*," Ruby said, her eyes glued to a young man talking to the receptionist at the front desk.

"Who?" Ella asked, but Ruby shushed her immediately.

"It's *him*," she said again, almost reverently.

"Who?" Ramsey asked, leaning over Ella and stealing a napkin.

"Chad Wolfson."

"With a name like that, he sounds like a valley boy crossed with a comic book villain," Ursula said, licking tapenade off her finger.

"He's the top food critic in the state," Ruby said, her voice in awe as she watched him talking to the concierge. "He usually stays in LA, but he's been here for the parties, and..." Without even realizing it, Ruby had wandered away from her friends, crossing the lobby before she finished speaking.

"I'm glad to hear you had a nice stay," the concierge told Chad. "Please consider staying here again if you ever return to Fairhaven."

Chad said something that Ruby couldn't hear, but the concierge's farewell hit her with full force. *Chad Wolfson, the top food critic in the state, is leaving.* A fierce determination struck Ruby like lightning. *Not without some of my food,* she thought.

She glanced down at her basket. This was perfect.

"Excuse me," Chad said.

Ruby hadn't realized she was so close to him—close enough to be in the way of his rolling suitcase.

"Chad Wolfson!" she said. Loudly. With the exclamation point.

"Ye-es?" he said, drawing the vowel out.

Ruby stuttered over a hello. "Um—I—er—"

"I have to go," Chad said, stepping around Ruby. "My cab's waiting."

"Wait!" Ruby called, grabbing his arm. His extraordinarily chiseled and well-tanned arm. She rubbed a thumb over his skin, then realized what she was doing—and how he was looking at her—and snatched it back.

Oooh boy.

"I work at the restaurant upstairs. The Enchanted Forest? I'm the sous chef. And we're doing a new thing. Box lunches. Here's one. And I want you to have it. I hope you like it. If you come back to Fairhaven, maybe you can write about our restaurant. My grandmother and I, we're the chefs. At the restaurant." She said this all in a rush, in one breath, and felt light-headed by the time she finished speaking.

"Uh...huh," Chad Wolfson said.

Ruby thrust the box lunch in his hands.

"Thanks?" he said, looking down at it.

"Thank *you!*" Ruby called, waving.

She watched as he wheeled his suitcase out the door before turning back to her friends. "Oh my gosh!" she squealed. "He took one! He took one of the lunches I made!"

"You're blushing!" Ella said, grinning at her.

"It's like you have a crush on him," Ursula pointed out.

Ruby's cheeks flushed as she recalled the way Chad's arm had felt, like it had been cut straight from granite. She wondered what it would be like to feed him—an odd sentiment for anyone but a chef. As a food critic, surely Chad would expect the best—and Ruby knew she could bring it. Something spicy but also smooth...chili-infused chocolate, maybe...

Ruby shook herself out of her reverie. She wished she'd had something better on hand to give Chad, but she knew her lunch boxes were an excellent taste of her talent. Her grandmother, the head chef at the Enchanted Forest restaurant, had been reluctant to give Ruby this chance, but a good write-up by Chad Wolfson in *Amuse-Bouche* magazine or maybe the *Times* would wipe out all those reservations...and could set Ruby up to opening her own restaurant...

Right. Enough day-dreaming. Time to get to work. Ruby smiled at her friends, bid them farewell, and headed to the door, ready deliver boxed lunches all down Main Street.

As the front doors to the lobby of Hotel Ever After slid open, Ruby's stomach sank. Sticking out of the top of the trashcan on the street was the boxed lunch she'd given to Chad Wolfson. The twine around the box was still tied in a perfect bow—he hadn't even bothered to open it and look inside.

Ruby felt her jaw clench. Well. She didn't need a food critic's approval, even if he had chiseled arms and an impish smile. She'd prove she was worth far more than being tossed away like that. And if she *ever* saw him again, she'd make sure he knew just how big a mistake he'd just made.

AFTERWORD

Thank you so much for joining me in Fairhaven at the Hotel Ever After!

These first four novellas are a part of a planned series. If you'd like to read the next story—or if you'd just like to help the author out—please consider leaving a review of this book! Liza loves rewriting stories with new, sexy twists, and has more planned for readers if they want them!

Speaking of retelling stories with a sexy twist...Liza has begun a new series of steamy romances with bestselling author Natasha Luxe. Liza and Natasha turn the world of super heroes and villains upside down, starting with the first book, NEMESIS.

This exciting new series of dark romantic novels will take you to new heights! Join Liza and Natasha as they explore the dark world of super heroes of villains...

~

BOOK ONE: NEMESIS

All-American Man: the Hero
Lillith Giles: his Fiancée
The Raven: the Villain out for revenge . . .

One year after All-American Man clipped my wings and left me for dead in the California desert, I've finally found the way to unseat the country's most beloved Hero: by getting to his less-than-happy fiancée. Lillith Giles may be all smiles for the paparazzi, but I know a trapped bird when I see one.

My nemesis took what mattered most to me, so I'll return the favor.

But then All-American Man tries to kill Lillith himself. Suddenly I'm her savior, and the more time we spend together, unraveling the threads of this golden-boy-turned-murderer, the more I have trouble staying a Supervillain who needs to take down his enemy.

I'm a Villain. She belongs to the Hero.

Do I want my revenge, or do I want her?

Perfect for fans of Katee Robert and Ivy Smoak comes a new romance series that stokes the heat on your most forbidden superhero fantasies.

Join the community on Facebook here: https://www.facebook.com/Heroes-and-Villains-103236091836912/

Subscribe to the newsletter here—and get free updates, novellas, and shorts! http://rarebooks.substack.com

Please consider reviewing this book at Amazon—nothing helps an author more than reviews and readers sharing the books they love!

ALSO BY LIZA PENN

Hotel Ever After Series

Heroes and Villains Series